VILLAGE
IN
THE
DARK

TITLES BY IRIS YAMASHITA

City Under One Roof

Village in the Dark

VILLAGE IN THE DARK

Iris Yamashita

BERKLEY

New York

BERKLEY
An imprint of Penguin Random House LLC
penguinrandomhouse.com

Copyright © 2024 by Iris Yamashita

Library of Congress Cataloging-in-Publication Data

Names: Yamashita, Iris, author.
Title: Village in the dark / Iris Yamashita.
Description: New York : Berkley, [2024]
Identifiers: LCCN 2023026673 (print) | LCCN 2023026674 (ebook) |
ISBN 9780593336700 (hardcover) | ISBN 9780593336717 (ebook)
Subjects: LCGFT: Detective and mystery fiction. | Novels.
Classification: LCC PS3625.A672227 V55 2024 (print) |
LCC PS3625.A672227 (ebook) | DDC 813/.6—dc23/eng/20230613
LC record available at https://lccn.loc.gov/2023026673
LC ebook record available at https://lccn.loc.gov/2023026674

Printed in the United States of America
1st Printing

For Tsuyoshi Yamashita

1927–2009

VILLAGE
IN
THE
DARK

CHAPTER ONE

CARA

THE FRIGID WIND WHIPPED UP EAGER SNOW EDDIES OFF THE knolls of the cemetery grounds in South Anchorage. Cara Kennedy tightened her knitted scarf around her neck and wedged her hands in the pockets of her parka in an attempt to keep warm. In summer, the parklike grounds offered a peaceful vista of green, rolling hills under the majestic, white-capped Chugach Mountains. Though the mountains were seven miles east, they were as much a part of the Anchorage skyline as the twenty-two-storied Conoco-Phillips Building on G Street or the twenty-one-floored Hilton Anchorage on Third. Even now in winter, despite having viewed the mountain vista a million times over, Cara still had to marvel at the unobstructed view of the giant, snow-coned peaks under glacier-blue skies. It's why she'd chosen this plot in the Angelus Cemetery for her husband, Aaron, and their son, Dylan.

Yet here she was watching their coffins being unceremoniously craned out of the ground from what were meant to be their final resting places.

Each click of the metal chains hoisting the caskets reverberated through Cara's bones. Aaron's walnut-stained, adult-sized box was raised first, casting a long shadow that blotted the patch of ground in front of her. The reality of what she was doing finally hit her. She felt suddenly queasy, and a wave of anxiety welled up within her. This felt sacrilegious. Was she making a horrible mistake by disturbing the dead?

OVER THE COURSE of a year and four months, Cara had lost her family and then been placed on long-term disability after failing a psych eval. It seemed like a lifetime ago since she'd been working as a detective for the Anchorage Police Department and Aaron was a manager at the research division of a pharmatech company on the edge of town, while Dylan had sprouted into a precocious six-year-old with an infectious smile.

Admittedly, it wasn't always a bed of roses. Cracks had begun to form in the looking glass of their picture-perfect lives. There was the stress of their jobs, the burdens of taking care of a child, and not least of all, the faithless thoughts that haunted Cara when Aaron slinked into bed in the wee hours after a long day at work. She had even secretly followed him once after a late-night call that he said was a work emergency, but it turned out he actually did go to his office. A getaway to the Talkeetna wilderness two hours north of Anchorage was the self-prescribed medication to fix their relationship. It was on the third morning of their trip that Aaron and Dylan had bundled up in their parkas, gloves, and hats, and headed out to look for snow-shoe hares while Cara slept in. They never returned.

There had been searches, of course—helicopters, dogs, and volunteers. But neither her husband nor son could be found . . . until nine months later when lightning started a multi-acre forest blaze and firefighters discovered a skull, a leg bone, a rib cage—everything in pieces at the bottom of a ravine. A man and a boy. Cara asked for a verifying DNA report to be sure. The scattered locations of their remains were explained as the work of wild animals—a suggestion that only added to Cara's pain and horror.

Aaron and Dylan had *probably* gone off trail and gotten lost, Cara was told. Or maybe Aaron had injured himself on the walk and couldn't make it back, while Dylan had stayed with him. There was only conjecture without any definitive evidence. In Alaska, where two thousand people a year disappear in the beautiful but vast and foreboding wilderness, few of the missing make the news.

Cara fell into a rabbit hole of unanswered questions and a well of guilt. If she had gone with them, could she have prevented them from getting lost, or helped Aaron if he was injured? Could she have found them sooner when there was still a chance to save them? Should she have forbidden Aaron to take Dylan into the cell-signal-devoid wilderness? Aaron's blue, dust-covered SUV, still splattered with the deaths of hundreds of insects, was found abandoned on a seldom-used gravel road with Aaron's expensive SLR camera gear and his driver's license still in the car. *Why would Aaron have left his camera and driver's license behind?* This last question made her begin to doubt whether the whole thing was an accident at all. Could there have been foul play involved?

At the station, she became obsessed with cases involving body parts and missing persons, including a slew of extremities washing up on the shores of the Pacific Northwest and Canada, and a couple that washed up near Anchorage. The mundane explanations revolved around the buoyancy of modern-day sneakers detaching from decomposed corpses of suicide and drowning victims, *not* the work of a maniacal serial killer. Still, Cara looked for possible connections to what might have happened to her family and began poking her nose into investigations that were not assigned to her. Colleagues began to avoid her. Cara felt herself breaking apart into irreparable pieces like the remains of her loved ones. Her developing anxiety manifested in claustrophobia and insomnia, and she was put on meds. Even now, she continued to be haunted by disturbing nightmares. After a mandated visit to the psychologist, she was deemed unstable and placed on disability.

NOW, WATCHING DYLAN'S half-sized coffin being lifted in staccato hoists, Cara had to wonder if she was just heading down another path to Crazy Town. But she had reason, she told herself. It had taken two months to process, but Cara was finally able to get a court order to exhume the bodies. No autopsies had been conducted, since there had been no suspected foul play, but now she wanted a full examination. She knew it would be hard to determine a cause of death from what was left of them, but she also knew that they could still discover evidence of blunt force trauma or bullet holes, or make the distinction between animal teeth marks and cuts by sharp metallic objects.

What had led her to commit this drastic act of exhuming the bodies of her own husband and son? Another case of dismemberment that Cara had investigated on no one's authority but her own. The case had led her to the remote city of Point Mettier—an odd town reached via a claustrophobic tunnel where all of its 205 full-time residents lived in a single, monolithic high-rise condo. In the end, Cara solved the case, a murder that was completely unconnected to the deaths of her loved ones.

Or was it?

Cara had walked away with a clue. It was on the cell phone of a deceased gang member she had never met before named Michael Lovansky: a photo of Aaron, Dylan, and Cara herself on the day they had left home for the Talkeetna wilderness. Why Michael Lovansky had this photo of her family was a tormenting mystery.

IN THE CEMETERY a sudden gust of wind picked up, coiling around Cara like a chilling, bodiless snake and making her shiver involuntarily. Was it a protest from the dead? Maybe she would never be able to get the answers she had been looking for. But she also knew that if she didn't try, she could never put the past behind her to rejoin the land of the living.

Cara was startled by a hand on her shoulder. She turned to find the tall, suited cemetery representative who was overseeing the exhumation. "Would you like to head into the office? I can take over from here. I'll make sure your family is properly handled and documented for the autopsy."

Cara nodded. She was relieved not to have to watch the rest of the process. Instead, she scuttled away from the gaping black holes in the ground and headed toward the beige administrative building near the cemetery entrance where she would plan her next move. She wanted to keep herself busy while she waited for results. She would start with visiting the gang that Michael Lovansky had belonged to.

Almost all the gang members were non-Native, but their leader had inserted himself into Chugach, an outlying Native village not far from Point Mettier, by marrying an elder's daughter. In Chugach Village—a town too small to have its own police force and too remote for Alaska State Troopers to keep an eye on—it would be difficult to extract answers from Lovansky's cohorts. But Cara had to try, and the only way to get to Chugach was to go through Point Mettier.

It was time to take a trip back to the city under one roof.

CHAPTER TWO

ELLIE

ELLIE WRIGHT PUFFED LAZY SMOKE RINGS INTO THE AIR AND patted her red bun wig while considering her poker hand at what she called her weekly "board meeting" at the Salty Pub. She was the owner of the Cozy Condo Inn, really a floor of small apartments in the building that was home to all 205 residents of Point Mettier. There were no guests staying at the Cozy Condo at the moment. Beyond September, few tourists came to visit an ice-boxed city in Alaska with no ski slopes or dogsledding tours, which could only be reached via a one-way tunnel through a mountain.

In high season, people flocked to the pier by the busload, boarding or exiting the cruise ships like gaggles of squawking geese. Motorboats lined up to launch off the slips for fishing or whale watching. Most of the people blew in and out the same day, but a good number of hikers and tree huggers booked overnight rooms. The temporary help who only came for the season also made for good business for Ellie's fourteenth-floor rooms. Ellie charged the tourists an arm and a leg, because, well, why not? But she gave the temporary help—the Summer People, as the kids liked to call them—a discount because they were just there trying to make a living, and their months-long stays didn't include daily maid service. Ellie could take in all of her year's earnings in the four months of high season. Not bad for a woman in her sixties who had grown up in the backwoods of Arkansas on the edge of poverty and had dropped out of high school not knowing diddly from squat.

But now, being February, Point Mettier was a bleak ghost town with temperatures cold enough to freeze a brass monkey. Most of the businesses along the pier were shuttered, except, of course, the Salty Pub, which was a goddamned necessity, and sometimes the petite Chinese lady, Mrs. Lin, kept Star Asian Food open, but most days, Mrs. Lin ran a take-out operation from her unit in the Davidson Condos, or the Dave-Co as it was known.

There were, at present, only eight people in the bar—the four of them playing poker, the tattooed bartender, and the two regular sots who spent most of their days drinking away the ghosts of their past. The eighth was the resident entertainer, Mariko Ishida, who, despite the lack of tourists and customers, was strutting her stuff on the little raised stage. Mariko was in her fifties and thought she was an Asian Madonna or something, shaking her little booty in a sparkly red dress that was looking a bit faded and waving a feather boa around. She wore a Barbarella-styled black wig—one of many in her repertoire. There were no hair salons in the Dave-Co, so it was a matter of practicality. She was singing some jazzy tune in Japanese and the only part that Ellie caught was an occasional "Woo-woo!" Nobody paid her much mind, but Ellie couldn't imagine the bar without her.

Ellie looked down at her cards. Two pair. A queen of hearts, a queen of spades, a pair of threes, and a throwaway. "Raise," she said, adding two chips to the pot.

Ellie knew people found it strange that anyone would want to live in a town that was packed into a single building, but there were some definite advantages to having everything an elevator ride away. It meant you didn't have to bundle up in your parkas, your scarves, your mittens, and your woolly hats, then break your back shoveling a walkway before driving through a goddamned snowstorm to some seedy corner store just to get a pack of ciggies. Ellie could just mosey on down in her housecoat and slippers to Chuck Marino's general store on the first floor. The post office, the police station, and church were also on the ground level. School for the kiddies was through a tunnel. Ellie would take this life over sitting in traffic in a smog-filled hellhole like Los Angeles or New York any day.

"Could you maybe not wave that thing so close to my face?" Chief Sipley asked, referring to Ellie's Marlboro that she kept dipping into the ashtray, before he sourly added "Fold" and put his cards down. There were only two police officers in town, Sipley and his young, pasty-white underling, J.B. Barkowski, who had come from some hinterland in Montana. J.B. was still a newbie, having just arrived a year ago, so he hadn't yet become a trusted member of the inner circle.

Officially, Point Mettier had a mayor, Sam Fossbender, who mostly kept to his office and acted like a building manager, making sure the plumbing worked and things were up to code. But he had been out of town visiting his sick mother in Idaho for a few months now, and nobody had really missed him. As far as Ellie was concerned, the people who *really* ran the town were all there at the bar, sitting at the table with her playing a round of five-card draw. There was Chief Sipley, of course. A big, burly man. He always put on a jolly face, but deep down, he was a calculating, conniving son of a bitch. Ellie knew she could always count on him to do what was necessary to keep the town safe whether it was legal or not.

Then there was Chuck Marino, the aforementioned owner of the general store. On first glance, Chuck looked like a simple, soft-spoken Black man with a grizzled beard who tended to keep to himself. But Ellie knew that there was much more behind the "quiet man" demeanor. He was, in fact, *Dr.* Marino, with a PhD in psychology. He was retired from both the army and being a practicing doc, but on Tuesday nights, he still counseled a group of battered women in the church space on the ground floor.

Chuck tossed in his two chips, as did Jim.

Jim Arreak was the toll booth operator; the gatekeeper, you could say. He was an Alaska Native whose main role in the town was keeping a list of all the people who shouldn't be admitted. The secret that outsiders didn't know about Point Mettier was that it was a place where women could hide from their exes. Ellie didn't feel a need to be one of Chuck Marino's counseled women, but she certainly preferred to have an alligator pit between her and her ex. If Jim suspected anyone might be coming to town to kick up some trouble, he'd make up some B.S. about the tunnel shutting down for maintenance, or he'd write down their license plate, ring Chief Sipley, and give him a heads-up.

Since Ellie was always on the lookout for her ex-husband, she also prided herself on being an unofficial neighborhood watcher who monitored the comings and goings of the Dave-Co through the big glass window of her check-in lobby on the ninth floor. The "whale watching" binoculars she always kept at her side weren't really for whale watching. Some might think of her as a gossip queen or the town snitch, but that was hogwash because Ellie only *gathered* info, never spilled. She knew everybody in Point Mettier had secrets to keep and she wasn't one to judge because she had her own skeletons that were better left in the closet. She always had the best interests of the townsfolk in mind whether they appreciated it or not.

Chief Sipley's phone jingled the theme to *The Good, the Bad and the Ugly*. He got up to answer, taking his mug over to the bartender for a refill. He was technically on duty since J.B. was still recovering from his recent injuries, and Ellie knew from the ringtone that it was a forwarded call from the station. It was probably about one of the elevators getting stuck again or maybe about the Samoan family's dog crapping in the sixth-floor hallway.

Chuck Marino splayed his cards out. A pair of aces. A good hand, but not enough to beat Ellie's, which she laid down, ready to cash in. Now it was just Jim, who was a hard son of a bitch to read because he always had that calm, steady look on his face as if he were some kind of Buddha, or maybe *shaman* was the right word, given that Jim was Indigenous. He finally flashed a toothy smile, showing his full house of three sevens and a pair of jacks before gleefully raking in his chips.

Before Ellie could say "son of a Red Wattle Hog–sucking bitch," Chief called to her, pointing at his phone with a stone-cold-sober expression. "Ellie, you gotta take this," he said, and he didn't add some kind of joke like "It's the debt collectors" or "Some guy says he's got a Tinder date with you," which was usually Sipley's style, so Ellie knew it must be something serious as hell. Even Chuck and Jim looked up in anticipation.

The immediate thought running through Ellie's mind was that it had something to do with her tax-fudging or maybe her ex catching up with her. She took the phone, preparing to do battle.

"Hello?" she spoke into Sipley's cell.

"We've been trying to reach you," the characterless voice on the other end said. Ellie didn't have a cell phone. She had a regular land-line where guests could leave a voice message that she could screen to decide whether she wanted to get back to them. Anyone else who would want to talk to her knew where to find her in person. "We believe Timothy Christopher MacCullum is your son?"

Ellie's pulse started pounding. MacCullum had been her married name, and Timmy was indeed her only son. But the last time she had laid eyes on him was six years ago. "Yes," she finally answered. "What has he gone and done now?"

"I'm so sorry to tell you this, but he was found dead in his apartment early this morning."

CHAPTER THREE

CARA

BEFORE MAKING HER WAY TO POINT METTIER, CARA MADE A pit stop to visit her unofficial tech helper, Angelo Fernandez. He owned a nondescript computer shop in a strip mall off Airport Road. The bubbly tech expert offered up a mason jar full of colored candies without taking his eyes off his blue light–reflecting monitor. "Jelly bean?"

"I'm good," Cara responded.

Angelo had the ability to make her smile with his always-friendly disposition. He had been born in the Philippines, landing in Alaska when his father took a job with a shipping company and moved the family from the tropics to the Arctic. Bright in both intelligence and personality, Angelo had found himself on the wrong side of the law when he used his computer hacking skills to add a couple of zeros to his bank account. It was all to pay for his father's medical expenses, he claimed, and in a plea bargain, he turned from black hat to white hat, doing jobs for the government. Cara had found that his gray-area methods were especially useful right now, since she wasn't officially working for Anchorage PD anymore. She found Angelo to be game as long as she was willing to fork over his usual rates.

"Remember those photos we found in Michael Lovansky's phone?"

"Oh yeah, the diced-up gang member with the voyeur pictures? Creepy." Angelo shivered at the thought.

"Is there a way to look up those photos on the Internet to try to identify them?"

"Oh, you mean a reverse image search? Of course. The free ones out there give results that are *meh*, but I have one that uses an advanced facial recognition algorithm."

The technology out there that could readily scour private information never ceased to amaze and alarm Cara.

"How soon do you need these?"

"Take your time. I'm headed back to Point Mettier, so I probably won't be back for a couple of days."

"Roger that."

THERE WAS AN ephemeral sense of déjà vu for Cara as she motored up Sanders Glacier Road in her Suburban toward the cragged tunnel leading to Point Mettier. She pulled up to the tollbooth. Jim Arreak slid the window open by a slice and peeked out, his face half buried by the bomber hat and fur-collared jacket he was wearing to combat the cold.

"Back so soon?" he asked. "Don't tell me there's been another murder." It had only been a few months since Cara had been there last, pretending that she had been sent by Anchorage PD.

"No, Jim. I'm here on a personal matter."

Jim looked at her and winked. "Got ya. J.B.'s on the mend. I hear he's up and about and getting used to those missing digits." Officer Barkowski had unofficially partnered with her when she was holed up there by an avalanche and started investigating the case of the dismembered body. He had lost two of his toes to frostbite after lying in the damp underground tunnels, incapacitated by a gunshot wound.

Cara was about to protest Jim's jabbing but decided to let it slide. After all, she would be lying if she said she wasn't interested in seeing J.B. Working in close proximity with him had done a number on her. After the sudden tragedy in her life, meeting him was like learning how to feel again after a long, numbing shot of novocaine. Cara thought she was finally ready to move on from Aaron, but now it seemed as though her deceased husband was calling her back from the grave by suddenly materializing on a stranger's cell phone.

"There aren't going to be any avalanches while I'm here, are there?" Cara asked Jim.

"Can't make any promises."

"Well, I packed a bag this time, just in case."

Jim nodded and gave her another wink. "Oh, you don't have to explain your sleepovers to me, Detective. That'll be thirteen dollars."

Cara's face grew red as she paid the toll, pulled up to the striped arm gate, and waited for the light to turn green.

If there was one thing she didn't miss about Point Mettier, it was the tunnels—the tunnel to get in, the pedestrian tunnel that led to the pier, the tunnel to the school, and the maze of tunnels beneath the city that had been built when it was a military base. It didn't help that Cara had developed symptoms of claustrophobia after losing Aaron and Dylan. It was like simultaneously experiencing vertigo and a certainty that she was going to die, hampering her ability to breathe. She was making progress on that front, she told herself. She had been seeing a therapist in Anchorage who had said that facing her fears head-on would help lessen her symptoms. But to be on the safe side, Cara had refilled her Xanax prescription before coming. She took a deep breath before delving into the two and a half miles of darkness through the mountain. To her dismay, she still felt her heart palpitate and her thoughts going to morbid visions of entering a tomb that she might not be able to leave.

Once on the other side, she was able to breathe normally again and passed a pier full of winterized boats and a sparse selection of hibernating shops and restaurants. At the end of the road, the Davidson Condos rose up, towering above the shipping warehouses like a Rhodian statue against a majestic mountain.

She parked and entered the lobby, then headed toward the twin elevators, but she paused when she came to Chuck Marino's general store, where the tall Black shopkeeper was at his usual seat, poring over the newspaper, the heads of mounted hunting game peering over his shoulder.

"Hello, Chuck." She waved.

Chuck looked up and stroked his salt-and-pepper beard. "Ah, my best customer," he said with a smile, referring to the fact that when Cara was trapped in Point Mettier last November, she had practically cleaned out his stock of touristy clothing, food, and sundries.

She showed him her duffel bag. "Maybe not so much this time."

"J.B. will be glad to see you," he said.

"I was actually going to check into a room with Ellie." Cara's face once again flushed.

"Okay," Chuck said, trying to subvert his tone of skepticism. "Ellie's gone to Anchorage but should be back soon. Her son died and she had to go ID the body."

Cara started at the news. "Oh, that's . . . I'm sorry to hear. I didn't know she had a son."

"Nobody knew."

Everyone in this town had secrets.

"I can check you in, if you want. She left me in charge."

"That's all right. I'll go see J.B. first and drop into the Cozy Condo later when she's back."

"Whatever suits you." With that, Chuck ruffled his newspaper and went back to reading. It was hard to believe this quiet, unassuming man had served in Afghanistan.

Cara took the rickety elevator up to J.B.'s floor. She had thought about calling him first, but given the reason for the visit she decided it was best to meet in person. She rapped at the door, feeling her pulse pounding despite willing herself to appear calm and collected.

She heard a hobbling toward the door and then J.B. answered. His hair was a scruffy mess, but he was still alarmingly handsome to Cara with his soft green eyes and square jawline. He leaned on a cane and looked at her with clear surprise.

"I know I should have called first, but . . ." She was stumbling for an explanation. Before she could think of what to say, he pulled her in and planted a kiss that left her feeling like putty. Then he smiled in a captivating ear-to-ear grin.

"Took you long enough," he said. Then he looked at her duffel bag. "Are you planning to stay a while?"

With all the heat generated from the innuendo and friendly teasing she had received since arriving at Point Mettier, Cara had to peel off her parka. "I came to see you, of course, but there's another reason I'm here."

"Not another murder, I hope."

"No. I mean, I'm not sure, but it has to do with Aaron and Dylan."

"Oh?" His brows raised and his smile disappeared.

She needed a breath. "Do you have any of that amazing coffee?"

J.B. HAD A siphon brewer that looked as if it had come from a nineteenth-century science catalog with its clear glass chambers and a Bunsen burner–like heating element. He hobbled over to his contraption and began the tinkering process. She already knew he had all but recovered from his bullet wound and that he was going to be fitted with prosthetic toes, so he was confident he would soon be back to one hundred percent.

While he made the coffee, Cara launched into what she had discovered—something she had delayed telling J.B. until now, even though she had visited him a number of times at the hospital, partly because she didn't want to stress him any further while he was on the road to recovery . . . and partly because she didn't know how the new information would affect their burgeoning relationship. Would it feel as if she were still obsessed with her dead husband and unable to move on?

But now she had to come clean, and explained to J.B. that she had found a set of photos on Michael Lovansky's phone that seemed unrelated to him or his gang, one of which showed Cara, Aaron, and Dylan on the day they had left for the Talkeetna wilderness, two days before their disappearance.

"My god!" was J.B.'s response. "Do you think he had anything to do with their deaths?"

"I'm having an autopsy done on their bodies to see if the medical examiner can determine a cause of death or whether there was any criminality."

J.B.'s jaw dropped. She could see the million thoughts running through his head and went to help him carry the mugs over to the coffee table.

"Do you have the photos with you?" he finally asked once they were seated. Angelo had transferred the photos from Michael's phone over to hers, so she showed them now to J.B. He lingered on the shot of Cara with her family, studying it intently—Aaron, the man who had been her husband, and Dylan, the child they had raised together. Cara only realized now that this was the first glimpse J.B. had had of either. It felt somehow wrong to be sharing a part of her intimate past in this context of possible murder.

J.B. finally moved on to the other one-off pics from Lovansky's phone—a heavyset man with a gray beard, a woman possibly in her fifties in a coffee shop reading a book, a younger man chaining a bicycle to a rack, a Native woman in her twenties . . . all of them engaged in everyday acts with no hint that they were aware they were being photographed. "Who are these other people?"

"I don't know, but I think it's an active list of some kind."

"Did you say *active* list?"

Cara pointed to a photo of a man in his thirties with a sandy-colored goatee leaving an apartment complex. "This one appeared on Lovansky's phone after he was dead."

"You're shitting me."

"I would wager that he's not the only one with this set of photos."

"Couldn't you trace who sent them?"

"My tech guy couldn't find out where the photo came from. It was hidden behind too many firewalls. I plan to go back to Chugach Village to see if I can suss out any info from one of Lovansky's pals."

J.B.'s countenance grew dark and, as Cara had predicted, he tried to dissuade her. "I don't think that's a good idea. They're not exactly going to put out the welcome mat and cooperate." That was an understatement given that Cara and J.B. were responsible for the death, wounding, or sentencing of every member of the gang they had encountered.

"I'll take my chances." She knew it would be difficult, but she needed to find out more.

"I'll go with you," J.B. said.

"With your foot—"

"It's just a limp. Otherwise I'm fine," he interrupted. J.B. was always trying to be the white knight, even now as he was trying to find his balance—physically, and in their relationship.

"If I counted correctly, with two dead and two still in jail, there should be only three thugs left and all of them maimed." She was referring to the shootout that Cara and J.B. had had with Lovansky's gang.

"I should go with you all the same."

"I'll ask Chief Sipley to come with me," Cara compromised.

J.B. still seemed unconvinced. "Let's sit on it for a night, can we?"

Cara nodded. "I wasn't planning to head over there until I had most of the daylight ahead of me anyway. Hence . . ." She lifted her duffel bag. "I'm checking in with Ellie once she gets back from Anchorage."

"Seriously?" He looked around the room. "I mean, I would have cleaned up if I knew you were coming, but there's no reason to check in with Ellie." He hesitated, still testing the limits of their relationship. "You can have the bed. I'll sleep on the sofa."

"N-no," Cara stuttered. "I don't want you to have to sleep on the sofa in your condition." J.B. seemed to have lost some weight, contributing to a look of frailty.

She wasn't exactly sure if she'd meant it as an invitation, but he moved in closer on the sofa and pulled her head toward him for a lingering kiss. All her caution about J.B.'s healing wounds was tossed aside, and Cara decided she would stay.

IN THE MORNING, Cara looked out the picture window of J.B.'s bedroom. The sun in winter stayed low, a hazy yellow blip over the horizon. In Point Mettier, it seemed to be perpetually hidden by mountains. Although it was past nine in the morning, the sky had not yet been lit beyond a weakish light, and she could only see the shadows of sailless masts in the harbor pointed toward the sky. Cara had been in J.B.'s apartment before, but this was the first time she had been in his bedroom. She perused the framed photos lining the sill, recognizing J.B.'s family members from a photo in the living room—his parents in Montana and his sister, Stacy, who now lived in Europe. The photo that stood out for Cara showed J.B. with his arm around a woman who Cara did not recognize. She had gently waved hair that framed a porcelain face and mesmerizing almond eyes.

"Oh, that," J.B. said, stepping out of the bathroom and toweling off his hair. Cara felt as if she had been caught in an illicit act as he crossed to take the photo from her and placed it face down. He had told her about the girlfriend he had planned to propose to before he caught her cheating with his station partner. "I should have gotten rid of this photo a long time ago," he said.

"Oh, I—sorry, I was just, um, looking," she stammered. "I didn't mean . . ."

"It's all right."

"You know, I should get changed so I can pop by Ellie's to express my condolences," Cara said, trying to thread her way out of an awkward conversation by switching subjects.

"Okay, I'll make coffee."

CARA AND ELLIE hadn't exactly been the best of friends. In fact, they were more like antagonists, but in the end, they had found a degree of mutual respect, and Cara could empathize with the grief of losing a son—a shockingly unfair and unnatural digression from the order of life.

She rode the elevator two stories to Ellie's check-in lobby. A CLOSED sign hung on the Cozy Condo Inn door, but she remembered that J.B. had said Ellie's residence was one door down. On the other side of that door, a dog responded to her knock by barking and yipping as if it had just discovered it was standing on a hot bed of coals. Ellie answered the door, and a little terrier bounded onto Cara's legs still barking.

"Down, Vlad!" Ellie said. Her eyes were puffy, and she didn't have her usual red wig on. Her hair was instead gray and thinning. But she still managed to exclaim, "Well, look what the cat dragged in! Are you here to arrest somebody? I hope it's not me."

Cara smiled. "No, I heard about your son and wanted to say how sorry I am."

"You didn't drive all the way over here for that, did you?"

"No," Cara confessed. "I just heard about it a couple of hours ago. I'm in town for something else."

"Come in," Ellie said, then chided, "Vlad, get off of her! We need to sit down to get Vlad to shut up."

They sat down, and Vlad did settle. Cara noted the style of decor that was not too different from the rooms Ellie rented out, with the same heavy drapery, dark wood, and furniture covered in doilies, except here, there was also an impressive display of guns on the wall and any pretense of "no smoking" was gone, evidenced by the multiple ashtrays full of spent cigarettes. In fact, Ellie was currently lifting one to her lips.

"Are you staying the night?" Ellie asked. "Need a room?"

"I, uh . . . I'm staying with J.B."

"Oh," Ellie said in a knowing tone that was akin to Jim's and Chuck's. "You two lovebirds are really hitting it off, aren't you?"

Cara sighed and determined to change the subject by noting the photo album that was splayed on the coffee table next to the ashtray. "Are those of your son?"

Ellie nodded. "Dug it up just now," she said. "We weren't exactly on speaking terms at the end." She was trying not to choke up.

"I'm so sorry. May I?" Cara asked.

"Go ahead." Ellie lifted the album and put it in Cara's lap.

Cara flipped through the pages. A young boy with sad eyes held on to his tricycle. "Dylan had a tricycle just like that, but it was blue. He loved that tricycle. Even gave it a name. Mr. Dodo. Don't know where he came up with it." She smiled in recollection then grew silent. They were two mothers now, tied together by loss.

There were pictures of the same boy in various school group photos. A birthday party. Around a campfire. Peeking from behind a tree. "Timmy looked happy here." Ellie pointed at one photo where the boy smiled beside a little friend. She sniffled as if she needed that glimmer of better times.

Cara continued looking through the photos, painfully reminded of her own tear-soaked album stuffed in a box in a storage unit because it had become unbearable. She froze as they got to a page of adult Timothy photos. "Is that . . ." She pointed to a photo where he sat looking distractedly out a window.

"Timmy? Yeah, that's the last time I saw him."

Cara pulled out her phone and found the last photo from Michael Lovansky's cell phone, of the man with the sandy-colored goatee.

Ellie turned to look at Cara with a combination of bewilderment and recrimination. "Tell me what in the bottomless pit of purgatory you are doing with a photo of Timmy?"

CHAPTER FOUR

CARA

KAI PETERSON WAS A TRANSPLANT FROM CALIFORNIA—A surfer turned Sea-Doo and snowmobile tour operator. His haze-filled room smelled of cannabis, and his bong sat prominently on the coffee table.

He had opened the door for her and Ellie in his perennial attire of flip-flops and board shorts and asked, "Who are you?" Cara was taken aback that he didn't remember her; just a few months ago, when she and J.B. had rented snowmobiles from him, he had called her pretty. But then he narrowed his eyes. "Oh, wait a minute. Don't tell me." He put a hand pensively to his forehead before looking up again and smiled in delayed realization. "You're that detective lady, right?"

"Cara Kennedy," she reminded him.

"That's right." He laughed, embarrassed. "Can't remember things like I used to since my injury."

Kai's days of pro surfing had ended when he was trying to ride a twenty-foot curler on the North Shore of Oahu, hit a reef, and suffered a debilitating concussion. Despite being in his forties, he still had longish blond hair and a California beach accent.

"We need a couple of snow machines," Ellie said, using the Alaskan vernacular. Ellie had insisted on coming with her to Chugach Village. At first Cara had refused, but J.B. convinced her it was a good idea. She thought Ellie's questionable past made her untrustworthy—she had once been a wanted criminal. But J.B. thought that would be an asset when dealing with the thugs in Chugach, and she was definitely spry for her age. He had witnessed her tackle a man in the parking lot—a guest who had tried to run off with something from the condo inn, J.B. couldn't remember what exactly. A piece of decor, maybe a carved wooden moose ornament. On top of that, Ellie regularly practiced shooting at her makeshift target range out in the woods, so there was no doubt that she was a crack shot. In the end, Cara begrudgingly assented to the innkeeper as a tagalong but didn't tell J.B. that she was forgoing having Chief Sipley with them as well.

When Ellie got over the shock of seeing Timothy's photo on Cara's phone, she figured the gang had dealt him some bad drugs and that's how he had died. But Cara didn't see why they would take a picture of someone they were dealing drugs to or what that had to do with Aaron.

"Are you sure your husband wasn't doing drugs too? The photos could be a sort of client list," Ellie had offered.

The thought had never occurred to Cara. It seemed doubtful. Regardless, both Cara and Ellie agreed that they needed answers.

Since they had both previously rented snowmobiles from Kai, they just needed to sign the disclaimers and rental agreements. Then he walked them out to the warehouse where the machines were stored, fitted them with helmets, and handed them the keys. Cara was impressed with the way Ellie, wearing a jacket over her heart-patterned sweater, climbed onto her snowmobile with ease and snapped the helmet over her bun wig. Her eyes practically lit up with the purr of the motor.

Ellie had decided to bring an arsenal of weapons. "We're not going there to shoot up the place," Cara warned, despite conceding that it wasn't going to be easy to get the men at Chugach Village to talk.

It was an hour and a half ride out to the village where the gang had set up camp.

Their den was distinguished by being the largest structure in the townlet—a two-story wooden house that loomed at the top of a hill, with a collection of menacing animal skulls proudly on display on its exterior facade. She wasn't sure who was now in charge since their previous leader, Wolf, had been shot dead by her own hand, but Cara suspected it was his brother, Victor, who had an uncanny glare that could make her skin crawl with just a gaze. But with most of the gang out of commission, there couldn't be more than a few men left in Chugach.

Still, Cara believed there must be someone higher up in the chain. "There's someone on the outside," Cara told Ellie. "Someone who feeds them information through a fax machine." She knew this because when she and J.B. previously clashed with Wolf's men, she had discovered fax messages warning the gang in advance. The key was to find out who was sending these messages and how they'd known that Cara and J.B. were coming.

———

CARA AND ELLIE parked their snowmobiles on the edge of the town, and Cara led them toward the house on the hill. She was armed with her Glock in her belt, while Ellie gripped her AK-47 as if she were part of a military op in a video game.

"So . . . we going to shoot first and ask questions later?" Ellie asked.

"No, we're asking questions first, but shooting later is a possible option." Cara had planned to threaten to file a report with the DEA to investigate their drug dealing unless they cooperated with her questioning. She knew where they kept their drug stash and had been planning to file a report anyway before she discovered the cell phone photos. But if the FBI or DEA got involved now, she would never be able to question them about their connection to Aaron and Dylan.

"You've gotta be shitting me," Ellie huffed. "Even I wouldn't answer the door if I saw people come storming up to my house with guns."

"Well, maybe you should put your gun away then—" Cara paused when she spotted something out on the water, beyond the ridge of the house, glinting in the bay. It was a ship—a freighter maybe a hundred and fifty feet long. Was it just passing through or was it transporting something to Chugach Village?

Before she could come up with a plan of advance, the snow in front of them exploded with an atmospheric river of bullets.

"Get down!" Cara dropped into the cold snowpack.

"Jesus!" Ellie yelled, also flattening herself. "Did you give them a call ahead of time? Let them know we were dropping in?"

"Of course not," Cara said through gritted her teeth. "They must have spotted us coming up the hill."

"I thought you said there were only three wounded men," Ellie rasped.

From the number of bullets crossing from various directions, there were definitely more than three gun barrels at the windows. Had the ship in the bay brought reinforcements?

"We're two dead ducks," Ellie said. "We should have charged in. Shoot first, ask questions later, like I said."

"That can be your epitaph," Cara quipped, but her voice was shaky, because she was also beginning to believe that perhaps she had made a grave mistake. Maybe it hadn't been the best idea to confront people whose family member she had just killed. But there weren't any other obvious leads to pursue, and she was desperate.

She covered her head with her hands as the bullets riddled the ground around her, none of them hitting their mark, as if the shooters were actually trying to avoid hitting them.

The barrage finally let up, and a door to the lodge creaked open. A dark-haired man emerged with one arm cradling an AK-47. It was Victor Volkov. His arm seemed to have fully recovered from the graze that J.B. had given him. His dark eyes and demeanor were as unsettling as she remembered. Cara stood up because she knew that if he meant to kill her, she would have been dead by now.

"Detective Kennedy," he said. "To what do I owe the pleasure of seeing you and . . ." He looked toward Ellie. ". . . your mother?"

"I'm the motherfucker who's going to avenge my son's death," Ellie said getting up from the snow and engaging her semiautomatic for emphasis.

"I just want to talk," Cara said.

"Talk? Given that last time you were intent on shooting off our appendages, I have little reason not to kill you on the spot . . . except the thought of a slow, torturous death."

Behind Victor, inside the house, Cara could see what looked like a shipment of boxes. One was sloppily opened, revealing bags of powder inside, possibly cocaine, and small bottles of what looked like the liquid form of fentanyl, the "it" drug of the decade.

Perhaps that was what the ship in the harbor had brought. Alaska was a high-value market for drugs, far greater than the lower forty-eight. Like most other goods, drugs were more expensive per kilo in Alaska's geographically isolated location. Even Mexico's Sinaloa Cartel had traffickers in Alaska.

"Look, I could have easily led the feds or the DEA up here and shut down that little operation you've got going on," Cara began, nodding toward the boxes. "But I don't have any interest in that because all I want is answers to why Michael Lovansky had photos of my husband and Ellie's son on his phone."

"Sorry, but I don't know who the fuck your family members are."

"Aaron Kennedy and Timothy Wright."

"Timothy MacCullum," Ellie corrected.

Cara thought she saw Victor's brow rise.

"And if you didn't know already, they're both dead," Cara added.

"Is that so? Thoughts and prayers."

"If you can just throw us a bone, it'll keep us from filing a report for a proper homicide investigation." Since they didn't as yet have any evidence of a homicide, Cara had to use a bluff.

At this point, Ellie aimed her gun straight at Victor. "Listen, sonny, I just lost my only child, and I'm in my golden years, so I think you've got a lot more to lose than I do, and I promise you I will take you down to the flames of hell with me unless you start fessin' up. Why did that prick have photos of our family members?"

Victor snickered in a way that sent shivers up Cara's spine.

"How the shit should I know what Mick did for kicks? Maybe he wanted to diddle them."

Cara's blood boiled. "Who do you work for? Who's keeping you on your best behavior here and telling you not to shoot us?"

"Maybe we just want to rough you up a little before we kill you," Victor sneered.

"Maybe without Wolf in charge, there's no one to call the shots."

"My brother was never in charge." Victor looked almost insulted. Cara thought she had pushed the right buttons, but he checked himself before revealing anything useful. He smiled again in that creepy way that didn't express happiness. "Wolf might've thought he was boss, but I was always in charge. Since we were young, I let him think he was in control, but this"—he pointed to his head—"is why I'm still alive and my brother's dead. You see, I'm my own free agent." He paused for a moment and his creepy grin reemerged. "Now I've answered your questions, so I get to ask one. Which cheek do you prefer?"

Cara looked at him confused.

"Shari, we have a visitor," Victor yelled, and a Native woman, whom Cara recognized to be Wolf's wife, now widow, emerged. She looked at Cara and her eyes turned to fire; she stepped out, took a running charge, and slapped Cara hard on the face. Cara hadn't answered Victor's question, but Shari hit her left cheek, then spat on her for good measure.

"Lucky for you I'm not allowed to kill you," Shari said before turning and going back inside.

Unseen men inside the house cackled with laughter. Even Ellie was trying to keep herself from grinning at the sight of Cara being slapped.

"You're free to go now," Victor said. "But you should probably watch your back, because when you least expect it . . ." He made a shooting gesture with his fingers. "Pow!"

Cara felt the sting on her cheek and seethed. She considered her options and decided it was futile to continue here. Reluctantly, she headed back toward the snowmobiles with laughter from Victor's men echoing behind her.

"Well, that went well," Ellie said sarcastically, following after her.

CHAPTER FIVE

ELLIE

ELLIE WAS DISAPPOINTED—ACTUALLY, *VEXED AS ALL HELL*—
with their little village venture. There had clearly been more than
three peg-legged men, unlike the story Cara had sold her and the
end-all of it was that the gang spilled nothing useful. Maybe next
time she would take Chief Sipley or Chuck Marino with her. But it'd
have to wait, because Ellie needed to get back to Anchorage to make
arrangements for Timmy's funeral and clean out his apartment.

Luckily, the roads were plowed and fit for driving, so Ellie packed
her clothes and brought her rifle, Woodie, along with her in her Jeep.
Ellie was proud of her collection of guns, which she had hanging on
her wall, including the AR-15–style Smith & Wesson rifle that she called
Scarface, and Woodie, her Tikka Roughtech WSM. She kept Bessie,
her Glock subcompact pistol, beneath the desk of her check-in counter.

Ellie didn't consider herself one of those yahoo gun crazies who thinks every numb nut should have assault rifles. She was a proud card-carrying member of the NRA, but she felt only people who knew how to handle guns and weren't hormonal or unhinged should be allowed to have one.

She assumed she'd have to spend a few days, maybe even a week in Anchorage sorting things out, so she left her terrier, Vlad, with Jim Arreak. Jim's German shepherd had just kicked the bucket, so he could use the company anyway. Besides, Jim was one of the few people Vlad didn't raise a conniption at every time he saw him.

The coroner's office had given Ellie the address of Timmy's apartment, and she figured she would stay there while she cleaned out his things. She received the key to the unit from the landlady, an old biddy named Felicia, who had discovered his body. "A shame what happened. OD, wasn't it?" the woman said. "Pretty common around here. I think I've even seen his dealers." Then she demanded a half month's rent before she handed Ellie the key. "Make sure you get all of his stuff out by the fifteenth."

IT WAS A real slum of an apartment building, with paint peeling off its flesh-colored exterior. Outside, a man who was clearly doped up on something was sitting on the ground mumbling to himself. The tiny studio apartment was maybe three hundred square feet, not even half the size of the suites Ellie rented out at Point Mettier. It had a hobbit-sized kitchen area, worn-out carpet, yellowed popcorn ceilings, and a musty smell. Timmy didn't seem to have much, but seeing his clothes littered on the floor and on the back of the chair, it looked as though he might waltz back in at any moment. That hit Ellie hard. She took one of his sweaters and put it up to her face. It smelled of weed and sweat like a grown-up Timmy, not the talcum-powder, sweet-baby Timmy she preferred to remember. But still, it was Timmy.

The last time they saw each other was six years ago at some yuppified diner in Anchorage where a pimple-faced waiter stopped by every ten minutes asking if they needed anything. Timmy had looked pale and thin and wolfed his food down. He started a jittery leg bounce before he launched into his usual song and dance about wanting to know how the "old lady" was and about how he was always thinking of her. But eventually, he got around to what he was really there for, which was to ask for some dough. Ellie said no, of course, but then he went on about wanting to turn his life around mixed in with some bellyaching about the cost of rent and *the man* trying to stomp him down, until Ellie finally gave him what he wanted. She supposed there was some part of her that knew this was how it would play out; she had, after all, gone to the bank to withdraw some cash before meeting him. Then he had disappeared, never to be seen again until he showed up deader than a doornail.

Now Ellie sat down on his bed and had a good cry, getting all of Timmy's clothes damp. "I'm so sorry," she bawled, not knowing whether he could hear her from the hereafter. Then she braved the cold for a good long smoke out the window to contemplate the ways she had done him wrong. Despite their treacherous relationship, she loved her son, and she knew she had failed him since the day he was born.

BY THE TIME Timmy turned five, he would look up at her with those sad doe eyes, as if he had the weight of the world on his shoulders every time they left him alone to go on a job.

35

"Now you be a good boy," Ellie had said to him when home was a double-wide in the armpit of Texas, otherwise known as Port Arthur. "Mommy and Daddy have to go to work now, but we'll be back before you know it."

"If you move from that sofa, I'll whip your hide off," Shane added. That was Shane for you—never having the good sense that God gave a rock.

"Now why'd you have to go and say that? You know he soiled his pants and ruined the sofa cushions last time because of your goddamn threats," Ellie huffed. Then she turned back to Timmy. "You can go to the bathroom when you have to, sweetie." But there was already fear stabbed into his soft blue eyes as he sat on the sofa in front of the TV. It made her feel guilty as hell.

"Time to go," Shane said, ignoring her. He already had his ski cap and sunglasses on and was restlessly shaking his keys at her.

They used to hit the banks around opening or closing time when fewer people were milling about. Ellie always cased the joint a few days earlier, checking to see if there were any guards on duty, if there were metal detectors, and where the cameras were. Then Shane would go in with a printed note that read, This is a bank robbery! I have a gun, so be quiet and no one gets hurt! Hand me all your 20s, 50s & 100s! Be fast & no alarms!!

Meanwhile, Ellie would wait outside in the getaway car they had rented with fake IDs. That was back in the day when driver's licenses didn't have newfangled security features. They made sure to ditch the rental before they got back home. They used two-way radios so that Ellie could keep tabs on what was going on inside, and she always carried her rifle, Bulldog, the precursor to Woodie, with her, in case something went sideways. Every few months, they moved to a different town.

One of Ellie's rules when they first started the operation was that no one got killed. "We can't be leaving a trail of corpses, 'cause someday that's gonna catch up with us, if not here, then in the flames of eternal damnation," she had told Shane.

"Well, that's up to you then," he had responded. "If you don't want anyone meeting their maker on your watch, then you'd better damn well learn how to shoot to maim."

So Ellie spent earnest hours learning how to be a crack shot, whether it was at the shooting gallery or in the woods to practice on moving targets—birds, squirrels, cottontail rabbits, and an occasional rattlesnake. She got so good at it, she could have shot the pip off a pair of dice if she had to. But at the end of the day, Ellie never had much cause to actually use Bulldog. There were times when she had to back up Shane, wave her rifle around a bit, and make some threats, but people were pretty yellow when it came down to it and hit the ground like they were told to. She and Shane were in and out before the cops arrived.

They were living in high cotton for a while, but when Timmy came along, priorities started changing. In the beginning, Timmy used to ride with them. He sat strapped in the back seat and sometimes Ellie breastfed him in the car while Shane was holding up tellers.

When Timmy turned three, Shane decided he could be left solo at home. Not that Ellie didn't try to put up a fight about it first. "We should at least have a sitter looking after him," she insisted.

"A sitter is a witness," Shane had countered. "It's only for a few hours. He'll be all right, woman." And in the end, he won that argument, not because he persuaded her with words, but because he had a pretty compelling fist.

She and Shane would fly off the handle over a lot of things, but mostly about Timmy. Things were especially bad when Shane went on his benders. Ellie always punched back. Hard to say who would end up more black-and-blue. Once, Ellie broke Shane's nose with a frying pan, and it stayed permanently off kilter.

On one of those boxing-tournament nights, after Shane had knocked out one of Ellie's teeth and her mouth was covered in blood, he got all remorseful. "I'm sorry, darlin'," he said then. "You know that everything I've ever done was for you and Timmy." Ellie took the opportunity while he was feeling soft to finally demand an end to their Bonnie and Clyde existence. "If you really love us, then you'll see that we gotta quit for a while, Shane. We need to make ourselves decent so Timmy can have a real life instead of running from town to town." Blood dribbled onto the carpet that she knew she would have to scrub later on.

Shane finally conceded with a caveat. "Okay, but we gotta do one more run and we gotta make it count."

That's when he came up with the bright idea to rob a jewelry store instead of a bank. "We can make a lot more money in one go," he insisted. "Maybe forty or fifty Gs."

Benson's Jewelers was in a sad-looking strip mall, sandwiched between a massage parlor and a Mexican fast-food joint right off the freeway for a quick getaway. The lot seemed mostly empty in the mornings and a little more scouting showed that there were no guards or metal detectors, just two people. There was a rosy-cheeked missy at the counter and an elderly man who Ellie assumed was the boss and who always came in an hour late. So they decided to make their hit when the store first opened. It seemed easy as pie. But still, Ellie was nervous about the operation because in the movies, it was always the last job before you called it quits that got you into trouble. She made Shane go over the plans with her at least ten times. She told him where the CCTV cameras were and the layout of the store. He would pretend he was looking for an anniversary gift, have the lady open up the display case, and then hand over a printed note, just like at the banks.

Ellie kissed Timmy's forehead before she followed Shane out the door, putting on her wig and sunglasses in the car. Once they got to the strip mall, she watched Shane stride into the store with his *I'm a fool who thinks I'm living in a Wild West movie* confidence and waited in the car with Bulldog by her side, listening in on their two-way radio. The clunker they had rented didn't have any A/C, and she was sweating like a sinner in church despite having the windows down. Eventually it got so hot, she had to pull her wig off.

"I'm looking for a present for my wife," she could hear Shane saying over the radio. "Something special for our anniversary. Can I take a look at this necklace?"

"Of course," the lady said.

There was a tinkle of keys and a sliding of the case. She could imagine that Shane was handing the gal at the counter the note they had prepared, because she could hear the woman gasp. But then an unexpected bit of commotion was followed by Shane yelling, "Shit! Ellie, get in here." This was followed by a loud pop that made Ellie literally jump in her seat. *Shit! Shit! Shit!* Ellie grabbed Bulldog and ran into the shop, rifle pointed in front of her.

Her adrenaline was in overdrive as she barreled into the shop and assessed the situation. The first thing she noticed was the blood splattered along the back wall, looking like one of those modern abstract paintings. At first, she couldn't comprehend whose blood it was since both Shane and the girl at the counter were still standing. Then she saw the man's legs sprawled on the floor. It was the possible–boss man lying in a pool of blood with a bullet through his head. It was his dumb luck to decide to show up on time that day.

Shane now had his gun aimed at the girl, who was shaking like a wet fawn and whimpering softly with her hands up. There was a cold look in Shane's eyes—the same look he had before he was ready to fly off the handle and use his fists.

"Shane!" Ellie yelled to distract him. "Let's just get the stuff and go!"

"Grab a bag and fill it up!" he said. He turned for just a moment to look at her and that's when the girl bent over and pushed the alarm button. The high-pitched sound was like a thousand wasps stinging her ears.

"Mother. Fucker!" Shane yelled. He cocked his gun and Ellie could see the madness in his eyes and that it was going to cost another body. The girl looked to be not quite twenty and barely out of braces. Ellie lifted her rifle and made a split decision—the decision that might have been what she had been practicing for all along. She shot Shane's arm before he could pull the trigger. "Goddamn it!" he yelled, dropping the pistol. Then Ellie shot his foot for good measure. She wasn't thinking so much as acting out of instinct. Maybe it was like one of those nature shows where a predator's motherly instinct kicks in and adopts its prey's baby.

"Holy mother of Christ!" Shane yelled in pain, falling to the floor, his eyes bulging at her in shock. "What the fuck?"

The girl at the counter looked at one and then the other in confusion. Ellie grabbed Shane's pistol. He was on the floor swearing up a storm, but for one split second, she thought she saw just a modicum of fear in his eyes. Maybe she was going to finally kill him for all his face-punching and pissing their money away on booze. She wallowed in that for a moment, then turned and hightailed it out of there.

She skidded out of the parking lot and made it home to Timmy, who was still sitting on the couch where she had left him, watching TV. "Where's Daddy?" he asked, and that's when Ellie finally broke down in tears.

The police came later that night, hammering at the door like they were the big bad wolves ready to blow the house down. Timmy started wailing when they put Ellie in cuffs and confiscated Bulldog. She had forgotten to put her wig and glasses back on when she had rushed in and walked in front of surveillance cameras. In the interrogation room, the police showed Ellie the video footage from the jewelry store. They had also connected the two of them to their bank shenanigans. Armed robbery crossing several states was a serious crime and now there was murder. The fact that she had turned on her partner, however, worked in her favor, and she was promised a lighter sentence if she cooperated. Her lawyer had even told her to make it look like Shane had coerced her with his abusive behavior so that she felt she had no other choice. Ellie wasn't going to go along with the plan until her lawyer said to think about Timmy. If she was going to get custody back, she needed to let Shane take the rap. Shane got handed a life sentence. Ellie was given three years and got out after two.

————

ELLIE MASHED OUT her ciggie in a coffee cup she had found and set herself to the task at hand, which was to see if she could find some kind of list of people to invite to the funeral. Having been out of Timmy's life for so long, she didn't have the foggiest where to start. Another reminder that she had failed as a mother.

CHAPTER SIX

CARA

CARA HAD MANAGED TO INVITE HERSELF TO THE FUNERAL for Ellie's son. "I'd like to see if anyone who shows up might know something more." The innkeeper had seemed to sour on their alliance after their botched trip to Chugach, but Cara gave her a good reason to trust her. "I'm the only other person who has something at stake here. We both want to find out what the hell happened to our sons."

That softened her up a bit. "Okay, but we do things my way from now on," Ellie demanded.

Cara didn't respond with a yea or a nay, but Ellie gave her the address to the church. A few months ago, she would never have thought the two of them would be teaming up on anything. But now here they were, a regular Cagney and Lacey.

As she pulled into the parking lot, Cara was shocked but somehow not surprised to see Ellie training her rifle on an elderly man who had his hands up, palms open in a defensive posture. She quickly put her car into park, unstrapped her seat belt, and hopped out of her car to intervene.

"What's going on here?" she said in her beat cop voice.

"This," Ellie growled with a tone that was somehow even scarier than the one she had used in her exchange with Victor, "is my ex."

Cara had previously investigated Ellie and was well aware of her and her former husband's criminal history. But she looked at the frail-looking man at whom Ellie was pointing her weapon and found it difficult to imagine him as the cold-blooded bank robber and killer she had read about. His more-salt-than-pepper gray hair had receded at the top to a small tuft while the rest surrounded his head in a bust-of-Caesar manner. His brows were similarly gray, though ample, and deep wrinkles etched his forehead. Could this man really be there to kill his ex-wife in revenge? Could he have anything to do with Timothy's sudden death?

"A man can attend his own son's funeral, can't he?" MacCullum said.

"You're supposed to be in prison," Ellie retorted, still pointing the gun. "Always knew you were going to try to fly the coop."

"I'm out legally. Got my release papers to prove it." He slowly reached for a folded piece of paper in his shirt pocket.

Cara took the creased form from Shane and gave it a once-over while Ellie continued to keep a bead on her ex. "It's good," Cara declared, but it did little to assuage Ellie.

"You're still not invited to the service."

"Timothy's my son as much as yours. I only came to pay respects. No other reason."

"Ellie, lower your rifle," Cara said. Despite his felonious past and the questions of intent, Mr. MacCullum didn't seem to be armed and had given a good reason to be there.

"This is a house of worship. Please be respectful." They all turned to see the robed priest, a young, dark-haired man who looked to be Hispanic, emerging from the church. He scowled his disapproval and nodded toward Ellie's gun.

"We can't let that man in here!"

"All are welcome in the house of the Lord."

"Frisk him to make sure he ain't packin'," Ellie said to Cara.

Shane MacCullum didn't protest, so Cara did as Ellie asked and found nothing. Ellie finally relaxed. Cara took the rifle from her just in case. "We'll be all right, Father," she said to the pastor, who nodded and headed back into the church.

Cara turned her attention to Shane MacCullum. "How did you find out about the funeral?"

"Saw the obit in the paper."

Cara turned to Ellie. "Did you post an obituary in the paper?"

"Yes, but what the fuck are you doing in Anchorage?" Ellie continued to glower at her ex-husband.

"I've been looking for Timothy for a while. Through my connections I finally found out he lived in Anchorage."

"Connections?" Cara's tone demanded an answer.

"Younger folks I met in jail who knew how to use the world wide web. Flew out here, knocked on his door to try to reconnect, but he didn't want nothing to do with me. Slammed the door in my face."

Ellie grinned slightly on hearing that. She had at least taught Timmy well on that score. "Would you have expected anything else the way you treated us?"

"I'm a changed man, Ellie. I just wanted to apologize to my boy. I stuck around in Anchorage, trying to think of a better approach. And then I saw the obit, so I'm sorrier than a steer in a stockyard that I was too late. What happened? OD?"

"How would you know that?" Cara asked, and Ellie seemed just as keen to know the answer.

"Just a guess based on the junkie-infested apartment he was living at. Now are we done with the twenty questions yet?"

"All right," Ellie said. "But you gotta sit in the front where me and the detective here can keep an eye on you."

A brow rose when he heard that Cara was a detective. But he complied, headed into the church, and took a seat in the front pew.

CARA HOVERED BY the entrance in order to greet the mourners as they arrived and grill them in the process. It was a small smattering of people, just seven others besides Ellie, Shane, and Cara. Ellie told Cara that she had found a list of names and numbers stuck to the fridge in Timmy's apartment. They turned out to be contact info for his rehab counselor and fellow group members, and she had invited all of them to the service. Some were Timmy's age, others older. Cara introduced herself as a friend of the family and asked them questions. *It was a shock to me, was it a shock to you?* Everyone thought Tim had been sober for a while. *But*—a knowing look—*it could've been any one of us.*

Were you good friends with Timothy? No one seemed to know him beyond a surface-level acquaintance. *Where did he work?* "I think maybe Keenan might've recommended him to a place" was someone's response, referring to the rehab counselor. But when Cara approached Keenan, he shrugged his shoulders.

"I don't recall making any work recommendations. Whoever told you that was mistaken," he said. "I . . . We all thought he was getting better. After fentanyl hit the streets, these funerals have become way too common." He shook his head sadly and added, "People think addiction can be cured, but we can only manage it."

Cara was no closer to answering any of the many questions about the photos in Michael Lovansky's phone.

The Point Mettier contingent arrived in carpools just before the service. Chief Sipley, Chuck Marino, Mariko Ishida the lounge singer, and the resident schoolteacher Debra Blackmon with her two sons, Spence and Troy. Mrs. Lin, the Chinese restaurant owner, and her daughter, Amy, also came. Chief Sipley apologized for Jim Arreak, who had to work the tollbooth, and J.B., who had to stay behind as the only other police officer in town. None of the Point Mettier residents had ever met Timothy, so it was a touching show of support for Ellie.

Once inside the church, the mass proceeded without incident. There was only one eulogy, given by the rehab counselor, describing Timothy as quiet and contemplative. "Always with a kind word." A speech as generic as the priest's. But Ellie, who sat on the opposite side of the front pew from Shane, nodded her head in agreement and sniffled into her tissue. The hardened woman's pain brought back memories for Cara of the bleak funeral she had had to oversee herself. She knew what it was like to put a son in the ground and the service sent tiny electric shocks pulsing through her body. Ellie's ex-husband, on the other hand, remained quiet and unreadable with only his back in view.

When the people filed out in a hushed line to express their condolences to the red-wigged innkeeper and her ex, Shane acted the mourning father and even wiped at his eyes, although it was hard to tell if the tears were real or fake.

When the attendees had all gone to the parking lot, Shane turned to Ellie. "We need to talk."

Ellie immediately stiffened. "I got nothing more to say to you. Funeral's over, so you can go back to whatever rathole you crawled out of." She was definitely not the most tactful person on the planet.

The heat of exasperation colored Shane's cheeks, and he looked ready to explode. But he pursed his lips, turned on his heels, and left.

"I don't trust the old geezer as far as I can throw him," Ellie huffed.

Cara had started to feel sorry for him. "Maybe he really did just want to attend his son's funeral, and maybe he is a changed a man, like he said."

"Well, it's all too late now" was the innkeeper's unforgiving response.

ELLIE HAD PLACED an order for canapés and veggie sticks at a place called Mo's Deli and asked Cara to pick them up for the reception after. She gave Cara the address of Timmy's apartment for the post-funeral gathering. "It's a tiny studio, but it's a small crowd, so it'll do." Most everyone from Point Mettier had returned to the Dave-Co, with only Chief Sipley and Chuck Marino staying on.

Cara was happy to oblige, glad to be of some use. Besides, a small, crowded studio didn't sound appealing to someone with claustrophobia, so any excuse to be outside worked for her.

Carrying the tray of food in one hand and drinks in the other, she noticed a young waif of a woman bundled in a faux fur coat, smoking an e-cig outside.

"Sorry about Tim," she said as Cara passed by on her way to the apartment.

"Do you live here?" Cara asked.

She nodded.

"I'm Cara, his mother's friend. We just came from his funeral. Would you like to join us upstairs?"

"No, I didn't know him that well."

But that didn't stop Cara from questioning her. It was almost a reflex. "We're still trying to get ahold of any of his friends who might want to be notified of his death. Did you know any of them? People who might have visited here . . . uh, I didn't catch your name?"

"Krista. And like I said, I didn't know him that well," she replied curtly.

She looked like she was ready to head back into her apartment, so Cara stalled her. "Want a canapé? I think we ordered too many, and I don't think there's going to be much of a crowd." Cara put the drinks down and lifted the lid from the tray as an enticement.

Krista took another deep inhale from her purple-colored e-cig and blew the smoke out before reaching in for an appetizer of salami and olive. "Thanks."

"Was he going to work as usual before this week?"

"I don't know if he had a job exactly. I think maybe he had part-time work."

"Why do you say that?"

"Every Monday and Thursday, he went regular. I know because it was about the same time in the morning when I left for work. I don't know when he'd get back though."

Cara mulled this. A part-time job that was only two days a week?

"Then I think he added hours because he started leaving at night too, sometimes when I was just coming home, he'd be going out and we'd say hi and shit."

"Do you know where he worked?"

Krista narrowed her eyes. "Who did you say you were again?"

Cara was aware that her detective self had overridden her "friend of the family" persona. "His mother's friend. I didn't know him too well either, so I was just curious. You know, I don't want to step on any landmines."

"Uh-huh. Well, I gotta go. I got something on the stove," Krista said, then hastily retreated into her apartment.

When all was said and done, Cara didn't feel any closer to answers, but she knew that with any case, it took adding up pieces before the bigger picture emerged. Sometimes it required going backward in order to move forward. Her plan was to retrace the last known steps of the people found in the cell phone once Angelo was able to muster any info.

CHAPTER SEVEN

MIA

"HE'S HERE AGAIN," LILY SAID. LILY WAS THE PERKY WAITRESS with cropped bangs who reminded Mia of the red-feathered finches she used to see in her village. Always flitting, never sitting still. Lily was untying her waist apron and nodding her head toward Table 5 where a tall man with moose-colored hair and a matching beard sat, pretending to study the menu.

It was the third night in a row that he had come to sit there. Lily leaned in toward Mia, who had just arrived to take over her shift, and said, "He's not here for the cuisine, I can tell you that." She gave Mia a wink.

Mia sighed as she made her way to the back where the smell of cooking grease, pickles, and mustard combined with the static-like sound of meat *hissssssing* on the countertop griddle, the *clickety clackety* of plates, and *pling*ing of utensils jarred her senses. She had been work-ing at the diner for almost six months, but the unnatural sounds and smells were something she still hadn't gotten used to.

Mia had always been attuned to noises because it was part of her life growing up in an unincorporated village in southwest Alaska comprised of fifteen off-grid and mostly self-sufficient households. The village could only be reached by boat or plane and sat along the south shore of a wide-mouthed lake whose official name Mia didn't know but that they'd always called Lake Unity. Standing still among the coniferous trees doing nothing but listening could tell you a lot. The alarm call of a bird warns of predators. A soft shuffle of brush could be a meal. The sound of the wind could foretell a heavy rain ap-proaching. And when the sun descended and a blanket of inky dark-ness covered the village, every sound and rustle could spell danger.

Mia clocked in her time card, *kachunk*, stowed away her parka and mittens, and tied on her apron. She had the evening shift at the Lonely Diner, appropriately named because it was the only diner for miles, in the town of Willow, Alaska, twenty-six miles from Wasilla and set back from the main road so that most people didn't even know of its existence. Not many people stopped in Willow because Wasilla to the south and Talkeetna to the north had a lot more op-tions for food and services. Willow mainly catered to visitors of the Willow Creek State Recreation Park. Most of the cabins in town were only used in summer, but once a year, the town swelled with tourists during the Iditarod Trail Sled Dog Race, which Mia had not witnessed yet and maybe never would. She wasn't sure how much longer she would be staying in town.

She pinned on her nametag, which read CAROL—the alias she was currently using—and went to the bearded man's table.

"What would you like to order?" she asked, pad ready, of the man who looked not much older than herself.

When the man had *clap-clopped* in the first night, he had immediately commented, "I like your hair." Mia didn't think there was anything extraordinary about her shoulder-length hair other than that it was jet black. "Thanks" was all she could say in response.

On the second night, the bearded man had told her his story, even though she hadn't asked for it. "Just moved out here for a job with Hills Petroleum. Was making eighteen dollars an hour in Utah in construction, but then a buddy of mine told me he was getting twenty-five in Alaska doing pretty much the same thing for an oil company, so I thought I oughtta give it a go here. Sold most of my stuff, which wasn't much, filled my truck with my belongings, and moved out to Wasilla." Mia wondered why he would drive all the way up from Wasilla two nights in a row for a not-so-special dinner but didn't ask. "Hard getting used to the darkness in winter, though," the bearded man added.

In December, they would be down to five hours of low-lying, skittish sun. Mia was born in Alaska, so it didn't feel like anything unusual to her. In summer, when the lake sparkled blue and the fireweed blanketed the fields, you had long days to play and work. In winter, when Malina, the sun goddess, was fleeing ever faster from her incestuous moon brother, Igaluk, it was still beautiful, with trees feathered in white and the hazy purple light coloring the sky. During the cold months, you simply tried to stay indoors most of the time. It was the way things had always been.

The bearded man had looked up at her as if he were expecting an answer to a non-question, so Mia had just nodded and poured his coffee.

Now, on the third night, the man was once again trying to start a conversation, even though Mia had done nothing to encourage him. "Are you Native Alaskan?" he asked.

Her story was too long-winded so she just said tersely, "I'm half-Indigenous."

He smiled. "No kidding? Did you come from an Indian reservation?"

There was only one "Indian reservation" in Alaska—Metlakatla, which was a gift from Alaskan Indigenous tribes to Indigenous people of Northwest Canada. The rest of Alaska's tribal lands were set up as Native villages. Each village was a corporation, and Alaska Natives were shareholders who received money from investments in things Mia knew nothing about, like space, energy, and computer companies. Mia's village, however, wasn't incorporated or receiving any shareholder money because it wasn't a legally recognized Native village, and only half the people who lived in Unity were actually Alaska Natives. Mia herself didn't have any Alaskan blood in her. Her mother, Ayai, was Ainu—an Indigenous people of Japan—while her father, whom she couldn't remember, was white. The way her mother told it to her, Mia's father had been studying in Japan on the northern island of Hokkaido, where Ayai was from. When they met, he promised her the sky. Then they got married, and he brought her back to Alaska. When she up and left him she didn't have the money to get back to Japan.

MAMA UNITY, WHOSE real name no one knew, had founded the village in the eighties and named it after a place in Kenya called Umoja, meaning "Unity." Just like Umoja, it was meant as a refuge for women who had suffered sexual assault or oppression. Alaska was, after all, the worst state for violent crimes against women. Rumor was that Mama Unity had killed her abuser, an elder, before she ran from her village, taking her younger sister, Niki, with her before she too became a victim, although Mia was never certain if that was true or not. Mama Unity opened the door to women who were not Athabascan like herself or even Indigenous. All women were welcome. Ayai got wind of the place and found it to be a safe haven for herself and Mia. Alaska Native ways and their respect for nature were not too different from the Ainu's, so she decided to stay. Besides, in Alaska, people seemed more accepting of Indigenous groups than in Japan.

Much of life revolved around the octopus-shaped lake with its thin river-feeding arms. When it was salmon run season in summer, the Unity women set their nets and buoys out across the lake and then hauled them in after the tide changed and the water was still. When the boats were full, they brought in their catch, and the women would gather around tables outside, cutting and gutting fish with the *swish splack* of their ulu knives. It was a community event, preparing the salmon to be hung and smoked for the sparse days ahead. Mia would marvel as the women pulled out the hearts, still pulsing and beating, as if they were holding on to the last throes of the fish's transitory existence.

In winter, the lake would freeze over, and the women concentrated more on hunting big game like caribou and moose, but there was still ice fishing, which Mia had always loved because it was more like a game.

"It takes a lot of patience," Ayai had said to Mia when she was seven. She had held a wooden jig stick, arced like a miniature bow, controlling a line with a silver lure tied to it. Much of the Ainu way and language was lost to Ayai after centuries of assimilation, so she melded many of the Alaskan practices with her own. Ice fishing was something Ayai learned after moving to Alaska.

Mia studied her mother's movements as she sat on a makeshift stool made of a sturdy plastic bucket, which would later be used to carry the fish home. Ayai batted her jigger, moving it as if she were slowly waving a fan up and down. "You can move the line. Act like a fish. But if you move it too fast, the fish won't come after it." Mia nodded her understanding. A minute later, the line grew taut, and Ayai jerked on the stick. *"Hora!"* she said excitedly in Japanese. "You see?" She pulled hard on the line, and the large head of a lake trout emerged, gasping and glaring at Mia with its glassy eyes. Ayai then grabbed the wooden whacking stick that was on the ground next to her and gave the fish a good blow on the head. The fish was large and took a lot of effort from Ayai as she heaved the whole of it onto the ice. "Now you try." Then she handed the line to Mia to give it a go. It took Mia several tries, but she did finally hook a fish that day and, with her mother's help, proudly added a six-pounder to their bounty.

The other women and their young ones were out there with them, wrapped in their caribou skin jackets and wearing their mukluks and fur mittens, sitting on their buckets and sinking lines into augured holes. Mama Unity had already pulled out five large fish before Mia caught her one. Marla and Sonia, the white couple, were singing to their holes, "Come on, fishy fishy. Come on." There was the Tlingit family headed by Nancy. She had four children—three girls and one boy. Carmelita was the Filipino lady who had two boys. Lorraine was Inupiaq. Her tall and handsome son, Alex, was two years older than Mia and already an expert at catching fish. All of the kids enjoyed ice fishing. It was like a fun outdoor festival, and as they grew older, they would compete to see who could bring in the biggest or the most fish.

Afterward, Mama Unity would gather everyone in a circle to bow their heads in prayer and give thanks to the fish who gave their lives and to the lake for providing the bounty. Unity beliefs were a hodgepodge of traditions and religions that were somehow melded together. So, while the Inupiaq gave thanks to Agloolik, the spirit under the ice protecting hunters and fishermen, the Tlingit thanked the Raven, maker of forests, mountains, rivers, and seas. Mia's mother thanked the *kamuy*; the white women had their Baptist god and the Filipinos their Catholic one.

They all had their various superstitions. Ways to ward off evil. Offerings made. False paths and ditches built to mislead malevolent spirits. Amulets carved to protect against disease or scare off mythical creatures such as the bloodthirsty Adlet—a race of people with the lower body of dogs and the upper body of humans.

Ayai told Mia to be open to listening to all of the gods. She also taught Mia to never forget the importance of being humble and respectful to nature. "We belong to the land and the lake," she said.

"Who does the land and lake belong to?" Mia had asked with genuine curiosity.

"No land or lake can belong to any man," Mama Unity had responded after overhearing the conversation, "just like us women. No man can own any woman."

The kids at Unity spoke a common language of English, which they learned from Lorraine, who had been a schoolteacher in the village she had come from. But they also learned Indigenous words from their moms and passed them on to others. Their conversations in the village were like a secret language, with sentences that would make no sense to anyone else. *Uvlulluataq*, a greeting in Inupiaq, followed by *Are you coming to the Ku.éex'*? A Tlingit word for a potlatch. Then, the response *E*, Ainu for "yes." Even the parents couldn't understand what they were saying.

Aside from school with Lorraine, Mia's education consisted of learning about the world outside the village, which Mama Unity called Man's World, by watching movies with Alex at Marla and Sonia's hut after supper. For a long time, Mia believed Marla and Sonia were twin sisters. But later she learned that they were partners who liked to dress the same and cut their hair the same way, even down to the same sideways part. They were always contradicting each other. "Well, that movie was full of clichés," Marla would say. Then Sonia would jump in with "On the contrary, I thought it was refreshing." Marla would roll her eyes with "Really? It's so derivative." Sonia would switch to Spanish to defend the movie, and all Mia could catch was "Meryl Streep." You would think they were discussing a historical drama and not *The Devil Wears Prada*.

Their generator-powered DVD player showed how the rest of the world lived—driving in traffic, working at offices, and not having to hunt for most of their food. People could just walk into a supermarket and find dozens of varieties of bread or cereal, and meat was laid out on display, already skinned, cleaned, and cut. From the DVDs, it also looked like most of the world was fair-skinned, so Mia was surprised to learn from Lorraine that the majority of the world population was actually Asian.

———

SCRIITCCHHH. THE MURDEROUS sound of the man's ceramic coffee cup rubbing against its saucer like a little scream sent a shiver down Mia's back and pulled her into the present.

Deciding not to confirm or deny the bearded man's question of whether she came from an Indian reservation, Mia answered, "Grew up near here." *Near* wasn't exactly true, but what did it matter? She lifted her pad and poised her pencil to encourage the man to place his order.

"I'll have the meatloaf and a cup of tomato soup, Carol," he finally said looking at her nametag. "I'm Derek, by the way."

Mia still hadn't gotten used to her current alias. Her name was just one of the secrets she had to keep.

She gave him a half smile. She always felt this aspect of Man's World to be odd, being expected to smile and say things like, "I'm fine," even when you didn't feel fine or feel like smiling. But Derek took the smile as an encouragement.

"What time do you get off?" he asked.

Mia had seen enough movies at Marla and Sonia's hut to know that "What time do you get off?" meant "Do you want to sleep with me?" Mia had had sex before, but the thought of an intimate act with this man made her grow cold inside.

"Eleven," she said—her second lie. The diner closed at ten. "And my boyfriend's picking me up," she added. A third lie.

"Okay," the man said and looked down at his plate.

Mia hoped that that would be the end of their interactions, but Derek didn't know when to quit.

———

AS SHE FINISHED stacking chairs at closing time, Mia could see neon green lights through the window, dancing across the otherwise dark sky. The northern lights were frequently on display in Alaska, but Lorraine, Alex's mother, had told her that the lights could be a bad omen. They were the restless spirits of the dead—humans who had died before their time or animals that had been hunted down. It was a bad portend.

Mia put on her parka and scarf and headed out toward the parking lot, stuffing her hands into the pockets of her jacket for warmth. Derek was waiting.

He came out of a truck parked in the shadows.

"Eleven, did you say?" he said with sarcasm, looking at his watch, which must have clearly showed that it was closer to ten.

Mia started to backtrack toward the diner, knowing that Anthony, the short-order cook, was still inside working.

"Hey, I don't want to hurt you. I just want to talk to you."

Mia felt all of her muscles tighten, and her breath quickened, exhaling visible clouds. She tried to will herself to run back inside and call Anthony but found herself instinctively frozen like a rabbit or a mouse that had spotted its predator. She wondered if he could smell the scent of her fear.

Mama Unity had warned her of men like Derek—men who were the reason why she had set up the off-the-grid village hidden in the woods. Derek was a dark shadow under the yellow lamps of the parking lot. "I didn't mean to scare you. I just want to talk," he said.

"I need to get back home. My boyfriend's waiting." An obvious lie.

"Come on, Carol."

He started to move toward her, and that's when Mia snapped into action, calling on what Ayai had taught her when they went hunting. In one swift move, she pulled the knife she always kept in her boot and lunged at him until the blade was up against his Adam's apple. She growled at him like an animal, and he took a step back, but she moved with him, keeping the knife at his throat. She could tell he wasn't expecting that.

"If you ever come here again, Derek," and she snarled his name, "I will fucking kill you. Do you understand?" She was careful to enunciate and draw out every word so that he *could* understand. *Do not show the wolf fear. Show your dominance.*

Derek seemed to recoil before he hustled back toward his truck and sped away with a frenetic *vroom* of his motor.

Mia heard the creak of the rusty spring in the door behind her and turned back to see Anthony locking up. She slid her knife back into her boot.

"Everything okay?" he asked as he watched the truck speed away.

Mia composed herself. "Yes," she said. "Everything's fine."

She wondered if perhaps she had overreacted. If there was just something in the night sky fueling malicious thoughts. Looking back up, Mia could now discern shapes in the aurora—two ghostly figures extending their arms, wavering with a kind of sadness. Mia could not help but think of the two souls who had died in the forest just over a year ago—a man and a boy.

CHAPTER EIGHT

ELLIE

ELLIE WAS GRATEFUL TO HER POINT METTIER NEIGHBORS who had shown up for the service. She hadn't done much right, but moving to the city-in-a-building where she knew people had her back had been a good move. Shane's appearance, on the other hand, had gotten her all worked up and it had been a rough night in Timmy's bed where she kept waking to strange clangings outside. She had bolted up several times to peer out the window but there was only the wind sending trash flying about in flurries of snow. Back at Point Mettier, Ellie wouldn't have batted an eye at any of the sounds, but with her ex possibly lurking out there, every creak and thud was a menace. By morning, she was plumb tuckered.

She knew Shane most likely wanted to kill her—first for plugging him at the jewelry store and second for lying about being coerced into being his abettor. But she got Timmy back and that was the only thing that mattered.

The truth of it was that Ellie was just as lousy a mom when she tried to be respectable as she was when she was holding up banks with Shane. She was rarely around for Timmy, working double shifts bagging groceries at the local Safeway or bartending at the Irish pub. Sometimes her job was cleaning filthy toilets or waiting tables for letches. It didn't matter. The jobs didn't last long because she wasn't good at any and hated all of them, so they were regular vagabonds. Eventually, Ellie moved them up to Alaska because if there was one thing Shane hated, it was the cold, and finding the most ice bucket-y place to live seemed like a good idea in case Shane got out of the pen earlier than expected.

It was no surprise that all the packing and U-Hauling made Timmy an insecure teen—easy pickings for bullies as the new kid in town. He started lashing out at his mom because she was the only safe target. The boy could start an argument in an empty house. Timmy the Terror was her nickname for him. "The apple don't fall far from the tree," she often found herself muttering to herself. He started running away from home when he was thirteen, but he always came back. Until one day he didn't. By then he was eighteen and legally an adult so there was nothing anybody could do about it, and Ellie stopped trying to look for him.

Probably the best day of Ellie's life was when she got hit by a car while crossing a street on her way to Value Liquor. She was laid up with a fractured hip and had to be on crutches for a few months, but she landed one whopper of a settlement. With her beautiful bonanza, she had enough money to buy not just one condo unit, but four in Point Mettier—a city she had been eyeing for a while as a perfect place to lie low in.

It was back in the day when the only land route was by train and the building was still half-empty, so it wasn't exactly prime real estate, but the views from the picture windows were something to write home about. With her three extra units, she started up her inn and found that she liked life in the town beyond the tunnel and being her own boss. In summer, some of the seasonal workers and shopkeepers rented her furnished units and after the road opened, her business boomed. Eventually, she bought out the whole floor. It was a shame all of this success was too late for Timmy.

Ellie had always intended for him to take over the business one day. Maybe it would make up for all the bellyaching she was sure she had caused him. She hoped to high heaven that he wouldn't just snort up her life's savings and wanted to wait for a day when he was sobered up to tell him of her plans. But now it was all too late.

ELLIE GOT HERSELF a cup of coffee at some little hippie pastry store full of sunny-faced kids barely out of high school. At first, Ellie scoffed at the labels of *organic, locally sourced,* and *gluten free.* Were they going to tell her next that the food was made by magical elves? She was sure she preferred the artificial, cancer-causing ingredients. But when she bit into one of their breakfast scones, she nearly broke into tears, because she couldn't remember the last time she'd eaten something so tasty, and the coffee was a far holler from her drip machine back home. It might as well have been brewed by elves.

The first thing she did when she got back to the apartment was to look for the car that matched the key with a Chevy logo she had found. It was an old-fashioned key without a remote; Ellie figured she was looking for a beat-up, secondhand truck.

Out in the lot, she scanned the rows for a car that hadn't recently had its snow scraped off. She spotted a blue Silverado that she tried first, but the key didn't fit. A sorry-looking woman with stringy gray hair rushed out from one of the ground floor units and scuttled over to her with a cigarette between her middle and pointing finger— Felicia Beadle. The old hag had probably been spying on Ellie since the moment she got there.

Puffing out a cancerous cloud, which reminded Ellie that she was due for another smoke herself, Felicia flicked the ashes on the porch and said, "It's the red Chevy." She tilted her head toward a late-nineties Tahoe that looked almost two-toned under the white blanket of snow. Ellie wiped some of the snow off the door, put the key in, and sure enough, it fit.

"I got a broom," Felicia offered, then scuttled back into her apartment and emerged with a push broom and handed it over to Ellie. She seemed to get a kick out of watching Ellie scrape the snow off the car without lifting a goddamn finger to help.

Inside the car, there were fast-food wrappings, empty soda cans, parking tickets, dirt-tracked floorboards, and other questionable muck. Clearly, Ellie had done a bad job of teaching Timmy how to clean up after himself. She turned the engine to see if the battery still worked. Amazingly, it sputtered a bit but kicked back to life.

Felicia shuffled over to the window and said, "I can take it off your hands for three hundred." So that's what she was after.

"Three hundred!" Ellie laughed condescendingly. "I say it's more like two thousand."

"That's ridiculous. It's dripping oil, the brakes squeak, and god knows what else has got to be fixed on the lemon. Tell you what. I'm feeling generous. I'll go up to five hundred."

"It's only got a hundred and thirty thousand miles on it. I can get a lot more for it if I put it on Craigslist." Which is what Ellie was sure Felicia was going to do with it. She stepped out of the car so she could look Felicia in the face and lit a ciggie. "A thousand," she finally said.

"Trying to fleece an old woman?" Felicia tried for a pitiful expression.

"Is that question for me or for you?"

"Seven hundred. That's my final offer."

They regarded each other, virtual mirrors in the way they flicked ashes on the driveway. The smoke from their respective cigarettes was leaving a bad taste in Ellie's mouth. She had to admit that not having to take care of the truck would mean one less headache. She could drive it off to a used car dealership and go through a whole rigamarole only to end up with the same offer. "All right," she said. "Only 'cause I'm a woman in mourning and you got me at a weak spell. But first I gotta get my son's stuff out of the car."

"I'll get my checkbook," Felicia said.

When Felicia returned with her signed check, there was something important Ellie remembered. "You said you spotted Timmy's supposed dealers—what did they look like?"

"Why? You think you can track 'em down?"

"I might. I suspect they're these tattooed goons that've kicked up trouble in the past. You know the mountain man–terrorist types who look like they crawled out of a hole?"

Felicia thought about it, flicking more ashes. "Don't think that was them. It was dark so I didn't get a good look at their faces, but these guys looked like regular clean-shaven Joes. Practically Eagle Scouts, but with sunglasses so I didn't catch a good look at their features."

"Maybe they were salesmen. What made you think they were dealers?"

"The van. You know those vans with the painted-out windows?"

Ellie didn't know that was a thing.

"I happened to see the guys come out of your son's unit and get in the van the night before I found him dead."

Ellie jolted at the new information. "Maybe they were his friends?"

"Maybe. Maybe not. But all I'm saying is that if your son OD'd and those guys were there the night before, just seems logical that they were his source."

Ellie didn't know what to make of this info, or whether she needed to pass it on to Detective Kennedy, but she was even more determined to find the sons of bitches responsible for her son's death.

Ellie returned to Timmy's room, facing the unwelcome task of cleaning it out. She came across condoms, needles, lighters, knives, a pistol. Ellie tossed the condoms and needles but kept the knives and pistol.

She thought it was odd that she couldn't find a cell phone or a laptop and was leaning heavily on the idea that the seedy landlady had stolen them, but Ellie couldn't report a crime that she couldn't prove happened in the first place.

She inspected every item of clothing to see if there was anything worth saving, making sure to check the pockets like when she used to do his laundry—jackets, pants, and a tattered raincoat. She found mostly lint, tissues, receipts, and a ticket stub. But she hit the jackpot when she found a debit card with a Visa brand mark on it in a pair of jeans. It was from a bank with a blue corporate logo she had never heard of: *Almagor.*

CHAPTER NINE

CARA

CARA'S RENTAL WAS A TOWNHOUSE IN A QUIET NEIGHBOR-
hood. There was nothing particularly remarkable about it other
than that it had an open plan and high, lofty ceilings. After burying
Aaron and Dylan, she had sold the house and placed most of their
things in storage. She hadn't yet been able to let go of their belongings but also didn't want to be constantly reminded of what she had
lost. As a result, her unit was sparsely furnished with only the
necessities—a microfiber sofa, a wooden coffee table, a dining set,
an end table with a generic lamp. It looked more like a characterless
Airbnb rental than someone's actual home.

Outside, the atmosphere was dark and bitter. A cold wind had
blown in, and snow had begun to gust past the window in speckled
sheets. It added to the feeling of emptiness in the apartment. What

was particularly hard on this night was that it was Dylan's birthday. Her boy would have turned eight. Cara had stopped by a bakery on the way home to pick up a single slice of cake. She placed a lone candle on its frosted top and lit it. She sang "Happy Birthday" to Dylan then blew the candle out. She had also found a bottle of wine in the recesses of her cupboard, which she popped open now and promised herself "just one glass."

The first time she was pregnant, it had felt like an exciting new chapter for Cara and Aaron. One filled with unknown challenges ahead but also with the joy and warmth of a family that she had always craved. That pregnancy ended in a devastating miscarriage that had put her in a slump of depression she wasn't sure she would crawl out of . . . until Dylan came. Her hidden fears that she would never be able to have a child were assuaged by his birth, with his perfect little toes and his tiny little fingers and his cherub face. She could spend hours just holding him and listening to his heartbeat. She loved the sound of his little footsteps plodding up and down the hallway and the gurgles of laughter. Those bursts of joy more than made up for the difficult times—his tear-soaked tantrums, those panicky nights when he came down with a fever or the drudgery of not being able to leave the house without either a plan for a sitter or a mountain of child gear. She would give anything to hear Dylan's happy giggle.

The wine did nothing to suppress her feelings of loss, the pain, or the stifled breathing that was rising within herself. This is what being alone with her thoughts did to her, she mentally sighed to herself—a drive down memory lane that ended up at a roadblock of bleak reality.

She decided to pop an Ambien. Perhaps that wasn't such a good idea because she blacked out—everything around her turning off like a light switch. She found herself in an unsettling nightmare of tiny flesh-colored worms inching along Aaron's arms, then crawling out of his mouth as he decayed before her eyes. The horrific image made her scream.

SHE DIDN'T KNOW if she only screamed in her dream or out loud, but she awoke to the sound of her phone buzzing. It was J.B.

"Hello?" she said, ragged in her breath, still immersed in a bath of fear.

"Oh sorry, did I wake you?"

"No . . . I was just . . . I'm tired," she lied.

"Just wanted to make sure everything's okay and to ask how the service went." He had been more than concerned about her after the unsuccessful trip to Chugach Village.

Cara summarized what had happened at the funeral—how, aside from Ellie's supporters from Point Mettier, there was only a smattering of attendees, mostly from Timothy's rehab group, and the appearance of Ellie's ex-husband.

"Isn't Ellie's ex a murderer? Maybe there's some connection."

Cara hesitated. "I don't know if he's connected to Timothy's death. It may well have been an OD."

"Maybe I should drive over there anyway," J.B. said.

"I'll be fine, and besides, have they even plowed the streets in Point Mettier after the snow?" Cara knew that they only plowed once a week.

J.B. admitted that they had not. "I just have to dig my car out from the lot. It's not like I haven't done that before," he said. "It certainly wouldn't stop me from getting to you."

Cara turned red and felt herself almost caving in and asking him to get to her as soon as he could, but seeing the lingering whiteout conditions, she would prefer that he didn't attempt to drive in this weather with a foot he was still trying to get used to. Since losing Aaron and Dylan and then watching J.B. get shot before her eyes, she was always quick to imagine worst-case scenarios. "Maybe when the weather clears" was her final answer.

Meanwhile, she decided that her next move was to visit Angelo, to see if he had made any progress investigating the photos she had found in Michael Lovansky's phone. She would pay him a visit in the morning.

CHAPTER TEN

MIA

MIA'S HEART RACED WHEN SHE SAW THE TWO PATROL CARS docked in the snow-covered lot of the diner when she drove in for her next shift. Were they here because she had pulled a knife on Derek? Or was it something else? A thought flickered in her mind of the bodies of a man and a boy in a gully. Had they found them? Whatever the case, she didn't think she would have the presence of mind to talk to them without giving something away. Should she turn around, call in sick? Her pulse was pounding so that she could hear the *su-wish su-wish* in her ear.

She felt a sudden yearning for Unity, the place where she had always felt safe and protected. She wished she could go back to the time when she was still an innocent and hadn't snaked out of the Eden of home.

―――――――

ALL THE WOMEN were expected to contribute in some way, whether it was learning to fish and hunt or using other skills, like Carmelita, the Filipino woman who used to be a nurse and now acted as the village's medic, or Lorraine, who acted as the schoolteacher.

Marla and Sonia ran their own flightseeing business, hoisting eager tourists over the vast and beautiful parks and uninhabited natural vistas. They provided the main connection between Unity and Man's World when the women had to go into town to get supplies or sell their wares—furs, handmade mukluks, or carved ornaments.

The two pilots had sometimes given rides to Mia and the other children for fun. At first, the guttural *brugga brugga* sound of the engine and the unsteady floor were overwhelming, and her stomach turned somersaults as they left the ground. She had gripped the seat arms wondering how such a metal beast could stay afloat in the air without plummeting them back to earth. But once she had gotten used to the noise and the movements, it was a whole new magical world, soaring like a red-tailed hawk over the tops of trees and the snowy white mountains that looked as though they had been dipped in bowls of whipped cream. Unity Lake below was a vast, reflective looking glass, and its rivulet arms were just tiny worms. Marla and Sonia had surely known what the real name of Unity Lake was, but since Mia didn't know at the time that Unity Lake had any other name, it never even crossed her mind to ask.

Mia knew that when she was old enough, she would also be expected to contribute to the community and needed to learn how to hunt, fish, and grow vegetables like everybody else.

The Ainu, Ayai told Mia, had traditionally been hunters as well as fishermen and had used bows and poisoned arrows before firearms were invented. "Ainu women have always hunted as well as men," Ayai said on one of their treks, leading her through the forest with her scoped hunting rifle. "The *kamuy* gives to us everything. When you see the caribou, that is the *kamuy* who gives its life to us as food." Ayai stopped Mia suddenly, pointing to the ground at a fresh set of caribou tracks and scat. They moved slowly after that so as not to disturb any leaf or make any sound, and Mia saw that there was clearly more than one set of tracks. They walked light as feathers, careful not to break any leaves or branches until they spotted the herd. This is when all of their senses were heightened. They slowed their breath and made themselves feel one with their surroundings, listening to what was told to them by the birds in their warning calls or smelling the scents that the wind carried to them.

Then Ayai lifted her gun, aiming for a bull. She took her shot—a single *PAFLACK!*—which hit its mark in the animal's neck, and the rest of the herd snapped to life, bounding away in a trail of dust. The bull went down on its knees and fell with a great huff from its nostrils. "Always aim for the neck," Ayai told Mia. "Then the death will be quick and it will not suffer." Then Ayai put her hand on him gently and bowed her head, giving thanks to *Hash-inau-uk Kamuy*, goddess of the hunt. In traditional Ainu culture, only men would have been able to participate in *kamuy* rituals, but Ayai believed the gods would forgive her for acting as both man and woman here where there were no men.

They would use every part of the gift the *kamuy* gave them. Aside from the meat, the skin would be used for clothing, the tendons braided to make nets, the antlers for bows and tools, its fat to fuel lamp lights, and the bones would be returned to the *keyohniusi* shrine that Ayai had built so that the caribou's spirit could be reborn. The hard part was gutting the caribou and transporting it on tree branches back to the village. It was impossible for the two of them to drag three hundred and fifty pounds of caribou, but all the women in Unity carried whistles with them to alert the others when they needed help. So Ayai blew the whistle three times in a request for help with cutting and carrying their bounty.

While waiting for the others to arrive, Ayai started preparing the caribou. Then the snap of twigs and brush alerted them to movement. The scent of the kill had brought another predator. Ayai froze and stopped carving. She motioned toward Mia to stay still. It was a wolf.

The wolf was gray and white with marks of reddish brown. Its hungry, yellow eyes regarded them and the meat, then it took two hesitant steps closer before baring its teeth in a low growl. Ayai scanned the forest for the rest of the pack, as did Mia, but they saw no others. That eased their sense of dread.

Ayai picked up a rock and threw it at him. "*Ike!*" she shouted. She lifted her rifle at it, ready to shoot. "The secret is to not let the wolf know you're afraid of him," Mia's mother always said.

The wolf stood its ground, and Mia swore the wolf could see that she was shaking in her boots. She had heard much lore about wolf spirits—sometimes they were protectors, sometimes adversaries. Today it was definitely an adversary. The large canine seemed to be looking straight at her and not at Ayai. It was almost taunting her. *I can see the fear inside you.* Ayai finally lunged toward it, screaming, "Go!" once again. "*Ike!*" The wolf finally turned tail and ran off.

Within minutes, the other women had followed their tracks to find them and were delighted to see the fallen caribou, because they knew they would all be sharing in the feast.

MIA COULD SEE through the frost-washed windows of the Lonely Diner that the policemen were seated at a booth, steaming cups of coffee in front of them. Relief washed over her. They were just there for a meal.

Mia put on her apron, glancing warily at the table of policemen. "Their plates are up, and coffees need refilling," Jessie said as she took off her apron for the shift change. Mia's hunting and fishing lessons meant nothing while living in Man's World, where everything was served up to you on a platter.

She parceled out the men's dishes and refilled their mugs with the dark, aromatic liquid, trying to be as unnoticeable as possible. She was almost able to walk away without saying a word when one of the officers, an older man, looked up at her.

"And who are you, darlin'?"

"I'm Carol," Mia said. "I'll be taking over for Jessie." She wondered if they could hear the nervousness and the slight shake in her voice. She hoped that was the end of the conversation and tried to walk away when the officer called her back.

"Just a sec, Carol."

Mia returned to the table. Now he seemed to scrutinize her for longer than was necessary. Maybe the officer had noticed how nervous she was. Maybe he could see the bead of sweat that trickled down the side of her forehead. Maybe he could see her fingers trembling. She stuck her hands into her apron pockets.

"I could use some ketchup," he finally said.

"Right away, sir."

Then he went back to chatting with his fellow officers.

Mia realized how far she had strayed from Unity, not just in the distance of miles but in the distance of her soul. She wasn't sure if she had found what she was looking for, and the many gods that had watched over her were surely dismayed and offended by her actions since joining Man's World. *Everything catches up to you someday,* she thought to herself. How long should she keep pretending to be Carol, and would she always have to keep looking over her shoulder for the police or someone else to come after her? She began to weigh her options.

CHAPTER ELEVEN

ELLIE

ELLIE CHOSE TO HAVE HER SON CREMATED AND HAD FOUND a nice little niche in a columbarium wall—a safe-deposit box in a bank of the departed, overlooking the parklike grounds. A couple of maintenance men came to open up a panel, shivving their putty knives into a crack and lifting off the front, revealing a square cubby—Timmy's new pad for eternity.

A buxom officiant in a long coat stood by and asked, "Will anyone else be coming?"

Ellie had decided that no one else needed to attend this part. "No, I wanted to keep it private," she responded.

"I understand. Did you want to say any words? Read a passage?"

Ellie had to admit she hadn't thought about a reading and was mulling whether to just recite the Lord's Prayer when a voice came from behind.

"Psalms forty-two."

Ellie froze. She knew Shane would show up again sooner rather than later. Now was not the time to confront him, but she thought for a second about grabbing the pistol she had found in Timmy's apartment that was now in her handbag.

Shane recited the verse. "As the hind longs for the running waters, so my soul longs for you, O God. A thirst is my soul for God, the living God. When shall I go and behold the face of God? I went with the throng and led them in procession to the house of God."

That was a lot of *God* for a man as amoral as Shane, but Ellie said, "Amen," and placed the urn into the hole.

The custodians replaced the marble face, closing the tiny space with a thunk of finality—like shutting her boy from the sun into a dark forever.

"I will take my leave now, but you are welcome to linger," the officiant said, then she scurried off to the warmth of her office.

Once she was gone, Ellie turned to her ex with venom. "What is it you want from me, Shane?"

"I don't want anything from you, woman, except a little respect."

"Respect?" Ellie let out a laugh. "That's gotta be the last thing in the world you want from me."

Shane's face grew red. "After all the years I gave you and Timmy, providing for you, putting food on the table. And for all that, all I got was a knife in the back!"

"I wouldn't exactly call stealing the same as providing for, and if you forgot, you had a partner you couldn't have done any of it without."

"Well, you sure didn't seem like a partner when I needed one the most. Are you forgetting how you shot me? Twice? And then stabbed me in the back at the trial?"

"So you looking for revenge? Or a payout? What are you hovering around like a vulture for? Timmy's scraps? He didn't have a pot to piss in. All he had was a crappy car, which I just sold. Here, take it!" Ellie dug into her purse for Felicia's check and threw it at Shane. Of course, she knew he wouldn't be able to cash it with her name on it. It was as if she were just egging him on to sock her one in the eye, like in the old days.

But Shane stooped down and picked the check up and handed it back to her all calm and quiet . . . which somehow scared Ellie more. "I don't want it," he said.

"Well, what the hell do you want?"

Shane seemed to suddenly grow soft, nothing like the rabid porcupine of old that Ellie had known. Just for a second, he looked tired. Spent. The fight within him gone. Then he straightened his shoulders and looked her in the eyes. "I got cancer. It's terminal. I'm saying my goodbyes."

THE TINY REDBRICK diner on C Street was full up with plus-sized patrons with plus-sized voices yammering away in the smoky bacon-colored booths. Ellie had sometimes met up with Timmy here. She liked the no-frills decor and the lack of hippie waiters wearing friendship bracelets. There were no mini sprigs of herbs or artsy sauces decorating the food that meant everything on the menu would be overpriced. Just regular burgers and sandwiches, in portions that made you feel like you were getting your money's worth, and free refills of coffee to boot. But the main reason she had chosen the diner was because she wanted to make sure they were someplace public for their talk.

"How much longer you got?" she asked. She wasn't sure whether to believe Shane about the cancer. He didn't look sick, and even if he was balding up top, she could see that he still had a good set of hair in the back.

"Doctors say it could be a year or it could be months."

"What kind?" She'd best grill him on the details. See if she could make him slip up.

"Colon."

"Well, shouldn't you be in a hospital bed, then?"

"I'm on meds. Doctor says I'm beyond chemo."

Ellie felt a teaspoon of pity despite herself. She took a bite out of her overstuffed corned beef sandwich so she wouldn't have to say anything.

"Jail food will mess up your innards," Shane said, but Ellie was figuring that it had more to do with the amount of alcohol he had consumed in his younger days. "It ain't pretty," he went on. "I was shitting through my pants, and my stomach hurt like a motherfucker."

Ellie could feel the pangs of getting old herself. The back pain, the arthritis, all the little anomalies that seemed to suddenly plague her after being mostly healthy as a horse. And the last time she saw a doctor in Anchorage, he had told her to stop smoking and prescribed her blood pressure medication. She stopped going to appointments after that because she couldn't quit smoking and didn't want to be guilt-schooled by someone half her age.

"I'm out of jail on compassionate release. The bastards probably just didn't want to pay my medical bills. Getting cancer ain't cheap."

Ellie sighed, wondering if this was going to be a plea for money like what she was used to with Timmy. Like she always said, *the apple don't fall far from the tree.*

"What is it you want from me?" she asked again.

"It's the other way around. I want to know what I can do for you."

Ellie narrowed her eyes at him. That was something she never in the gates of Hell expected to hear from Shane's lips.

"I was too late for our son. But I want my last spell here to be in amends. Now, I ain't rich at the moment, but if you're in need of money, I can find a way to get it. Or if you got some repo rat harassing you, you know I can definitely take care of that."

Ellie laughed. "You sure got a strange way of making amends. And you aren't the spry thief of yesteryear. In case you haven't looked at yourself in the mirror lately, you're an over-the-hill codger with an expiration date, and you just got done telling me how you've been shitting yourself because of your cancer."

"Some days are better than others," he admitted. "But look at it this way, I got nothing to lose. I mean, the worst that can happen is that I get sent back to jail and then I've got free health care, right?"

Ellie debated whether to fill Shane in on what Detective Kennedy had found. She looked into Shane's eyes and decided he was being earnest. "Okay, maybe you can find out who killed Timmy."

The burger Shane was about to bite into nearly fell from his hands. He put it down on his plate and looked at Ellie to see if she was being serious. "Somebody knocked Timmy off? I thought it was an OD."

"Maybe it was. Maybe it wasn't."

"What do you mean?"

"A detective lady tipped me off that some thugs from Chugach

Village might have been involved somehow, maybe dealt him some bad drugs. We're not sure exactly but we found Timmy's photo in one of their cell phones."

Shane looked riled up. Luckily, his anger was directed in the right direction. "We gotta pay a visit to this Chugach Village. Find out what those motherfuckers were doing with his photo. I swear, if they had anything to do with his death—"

Shane's volume had gone up a notch and the other customers were turning to stare, so Ellie stepped on his foot to keep him from announcing his murderous plans.

"We already tried that," Ellie hissed. "Got us nowhere."

"Well, what was your game plan when you went there?"

"We didn't have one," Ellie admitted.

"Come on, Ellie. I taught you better'n that. You always gotta have a plan, and that's why we were so successful."

They weren't so successful on their last jewelry heist, Ellie thought to herself but kept quiet.

"You and me, we're partners. We're better together." He gave her a sly wink.

For a moment, there was the old Shane back. The one who wasn't menaced by the bottle. She squinted at him, trying to see his angle. "You haven't earned my trust back yet."

"I'm a changed man, Ellie. But you tell me what you want to do. You want me to help you? Or do you want to sit on your haunches and let Timmy's death go unavenged."

Ellie had to think about that one. "All right, I'll put you up in one of my rooms in Point Mettier so I can keep an eye on you."

"Rooms? You live in a mansion now?"

"I got an inn. I rent out units."

"Sounds like somebody's been doing well for themselves. You been flyin' solo? Keeping up the family business and cashing in?"

"No, you big lug. It's all legal. I'm a bona fide entrepreneur." Ellie took a moment to preen. "I've got rules, though. First sign of the drink or your lip-splitting shenanigans and you're out. You got a week to come up with a plan, and if I don't like it, we're not doing it."

"Fair's fair." He grinned like they were back in high school and he had just managed to convince her to be his date to the prom.

CHAPTER TWELVE

CARA

"PHOTOS, PHOTOS, PHOTOS . . ." ANGELO LOOKED THROUGH a messy heap on his desk.

His shop could use a thorough Marie Kondofying, Cara thought to herself. Nothing in the space *sparked joy* for her as she glanced around the claustrophobic mess of racks stacked with wires and hard drives, and despite his digital capabilities, Angelo seemed surprisingly analog, with notepads and sticky note reminders littering his desk and monitors. Each time she came to visit, the paper seemed to compound.

"You need a haul-away service?" she asked as a hint and pointed to a graveyard of nineties-era machinery piled in a corner. "'Cause I know a guy."

"No, no, those are collector's items," Angelo insisted. "Besides, I have baby boomer types always looking for replacement parts for their old machines. Ah, here they are," he said, finally finding his buried notes. "I've got the four-one-one."

Angelo started with the older man with the beard, throwing his picture up on the screen and simultaneously pulling up photos that came up on a search. A random shot from a building site and a Facebook page. "His name is George Apernathy. Looks like he was part of a construction crew."

Cara peered over Angelo's shoulder to get a closer look. "When was the last Facebook entry?"

"Over a year ago, but he didn't seem to be a regular Facebook poster. Didn't find any photos of a family."

Angelo moved on to the photo of a woman in a coffee shop. The reverse search revealed that the woman's name was Rebecca Taylor and that she had worked as a librarian. "At least, it looks like she had a job as a librarian," he corrected. "But, um, not recently. Single. No kids as far as I can see."

Cara knew that she could do a deeper dive using her police resources now that she had names to go on.

The man chaining the bicycle turned out to be Jorge Salazar, a man who had been reported missing by his parents, who lived in Arizona. He had been a student at the University of Alaska Anchorage.

"What about the young woman?"

Angelo could only pull up one photo from his search. "This woman has no Facebook, Instagram, nothing."

Cara thought that if she were a Native from a remote village, that might not be too unusual.

"There's just this one photo from a cleaning place on their employee site. Anchorage Pro Cleaners. Her name was listed as Jennifer

Maliki. I couldn't find any info on the man at the apartment complex either. Turned up nothing. I don't think he had any kind of social media."

"I already know who he is," Cara explained. "Timothy MacCullum. He's dead. An OD is the official cause of death."

"No shitting!" Angelo's eyes grew wide. "So who do you think these people are?"

"Well, the only thing they have in common is that they all seem to have died or haven't been heard from recently."

"Do you think they're all dead?"

"I don't know, but I'm going to find out. Maybe we can dig up car registrations. See if they're still being registered."

"It might take a little more time, and it'll cost ya."

"You know I'm good for it."

Angelo popped a jelly bean into his mouth and smiled.

ARMED WITH THE names, Cara drove back to her apartment ready to do a deep search. She created a file for each name and photo she had, pulling them all up one by one. She knew what had happened to Timothy MacCullum. Then there was the photo of her own family. She lingered all too long on it, taking in how happy they had looked on their way to their mini-vacation.

Aaron looked as handsome as the day she had met him in the express checkout line of a grocery store.

There was a lot you could tell from a person's grocery haul. Aaron, for instance, was a wine kind of guy. He liked fish, and he was probably single given the small portions. His selection of blueberries and shiitake mushrooms showed some health consciousness, but there was also a bag of chips to show that he was human. Cara could see from his physique that he was someone who worked out, and his suit said he was white collar.

"Is that any good?" he had asked, pointing to her bottles of Leinenkugel Craft Beer. *Checkout* line was right; that's what they were both doing to each other. Cara looked down at her basket and turned red with embarrassment—beer, chocolate, frozen dinners, and a romance novel. She must have seemed like a sad character. She was dressed down in tatty jeans, a T-shirt, and a hoodie.

"It's fruity," she said. "You might not like it."

"Well, you never know whether you'll like something until you try it," he said with an inviting smile.

Outside in the parking lot, they exchanged numbers.

His proposal came on a hiking trip in Denali National Park. In his nervousness, he dropped the ring on the trail, and they spent the better part of an hour searching for it in the grass. But it was romantic nonetheless, with a clear sky revealing the white-topped mountains in the distance and the vast and achingly beautiful valley spread out before them as if the world were theirs for the taking.

CARA WAS WOKEN from her reverie when her cell phone buzzed, and she saw that it was a call from the private lab she had sent Aaron and Dylan's remains to for the autopsy. It was almost as if thinking about him had summoned the call.

"We will send you the official report, of course," the voice on the other end said, "but we felt we needed to discuss the results with you first."

"Okay," Cara said, finding herself suddenly shaking.

"There wasn't much left to examine of the male youth. However, in the adult male, we found a metallic fragment in the left thoracic cage."

Cara took a deep breath and had to sit down, contemplating the meaning of a piece of metal lodged in Aaron's rib cage. "Would it be consistent with a bullet fragment?"

"Yes."

Foul play was something Cara had worried about all along, otherwise she wouldn't have asked for the autopsy, but to hear it out loud still felt like an ice water plunge for her entire being. "So Aaron was shot?"

There was a pause. "Possibly. The adult male might have been shot. There's . . . something else we need to discuss."

Cara braced herself.

"We also did some DNA testing as you requested. And, well, we just wanted to make sure you submitted the correct samples."

"Why do you ask?"

The woman on the other end of the line hesitated. There was an intake of air. "Because the DNA of the bone fragments does not match the samples you sent us of either Aaron or Dylan."

CHAPTER THIRTEEN

MIA

MIA HAD MADE THE DECISION TO LEAVE UNITY NOT TOO long after Alex left. Mia had always thought of Alex as her big brother. Then he became her best friend and then something more.

On a star-glittered evening, when there was a kind of orange glow on the horizon, enough to see the crisp outlines of the trees and the sleeping mountains across Lake Unity, Alex and Mia sat out on the pier where Marla and Sonia's float planes were docked. They had just left the two pilots' hut after watching the movie *Big Fish* for the third time on their DVD player. Before going back to their own huts, Alex said he wanted to talk to Mia alone. He'd been uncharacteristically silent that night; usually they were full of banter, critiquing movies they had seen many times over. It was that perfect time of year in spring when days were starting to get longer but hadn't yet consumed the hours. They sat snuggled together, hugging their legs for warmth.

"So what's up?" Mia asked turning toward Alex, and it dawned on her how much taller he had gotten. She used to look at him at eye level, and now she had to tilt her head upward to scrutinize his face. He had grown his hair long, past his shoulders, and the breadth of his chest was now twice the size of Mia's.

Alex studied the lake that lapped below in *swish swosh* sounds. "I got a scholarship to a college," he finally said.

Mama Unity said the boys who grew up there would be allowed to stay as adult men, so Mia had never thought about Alex leaving. Mia knew she should be happy for him, but it was like a cinder block dropping on her soul and sinking it to the bottom of the lake. "To where?"

"A tribal college. Northwest Indian. It's in Washington."

Washington was the closest of the lower forty-eight, but once when Mia was looking at a map in class, Lorraine had told her it would be a two-day drive without stopping to get there. For someone who had never left Unity, it seemed as far away as the Sahara Desert.

"You can't go. Who am I going to talk to? Who am I going to watch movies with?"

"You've got all the other kids here. José, Kyle, Tida, Kiana—"

"*Hadláa!* They're just kids!" Mia interjected with Tlingit. There was no one who could take the place of Alex.

"I have to discover life beyond Unity, Mia. But I'm sure I'll come back."

"No you won't. You'll forget all about me, and you'll find someone else." She was sure that Man's World would entice him to stay and never come back.

"I promise I'll never forget you," he said, then he kissed her eyelids and then her cheek and then her lips until she had forgotten what they were arguing about.

Two days before Alex left for Washington, they decided to consummate their love. Ayai wasn't comfortable with teaching Mia about sex, but Marla and Sonia had prepared her for her first time, showing her diagrams and explaining how the anatomy worked. But they also told her not to "give it up" to any man—or woman, for that matter—unless she really wanted to. They taught her about contraception, sexually transmitted diseases, and the kinds of things someone in Man's World might say to get her to sleep with them. Marla made sex sound like something frightening, so Sonia had to add, "On the contrary, it's pleasurable and beautiful and precious with the right person at the right time." Marla and Sonia exchanged a look and touched hands.

Mia wasn't sure what kind of instruction Alex had received, but it looked like Marla and Sonia had given him a similar talk, because he came prepared with a condom and treated her respectfully. It was the edge of summer, and they had found a moss-covered spot on the edge of a serpentine rivulet, far from the village huts.

He was tender, finding the spot on her neck that made her sigh and grow damp in her nether region. He entered her, and she could feel their *anirniit* spirit breaths combine, melding like the various beliefs and gods of Unity that all coexisted in harmony, overlapping, overflowing, all-accepting, and embracing. All that surrounded them— the trees, the stars, the rocks, the water that flowed beside them, and the crickets that chirped in the night were filled with godliness. She believed she had found Sonia's version of sex instead of the toxic version Marla had warned her of.

When Alex left Unity to join Man's World in pursuit of knowledge, Mia felt as if part of her had been ripped away. Life went from color to black-and-white. She never knew she could be so heartbroken.

Ayai had not been oblivious to Mia's feelings for Alex. She told Mia that first love always seems the hardest, but with time, the pain would lessen. But who else was there for her in Unity? All the other boys were younger—just children in her eyes. Mia saw only a vast, empty plain of loneliness ahead of her. She felt the hole in her heart grow even bigger when Alex didn't come back the next summer. It was then that she decided she had to leave the village.

WHEN MIA INFORMED everyone of her decision, Mama Unity oversaw a potlatch feast in the Clan House—the big building where the community often gathered—for Mia's sendoff. Ayai, of course, was unhappy with the idea of Mia leaving, but Marla and Sonia fought on her behalf, saying she could always come back if she wanted to, and that Unity was meant to be a safe haven, not a prison.

Mia wouldn't be able to get a scholarship like Alex had. Even though Lorraine had told her she was a quick learner and could go far if she applied herself, Mia wasn't studious like Alex. She had floundered on the high school proficiency test that Lorraine had administered. But she didn't mind getting a job that required using her hands. She regularly hunted, skinned her food, and cut and hauled firewood. Hard work didn't scare her.

At the feast, women wore their finest shawls and cedar bark hats and entered to the sound of drums played by the children. Mama Unity asked everyone to pray to their gods or spirits to watch over

Mia. They had a feast of caribou stew, potatoes, baked salmon heads, and spruce beer. There was singing and dancing, and the women told stories about Mia. Ayai recollected the day Mia had caught her first trout, and how proud she was that Mia never once complained about the cold and wasn't squeamish about the fish that the *kamuy* had brought her. Mama Unity talked about the time when she was horrified to discover Mia covered in blood, only to find out that it wasn't blood but a stash of berries she had discovered and eaten to messy excess.

Potlatches were also a time of giving. Marla and Sonia had given her leather gloves. Carmelita gave her a wool sweater. She received a knitted hat from Niki and an all-purpose woven cloth bag from Lorraine. Ayai gave Mia five hundred dollars, which she had made from selling fur mukluks and moose antler pendants, preparing for this day. She also gave Mia a knife similar to the one she used to gut fish; it was clean and sharp, the light glinting off its blade. "Always keep this on you or near you, no matter what, day or night," she said. "It may prove useful." Then she repeated the warning that Mia had heard often. "You will be alone in Man's World, without neighbors you can run to when you need food or help," Ayai said through tears. "But you are smart and know how to look out for yourself. So you must survive and remember all we have taught you."

In order to give her own thanks to everyone who had looked out for her and helped her grow up, Mia then went around the circle of women and gave each of them wild berries she had gathered and sprigs of mint leaves she had been growing behind the hut.

In the morning Mia packed her clothes and a photo of Ayai into the cloth bag Lorraine had made, along with all the moose and salmon jerky she could carry. Then Marla and Sonia flew her to

Anchorage. There, the two pilots took Mia to the women's shelter that had helped Mama Unity in the past. Mama Unity had said she could find a job and a place to stay from there. Even though she didn't own a cell phone, Mia took the number for Marla and Sonia's tour operation in case of an emergency.

THE WOMEN'S SHELTER was a wooden building that looked as if it were made of giant crates painted the colors of currant jam and river pebbles. Inside, there was a large room, bigger even than the Clan House. It was filled with long black tables and benches in the front and rows and rows of cots behind. The beds were covered with clothes, jackets, shoes, plastic water bottles, and bags—the sum of each woman's belongings laid out on the shelter-provided quilt covers. On the center of the wall was a giant cross that stretched from floor to ceiling. Mia was familiar with some Catholic and Christian beliefs but was disappointed that they only honored one god here.

The lady at the shelter who greeted her and checked her in was an Indigenous woman named Sandra. Sandra gave her a form that asked for a lot of information Mia couldn't give, including her permanent address, phone number, and social security number, whatever that was. She put down her name as Jennifer Maliki—Ayai had told her to use a fake name in case her father was still looking for them, so she picked two names she saw on the volunteer board outside. For race, she wrote Alaska Native with Athabascan heritage. Even though that was a lie, her mixed Asian and white DNA gave her a pass in the looks department. Sandra looked at the form and sighed at all the empty spaces but clearly that wasn't anything new to her. "You're lucky," she said. "We usually don't have any openings. But last night, someone *oh deed*, so you can take her spot." Mia didn't know the meaning of *oh deed*.

Then Sandra showed her her cot. Women's voices buzzed throughout the room in an echoey sound that felt unnatural and eerie to Mia. Every chair-scraping *scritch* and pen-dropping *plink* made her feel hollow and empty inside. But she reminded herself that she had chosen to be here, and she was grateful for the kindness of food and shelter. At least here she would still be part of a women's safe place before she fully entered Man's World.

Many of the women were gone at the moment, Sandra told her, because everyone there was expected to work or be looking for a job. The center was only meant to be a temporary shelter, for up to thirty days. At four thirty, the women started filing back in so that the space was brimming. At six, everyone lined up for dinner, which was a crusty bun, a casserole with some kind of meat Mia didn't recognize, and green beans. Someone led a Christian prayer and Mia bowed her head, saying her own internal prayer thanking the unknown animal *kamuy* that had given its life.

The women looked as diverse as the ones at Unity—Indigenous, white, Black, Asian, older, younger, and they all had different walks—slow, fast, hitched, deliberate, limping, or plodding. Mia could tell much about someone by the way they walked. Some of the women looked pale and sad, others were cheerful and chatty. There were a few children.

Mia was already awake at six in the morning when the lights switched on and a loud buzzer sounded. It scared her, not knowing what it was or where it was coming from, but she quickly realized it was a wake-up alarm, and the other women responded by grumbling and complaining before pulling themselves out of their cots.

At breakfast, most of the women ate in silence, but there was one white woman who looked as old as Mama Unity, her gray-and-white hair in wild frizzes, the skin around her eyes sagging in folds. She sat opposite Mia and started talking nonstop. Mia couldn't understand much of what she was saying because of all the cuss words.

"I'm fucking tired of the shitty radio songs you keep playing all the goddamn day," she growled. Mia didn't have a radio or anything else that played music. The woman kept going. "So what are you gonna do about it, bitch? Huh? What the hell are you gonna do about it?" Mia looked around to see if she was actually talking to someone else, but there seemed to be no one.

After the lady got up and left, one of the other shelter residents made circles in the air around her ear with her index finger, which Mia knew meant "She's crazy."

Since Mia didn't have a job yet, Sandra asked her if she had any skills for employment. Mia told her she could hunt and fish, and Sandra sighed, which she seemed to do a lot. Then Sandra asked her to be truthful in telling her about any criminal record or addictions, because they would find out eventually. Mia said she had none of either. Sandra scrolled down a list on her computer and stopped at one before turning back to Mia. "How do you feel about working for a cleaning service?"

CHAPTER FOURTEEN

CARA

CARA WAS UNABLE TO PROCESS WHAT SHE HAD JUST HEARD. A myriad of thoughts and questions flashed all at once, so that she needed to mentally reverse. "What did you say?"

"The DNA is not a match with your husband's. Nor do any of the remains match your son's."

The words were implausible, incomprehensible, and nauseating all at once. This must be some kind of cruel and misguided joke. "Are you sure? There must be some kind of mistake. Can you run the test again?"

"Because of the unusual circumstances, we did rerun the tests on both samples, and the results were the same."

"But there was a DNA test conducted before they were buried." Cara felt both her tears and her anxiety welling up.

"There is no record of us ever having done a DNA test for Aaron Christopher Kennedy or Dylan Lucas Kennedy in the past, so you'll have to corroborate with the lab that was used then. I'm so sorry, Mrs. Kennedy."

How could this happen? Whose bodies had she buried? And what had happened to Aaron and Dylan? Were they still in the forest somewhere? Or were they possibly still alive? After she hung up, Cara ran to the bathroom and retched the contents of her queasy but mostly empty stomach.

THE HEADQUARTERS OF the Alaska State Troopers was a maroon-colored U-shaped building. It was a place she had frequented after Aaron and Dylan had gone missing and now she barged through the glass doors and made her way to the front desk where a fresh-faced receptionist sat.

"Can I help you?"

"Detective Cara Kennedy here to see Lieutenant Branson."

"Did you have an appointment?"

"No, I don't. But Lieutenant Branson should remember me."

The woman looked at her skeptically "And this is concerning . . . ?"

"It's about DNA tests that were done for a missing persons' case. My husband and son."

"Hold on," the woman said. She dialed a number and spoke softly into the phone. "Have a seat, please," she said after hanging up.

After thirty minutes of waiting, the man who had been in charge of her case finally appeared in the lobby. The stalwart officer with gray sideburns was the one who had informed her of the DNA results. "Detective Kennedy," he said, all smiles. "Come on back." She wasn't sure whether he had already forgotten who she was, but there was no "Great to see you" or "How've you been?" Instead, he led her in silence to his office.

The room was spacious and bright, with a tall glass window. Cara recognized the fake fern listing unevenly on the sill and a photo of the lieutenant posing next to a prize-catch halibut hanging on the wall from a past visit. Once they were both seated, Cara placed the printed DNA results of her private autopsy in front of him.

Branson looked down at the innocuous-looking sheaf of paper. "What am I looking at here?"

"I had an autopsy done on the remains of my husband and son."

He looked at her, perplexed. "Didn't they get lost hiking in the woods? Their remains were found after a fire, if I remember correctly." So he *had* remembered her.

Cara nodded in confirmation. "Only they're *not* the remains of my husband and son."

Branson stiffened at that. "What do you mean?" He began to read the report and Cara could see the moment when his brows raised: DNA eliminates A. Kennedy and D. Kennedy as the John Does of the male skeletal remains.

"Whoever's DNA reports these are, they're not my family's."

"Now that's odd. There must be some mistake."

"Clearly. But I don't know on whose end. I want to see the original lab work that was done when the remains were found."

"We'll look into this. I promise. I'm sure it was all just an honest mistake."

"An honest mistake that had me burying the wrong bodies. Holding a funeral for people I didn't even know. There is a potential lawsuit here and I'm not leaving until I get some answers."

Branson frowned, the wrinkles on his forehead converging into Vs. "I understand why you're upset but there's no need to be combative. I want to know what happened just as much as you do." True, it was premature to direct the blame on Branson, but she couldn't be brushed off so easily. He finally pressed a button on his intercom phone. "Tom, could you get me the file on the Kennedy case? Missing persons. The names were . . ." He looked to Cara for help.

"Aaron and Dylan."

It wasn't long before a freckle-faced young man with a crew cut walked in with a file, gave a slight nod to Cara, handed the folder to Branson, and walked out as quickly as he had come in.

The lieutenant shuffled through its contents. Inside were the reports and evidence photos of the human remains found in a gully in the Talkeetna forest. Cara thought of how utterly devastated she had been when she first saw them, but now, her feelings were different. Knowing that they did not belong to the people she loved, the pieces were now a case to be solved. *Who were these people? And where were Aaron and Dylan?*

"Ah, here it is," Branson finally said, pulling one of the pages. "Here's the summary."

Cara perused the report, which indicated that the DNA testing lab, AADC—Anchorage Advanced Diagnostic Center—had concluded the "probability of match" was 99.9 percent for A. Kennedy and D. Kennedy.

Branson looked vindicated. "You see? It wasn't our mistake. This is what was reported by the lab. You best take it up with them."

"Can I see the actual report from the lab?" Cara asked. "The one with the seal and signature of the doctor?"

Lieutenant Branson riffled through the papers again, his frown reappearing. He paused on a typed note. "Looks like the original report was sent to APD." Cara was perplexed by this. "That's not protocol, is it?"

Branson looked indignant, or perhaps he was just trying to cover for the faux pas. "Look, this is between AADC and your colleagues at APD. It's not the first time they've overstepped."

Cara took the dig in stride since she was still part of APD.

"I'm sure we would have raised a fuss about having our own copy on file, but as you know, getting anything through AADC is a tough row to hoe right now."

Branson was referring to a relatively recent Alaskan state law requiring DNA samples to be taken from all people charged with a crime against another person or a felony. A number of police departments dropped the ball, failing to collect, and after missing DNA evidence made the headlines, police were frantically backtracking and collecting DNA samples from people with prior convictions. As a result, the AADC staff was backlogged.

Branson looked down at the note again. "A Ms. Wanda Doyle requested the report to close their own missing person's case. See if you can talk to her."

Cara was startled to hear Wanda's name. She knew the administrative assistant well. Her son had attended the same preschool Dylan went to. She had been the one who had sympathized with her the most over the loss of her family.

The lieutenant stood up. "Now, I'm a busy man, Detective Kennedy. It was just blue line courtesy that I saw you without an appointment."

After leaving the trooper station, Cara immediately called the DNA lab, only to get an automated recording instructing her to leave a message and callback number. She resisted her urge to throw her phone at the wall and headed to Anchorage PD.

CARA REMEMBERED WANDA as having a retro feathered haircut, but now she had toned it down, gotten a shorter 'do that suited her and made her look more professional, more dynamic. Her whole demeanor and the way she carried herself had seemingly altered because of it—more confident and secure. "Cara!" she said in surprise.

"How *are* you?" Wanda chirped in a long-lost-friend tone once they were seated at her desk.

"How is Theo?" Cara thought to ask.

"Oh, he's getting into his talking-back age," she said. "You know, when they start thinking 'I don't have to listen to mommy anymore.'"

Cara felt a sharp pang, similar to the one she felt at Timothy's funeral. She had been cut off from seeing the next stage of her own boy's growth. The little moments. The messes he would have made stomping in from the snow and mud. The occasional brilliant things he might say out of the blue. The way his contagious laugh at the smallest of things would get them all into hysterics.

She pulled herself together and showed Wanda the autopsy report of mismatched DNA.

"Holy cannoli" was all Wanda had to offer as she stared at the report.

"AST informed me that you may have gotten the original DNA report from the lab. I'd like to see it, please."

"Funny, I don't remember receiving the test results, but let me look into it," she said.

Wanda went to a back room, and Cara sat feeling the stares from the other officers even as they pretended not to see her. A year ago, she had been widely known as "the crazy lady" who had been taken off duty by a psychologist. No one wanted to stick their foot into that pile.

Wanda returned, flipping through the documents, her expression casting into consternation. "Sorry, hon, I don't see anything here. Maybe AST was mistaken," she finally said.

"Somebody either lied or fucked up. The lab, AST, or APD. And someone's got to answer for this." Cara's voice had risen a couple of decibels and the room seemed to go silent. She could feel her cheeks burn with frustration.

Wanda tried to take it down a notch by lowering her voice to a whisper. "You know, it was a pretty chaotic time. We were moving offices when your family . . . I mean, the remains . . . were found and I imagine AADC has their own problems. I'm not saying it's an excuse or an explanation, but maybe there was some kind of mix-up? Lines crossing. That sort of thing. I'll leave a message with AADC and I promise I'll update you as soon as I hear anything. All right?"

Cara wanted to scream in frustration, but with darkness already setting in, she had no other recourse than to head back to her apartment.

CARA COULD FEEL herself growing increasingly tense on the drive home. Not knowing what had happened to her family would consume her until she had answers.

She parked in her designated spot in the alleyway behind her unit, then headed to her apartment using the paved walkway between the two-story townhouses. Cara stopped short when she noticed a small splotch of red in the snow under the dim light of a mansard lamp-post. *Blood?* She bent down to take a look, flashing a beam from her cell phone at the discolored drops, but she couldn't be sure.

Cara froze again when she saw that the door to her unit had been broken open. She went into police mode and scanned the immediate area for anyone in the vicinity. Cara had an end unit, away from the street, but the alleyway behind made it easily accessible without her neighbors noticing. Her breath quickened as she returned to her front door, grabbed her Glock, and listened for any activity inside. She finally kicked it all the way open and entered with the gun pointed in front of her, ready to do battle.

While she didn't have much in the way of furniture or anything of value, it was clear that her living room had been ransacked—chairs upturned, house plants and vases smashed on the floor; the lamp on the table was in pieces as if someone had taken a bat to it. But the most chilling detail was the phrase in red paint weeping down the living room's white wall.

Curiosity killed the cat

CHAPTER FIFTEEN

ELLIE

ELLIE DROVE HER FIRECRACKER-RED JEEP TO JIM ARREAK'S tollbooth. She didn't know how Jim could sit in that frigid booth all day without being bored out of his mind during the tourist-scarce low season. When he looked out the window and saw Ellie and Shane, he seemed to fall out of his chair for a moment. Never in her entire twenty-odd years in Point Mettier had Ellie ever brought a visitor back with her.

Jim slid open the window and squinted as he inspected the man in the passenger seat. "Is that . . . ?" Jim's unofficial job, after all, was to be on the lookout for her ex-husband and to not let him through.

"Yeah, this here's Shane. The one who I've been telling you was going to kill me unless I killed him first."

Shane smiled and waved at Jim without contradicting the narrative.

Jim scratched his head under his bomber cap. "Okay . . ." From somewhere behind him in the heated booth came high-pitched yaps. Jim turned and disappeared for a moment before putting Vlad's head through the window. "Want your dog back?"

Vlad yapped and wagged his tail, but when Ellie pulled him through the window, he went into a deep growl and bared his teeth at Shane. "Keep that mutt away from me!" Shane yelled.

Why a former bank robber and killer would be afraid of a little Jack Russell terrier was beyond her, but Ellie handed Vlad back to Jim. "Better keep him a bit longer. I'll come by your unit after you get off."

Jim nodded. He was one of two people in Point Mettier besides Ellie whom Vlad didn't have a problem with. The other was Lonnie, Chief Sipley's daughter, who had a mental disability that Ellie didn't know what to call. She had a way with animals.

As they drove through the seemingly endless dark hole through the mountain, Shane had to comment. "So what made you decide to live in a hellhole of a place where you have to drive through a goddam tunnel?"

"You did," Ellie replied flatly.

When they finally parked at the lot in front of the towers, Shane got out to stare at the fourteen-story behemoth of a building. "Who was the fuckin' genius who decided to build this huge monstrosity in the middle of goddamn nowhere?"

"The military built it back in the fifties."

"Where are the rest of the houses?"

"This is it. Everybody lives here in the Dave-Co."

"Everybody?" It was as if the idea couldn't penetrate Shane's thick skull.

"Yup."

"Well piss my leg, you sure picked a strange place to live. Why's it called the Dave-Co?"

"Short for Davidson Condos, and if you don't like it, you can leave. You're the one who gave yourself an invitation."

A woman with an olive-green beret walked by, leading a moose by a leash. She stared at Shane for a moment. "Outsider, stranger, intruder, pariah, vile, evil," she said before continuing to the barn.

"What's the matter with her? She soft in the head?" Shane whispered.

"That's Lonnie and her moose, Denny. She suffered some trauma in her younger days." Lonnie had witnessed her mother's murder by her stepfather, after which she was sent to an institution. Her biological father, Chief Sipley, finally took custody and got her out of there. Ellie wasn't really sure if Lonnie had been born with her condition, but the trauma sure hadn't helped. "She's a heck of a lot smarter than you, though. She didn't mess up her life doing something stupid enough to land her in jail."

Shane sighed. "You gonna keep throwing barbs at me? 'Cause if I remember correctly, the dumb thing I did that landed me in jail was putting my trust in you."

"All right then, if you don't want to listen to me mouth off, how 'bout we both just keep our traps shut? I like the sound of silence."

Lonnie must have sensed the conflict between Ellie and Shane because she doubled back and walked right up to them. "Is the old man bothering you, Mrs. Wright?" she asked in a concerned voice.

"No, Lonnie, I'm fine. I don't need any help." Considering that the last time Lonnie was "helpful" she had knocked two men unconscious, it was probably better that she kept her distance.

Lonnie gave Shane a cutting glare, which made him shift in his boots. "I gotta take Denny back to the barn before the cold, frost, snow, storm. Stormy weather. Storm the castle. There's a storm coming."

Shane's mouth gaped an O.

"You do that, Lonnie. Make sure Denny's warm and dry," Ellie encouraged.

Lonnie took her cue to go back to leading Denny to the barn.

Ellie and Shane entered the lobby, passing Chuck Marino's store filled with tourist tchotchkes and overpriced sundries on the way to the elevator. "Does he sell smokes?" Shane asked, and Ellie nodded, so he decided to make a pit stop. Chuck looked up from his paper and had the same slack-jawed reaction as Jim.

Ellie hitched a thumb toward Shane, who was staring at the various animal heads on the wall seemingly watching his every move. "This is my ex," she said by way of explanation.

"The same ex that—"

"Yup," Ellie cut him off and nodded. Chuck gave Shane an evil-eyed look in response.

"Have you been tellin' everyone I'm the Devil?"

"Pretty much."

"You know the condo rules," Chuck said. "Visitors aren't allowed to bring firearms on the premises. Want me to give him a pat down?"

Ellie grinned. "I'm sure he'd like that."

Shane took a step back, got in a fighting stance.

"It's all right," Ellie said. "I took his weapons before we got in the car. He just wants to buy smokes."

Shane pointed toward a pack of Marlboros behind Chuck.

"Just holler if you need me," Chuck said to Ellie, continuing to give Shane pointed glances while he paid for his pack.

Once they got to her apartment, both of them lit up their ciggies. A habit neither of them had ever been able to kick, which had probably contributed to his cancer.

Then he gave the unit the once-over, inspecting the kitchen, the bathroom, and the bedroom as if he were casing the joint. "Bed looks comfy."

"You're not staying here," Ellie said. "After we go over a plan, you're heading to one of my rentals on the fourteenth floor. No maid service, though, so you gotta clean up after yourself."

Now he was examining her display of firearms, getting his grubby hands all over her weaponry. Woodie was still in the trunk of her Jeep but Scarface, her AR-15, was displayed on the wall as well as some more decorative handguns. "Sure brings back memories," he said, stroking Scarface. They were mostly memories that Ellie preferred to forget.

"How 'bout some grub? We got a Chinese food delivery service in the building."

"I don't eat Chinese," Shane said.

"Well, you do now because it's our only option. What do you want?"

"Okay, get me some of them noodles. Whaddya call them? Chow chow?"

Ellie rolled her eyes at Shane. "You mean chow mein?"

"Yeah, get me that."

A FEW MINUTES later, Amy Lin, the teenager who helped her mother run Star Asian Food, knocked on the door. Ellie opened the door and Amy peered in like a timid mouse, her squeaky delivery cart poised behind her. She was deathly afraid of Vlad, but when Vlad didn't appear, she seemed to relax a bit—then got startled again, this time by the presence of Shane.

"Oh," she said, halting at some invisible line on the carpet and refusing to come in any farther. The poor kid. She had been through a lot recently. Everything seemed to scare her these days and anyone would be scared by Shane's grouchy mug.

"Don't worry, he looks worse than his bite," Ellie said. She chuckled inside, thinking it was something similar to what she would have said about Vlad. She handed thirty dollars to Amy, who was now coughing from the extra cigarette smoke. "Keep the change." Amy's eyes lit up at that, and she retreated into the hall to her cart.

After their food was unpacked and Ellie got Shane a fork because she didn't want to see him even attempt to eat noodles with chopsticks, they sat down at the dining table.

"Just like old times," Shane said.

"Don't get used to it."

She stubbed her cigarette in the ashtray. "Now let's talk about the plan."

"How many men are at the lair?"

"There were only supposed to be three injured men and some women and children, but it seemed like they had gotten some reinforcements."

"How many?"

"Couldn't say, but there sure was a lot of firepower. Not going to be as easy as bank robbing."

Ellie could see the wheels spinning in Shane's head. This was a new kind of operation. "We still got the element of surprise. How about numbers? We got anyone else joining our team?"

Ellie ran down her list. "Well, there's Chief Sipley, but if I have to be honest, his aim ain't that great and there's no upside for him to head out there given he's on a short leash with state police. J.B.'s the junior officer, but he's still recovering from being shot, plus he's lost some toes."

"Jesus, this sorry-ass place is full of sorry-ass people," Shane interjected.

Ellie took offense to that. "What did I say about you and your snide comments?"

Shane piped down.

"I could call up Detective Kennedy. She's got a stake in this too."

"That wispy little woman at the funeral?" He guffawed. "Didn't you tell me how she nearly got you killed on your first go-round?"

Ellie had to agree on that one.

"What about your friend in the tollbooth?"

"Jim? He's gotta man the booth. Plus, he's no use to us when he gets the shakes." Ellie didn't know the full tragic story, but it had something to do with his coastal Native village disappearing under water. She would admit that, for a long time, she believed her favorite news show when it said climate change was a big fat hoax, but up in Alaska, they could see what was happening with their own eyes. On the other hand, oil was Alaska's lifeblood, and every Alaskan got a royalty check from the drilling, so nobody was going to clamor to stop it. Anyway, Jim Arreak lost his home and took to drinking, which also lost him his family. He somehow wound up in Point Mettier, where he more or less sobered up except for the occasional binge.

Shane was about to say something but checked himself. "So, who else you got?"

"That leaves Chuck Marino. He's a guy I can count on, and he served in Afghanistan." What Ellie admired most about Chuck was that he could shoot like a regular Buffalo Bill in a Wild West show. The only person who could shoot better than Chuck was probably Ellie herself. If he was Buffalo Bill, she was Annie Oakley, and everybody knew that Annie Oakley was the better shot. "But he's opposed to doing anything illegal, so it'll take some convincing."

"Well, we should have a talk with him."

A thought crossed Ellie's mind like lightning striking her mental tree. It was an outlandish idea but suddenly seemed like a good one. "You know, there's another person who's usually game for anything. She's not a likely suspect for being backup on a raid, but I tell you, this woman's fearless, and I've been teaching her how to shoot out on my range in the woods. She learns quick, and with a little more training, she'd be up to par. Her name's Mariko Ishida, and she's a lounge singer at the bar."

"Doesn't sound like much of a team," Shane scowled. But without a whole lot of options, Shane agreed that he would at least meet with Mariko.

CHAPTER SIXTEEN

MIA

ANCHORAGE PRO CLEANERS WAS A JANITORIAL SERVICE headquartered downtown. A portion of Mia's wages would go directly to the shelter and the rest she'd receive in cash. Mia didn't have a car, so Sandra asked one of the women at the shelter who also worked at the cleaning service to show her the bus route. The bus system was called People Mover, which sounded appropriate. Mia felt excited to get on one of the big, white-and-blue vehicles that rumbled, screeched, and hissed when they stopped. She was fascinated by the images she saw through the impossibly large windows of each People Mover.

Mia had been to some of the smaller towns near Unity, but what she saw through the panes showed Anchorage to be huge in comparison, with tall buildings seemingly made of glass, traffic signs, utility poles, and vehicles that whizzed by. It was a chaotic blur of images as the bus passed people, houses, and strip malls. Bigger cities had been the setting of many of Marla and Sonia's DVDs, but to experience one in person through all her senses was startling. The contrast was even more noticeable after the sun went down. In Unity, when darkness descended, activity slowed, and people retreated into their huts. But here, darkness was hardly an impediment. Mia had to adjust to the almost blindingly bright indoor illumination and the streetlamps and headlights outside that kept the streets bustling with activity.

At Anchorage Pro, Mia was given a uniform and an ID badge and was shown where she needed to clock in every day before she went with a crew in a van to her designated location. Mia's first location was a high school, and for the first few days, she trained with a woman named Sofia.

Mia thought she knew how to clean, but in Unity, they mostly cleaned with water and rags. Here, everything had regulated steps they needed to follow, such as putting up a yellow plastic sign that said CAUTION WET FLOOR when they started mopping. The broom was to be swept in imaginary garden planting rows. When they cleaned the bathrooms, they knocked first and announced themselves, then put out another sign that read RESTROOM OUT OF ORDER. There were all kinds of toxic-fumed cleansers, disinfectants and polishes, paper towels, microfiber cloths—a whole cart full of tools whose wheels grumbled on the floor.

The school was dirtier than any place Mia had ever seen. The students left toilet paper, feminine pads, cigarettes, and even needles everywhere, and gum all over the floors and the lockers needed to be scraped off. When students or teachers passed them, Mia was surprised that they never paused to greet her as people did in Unity. It was as if everyone from Anchorage Pro Cleaners was invisible. But Mia did as she was told without complaint. She didn't take endless smoking breaks or cuss and complain like some of the other people on the crew.

It wasn't long before her supervisor told her there was an opening at another location. The coveted spot at the medical building was like a promotion, he said, with only the best and most responsible workers chosen. And it included a pay raise.

Her first day at Almagor Tech, Mia was dazzled by all the floor-to-ceiling windows and glass doors. She had never seen such a building as this before. It already looked and smelled cleaner when they arrived than when they were done cleaning the high school, but the crew had more duties. Everything had to sparkle, and everything needed to be wiped down with disinfectant. Mia liked working there. She was delighted—if startled—to discover that the light in the bathroom turned on automatically, blinking in a chorus of *tinkles* before it remained steady. At first, she couldn't understand how the faucets worked. She thought they were all broken. But when she started wiping the first wash basin, the water turned on by itself. She spent five minutes in awe, passing her hand back and forth underneath, watching the faucet turn on and off on its own.

WORKING AT ALMAGOR, Mia made enough money to apply for her own rental apartment instead of staying at the women's shelter. She was happy to be out of the big red box house where the women looked sad and the frizzy-haired lady argued with invisible spirits. Sandra was proud of Mia and said she was a "bona fide success story," which meant that she was someone Sandra could put on the fund-raising poster board at the women's shelter as a star example. With housing assistance, Mia found a furnished studio in a three-story apartment building downtown. It had a tiny kitchenette with a half-sized refrigerator, a microwave, and brown carpeting. Mia had never experienced carpet before, so the first thing she did after moving in was to take off her shoes and walk around the apartment, feeling the softness under her feet, like forest tree moss. There was also a community kitchen with a proper stove and a shared lounge with a TV and books. In addition to her apartment, she needed a key for the building and the elevator. It seemed that in Man's World, keys were needed for everything.

Mia didn't go out of her way to make friends with other residents in the building. She felt intimidated by the cadence of English in Man's World, which was much faster than what she was used to. But she did make friends with one of her neighbors after she opened her door one day to a scratching sound and found a black kitten outside. There was a no pets policy in the building with signs posted everywhere, so when a young Black woman came running out of apartment 302 and quickly stammered apologies, Mia could tell she was worried that she might report her cat to the manager. So Mia bent down and stroked the feline and smiled, to assure both the kitten and his owner that she was on their side. "That's a good kitty," she singsonged.

"He seems to like you."

The cat rubbed against her legs and looked up at her with playful green eyes.

The woman looked relieved. "I'm Diedre," she said.

"I'm Jennifer," Mia said, using her alias, and they were instant friends.

A government-sponsored program also got Mia a cell phone with a reduced-rate data plan. She discovered there was much more that she could do on the phone besides make calls. Diedre showed her how she could search the Internet and even watch movies, but Diedre warned her not to do that because the amount of data she was allowed to use on her plan would be gone too quickly. Mia became comfortable using her new phone for everything from paying her bills to learning bus routes. She was given one thousand minutes for voice calls, which seemed an enormous amount, considering there was no one she could think of calling except Marla or Sonia. But then she thought of Alex.

She knew he was at the Northwest Indian tribal college in Washington. There were only two residences there: one for families and the other for singles, so she called the number listed for singles and asked for Alex Arnatsiaq. She said she was visiting from his Native village where there was no cell service, and she didn't know his phone number.

The electronic *trrrrill trrrrill* of the phone rang three times before Alex's muffled voice said, "Hello?" It sounded like he was far away, in a box.

"Alex?" She had to confirm it really was him.

"Who is this?" came the voice on the other end of the line.

"It's Mia," she said. "I left Unity. I live in Anchorage now, and I have a job."

"Mia!" He sounded more than a little surprised. "Wow! That is . . . that's awesome." She wished she could see his face. She didn't like the distance in his voice, her inability to touch him.

Mia went on to tell him about her job at Anchorage Pro Cleaners and her new apartment. He responded with "Yeah?" several times, but didn't ask her any questions or talk about his life at the college. She asked when he was going to visit Unity again. She knew he would have to fly in to Anchorage first, and she was excited to see him.

"I don't know," he responded. "I don't want to spend too much on plane fare, and I've lined up a job for the summer." Mia thought she heard a girl tittering in the background. When Mia asked about school, Alex said, "Actually, I've got to get to class pretty soon. Can we talk later?"

Mia felt stunned. She had been watching the clock to see how much of the thousand minutes she was using. It had been less than twenty. Back at Unity, they could talk for hours.

"Okay. I'll tell you my phone number."

"Your number automatically shows up on my phone, so you don't have to worry about that."

After they hung up, Mia felt an emptiness she hadn't felt before. She waited for a call that night, but there was none.

Finally, in the deep night hours, a *ping* sounded on her phone and Mia picked it up excitedly to say hello before she realized it wasn't a call but a text from Alex saying he was sorry that he had gotten busy and couldn't call back. Despite being in her new apartment with a soft bed and soft carpet, Mia felt a sense of loss and sudden loneliness.

In the morning, Mia pulled herself off her tear-soaked pillow. An expression she had often heard in movies was *There are plenty of other fish in the sea.* But what did it matter if it wasn't the right fish? And although Mia knew plenty about ice fishing, she knew nothing about how to lure a "fish" in Man's World.

———

AT FIRST MIA didn't know what kind of company Almagor was. She came to understand it was a pharmaceutical company, but she didn't know what exactly it made. What she did know was that there was so much glass to clean—glass window panes, glass elevators, glass bottles, and glass tubes. She always felt as if she had to tread lightly so as not to bump into anything breakable and hated the *screeeech* her squeegee made against the shiny surfaces. Nothing at Almagor felt natural. The building reminded her of the science fiction films she had sometimes watched with Marla and Sonia.

The only part she really disliked was an expansive room in the basement that was as big as the cafeteria at the high school she had cleaned. It was filled with reclining chairs made of blue plastic, shaped like seals arching their hind flippers up. They were lined up in rows, and in between were large, white ice chest–like machines bristling with tubes and dials. The *schizzling* buzz of the fluorescent lights sounded like mosquitos. She recognized the dark red splotches that she sometimes had to scrub out of the floors and machines to be blood, and that was creepy. She was always generous with her use of the toxic-smelling bleach in this room.

One day while cleaning the Room of Doom, as Mia referred to it in her mind, a man in a white lab coat said hi to her as he retrieved a clipboard full of scribbles. Mia was surprised that he actually stopped to speak to her as if she were a human being and without the air of superiority that most people had, including some of her fellow workers at Anchorage Pro.

"I'm Aaron Kennedy," he said introducing himself. Mia was unable to look him in the eye.

"Jennifer."

"You're new, aren't you?"

She nodded, finally venturing to look up. His eyes were the color of the feathers of a great blue heron, and his hair was a silky gold. "You're probably wondering what we do here."

Mia found herself still unable to talk, but he continued.

"It's where people donate blood. It's for a good cause. It helps a lot of sick people."

"Oh?" She finally found her tongue. Her opinion about the Room of Doom shifted slightly.

"I work a lot of late nights, so guess I'll be seeing you around," he said.

"Okay, Mr. Kennedy," she said, focusing on running her mop across the glossy floor so that he wouldn't see her cheeks burning.

"Aaron's fine. See you around, Jennifer." He smiled at her and went out the door.

Mia found that her legs had inexplicably turned to jelly. She couldn't understand why her heart had started galloping or why, when she got back to her apartment, she ran the conversation over and over in her head, remembering the smoothness in the tone of his voice and the refined way he had of holding himself. He wasn't awkward like Alex sometimes was. He was more assured, more adult, but still friendly and down to earth. Aaron seemed, in a word, *perfect*.

CHAPTER SEVENTEEN

CARA

CARA SURVEYED THE WRECKAGE OF HER APARTMENT. THE "curiosity killed the cat" message on the wall did little to discourage her. Instead, the desecration of her apartment made her even more determined to find out who was responsible for the damage and possibly had answers to what happened to her family. Not only would she have to repaint the wall, but the sofa and dining chairs were ripped and rendered unusable, there were shards of glass everywhere, and she would have to call a locksmith. There was a modicum of relief in knowing she could still deadbolt the door from inside. Inspecting the door handle and places the vandals would likely have touched, Cara didn't find any usable prints. They had worn gloves. The bedroom, thankfully, had been left largely untouched, and her laptop was still in her briefcase. Clearly, this was not a case of robbery, but an act meant to threaten her.

Given her visits to the law enforcement agencies, maybe this was intended to scare her away from investigating Aaron and Dylan's disappearance. The message was clear. Whoever these people were, they knew where she lived and had the means to enter and violate her space. Were these the same people who had been feeding information to Wolf's gang that was now led by Victor?

Cara's mental notes were interrupted by a loud rap at the door. She drew her Glock and flattened against the wall. "Who is it?" she yelled, with both hands on the gun.

"It's me. J.B.," the voice came through the door.

Cara relaxed but took a look through the peephole before opening the door.

On the other side, J.B. stood with a fragrant bouquet of flowers— pink roses, white daisies, pastel carnations. "I had an appointment to be fitted for my new toes, so I thought I'd swing—" He halted mid-sentence, and his smile faded as soon as he stepped inside and saw the ominous words painted on the wall along with the carnage of furniture. His hand instinctively went for his gun, although he didn't pull it out. "What happened here?"

"It's okay, they've gone."

"Have you called the police?" Cara shook her head no while J.B. instantly went into crime scene mode, cautiously scouring the room while being careful not to step on or touch anything.

"It's just a scare tactic. Taking a stab here, but I suppose it's because I've been investigating Aaron and Dylan's disappearance."

"Disappearance?" J.B. had a puzzled expression. "You mean deaths?"

"I'll explain everything," Cara said, taking J.B.'s cue and dialing 911.

WHILE THEY WAITED for police to arrive, Cara found two chairs that weren't destroyed and placed them upright. "Thank you for these," she said, taking the bouquet and putting it in a glass that hadn't been shattered. Then she sat down and explained everything she had learned since she had last talked to him. With every detail, his eyes grew wider and somehow darker. "So whose bodies are they, and what happened to your family's?" he asked.

"I don't know, but I'm going to find out."

"I don't think it's safe for you to stay here alone," J.B. said. "You should come back with me to Point Mettier."

"I can conduct an investigation better from here."

"All right, then I'm staying here with you. I'm on paid leave until a shrink clears me for duty."

Cara hesitated. She didn't mind J.B. staying there, but the air was thick with unspoken thoughts. If there was a possibility Aaron was alive, was she still a married woman, even if Aaron had been legally declared dead?

J.B. seemed to read her mental calculations in her lack of a response. "Or I can book a room someplace nearby. I have to go in for PT tomorrow anyway. Maybe I can stop by Anchorage PD. Sniff around a bit. Talk to Charlie Wilkes and see if I can shake anything out of him." Charlie Wilkes, whom J.B. knew from the National Guard, also worked at Anchorage PD, and J.B. had once suspected he might be the one on the inside feeding info to the gang in Chugach Village.

Before Cara could answer, two officers arrived to investigate the break-in. She didn't recognize either of them. One was E. Hoover, according to the name stitched on her uniform. She had a sandy blond ponytail and an all-business demeanor. Her partner, G. Elliott, a heavyset man in a ski cap, was fixated simultaneously on his cell phone and a little memo pad. They grilled Cara as if she were the suspect of the crime she had called in, but their tone softened when they discovered that Cara was a member of Anchorage PD, albeit on disability, and that J.B. was an officer in Point Mettier.

They asked if she had installed any security cameras in her apartment, which she had not. The complex had a few strategically placed cameras, but Cara knew they were easily avoidable if the vandals had come from the dimly lit alley to her end unit. She thought there might be footage of a license plate, if they had driven into the alley. So Cara called the property manager about the footage only to have him sheepishly admit that the camera in the alleyway had not been working for over a month.

Predictably, there wasn't much the officers could do, other than write up a report and suggest she install cameras in her unit. "Probably a disgruntled ex," they said, based on the personal message and lack of stolen items. Despite Cara insisting that no such ex existed, she knew there was little hope of a proper investigation unless this was followed by more break-ins in her neighborhood. APD was always short-staffed and needed to focus on more serious crimes.

After the officers left, Cara was able to find a handyman who worked into the night to fix the door. Despite the new lock, she and J.B. agreed it was better to stay at a nearby inn instead of being continually on edge at the defiled townhouse.

The basic chain motel was clean and functional. She booked a room for two nights, thinking that would give her time to clean up the mess, paint over the wall, and maybe find some replacement furniture. Cara fell asleep as soon as her head hit the pillow, exhausted from the day's ordeals and comforted by J.B.'s presence.

In the morning, J.B. helped Cara clean up her apartment, sweeping up and putting everything back together so that at least it was tidy again. He also made a trip to the hardware store for paint and a set of security cameras. J.B. seemed to be all the king's horses and all the king's men, picking up the pieces of Cara's broken life. She appreciated him, maybe even needed him at this juncture in her life.

He then headed out for his scheduled physical therapy session while Cara dug in to research the people whose photos Angelo had helped identify.

SHE COULDN'T FIND much on George Apernathy. His last known place of work was at a construction company. When Cara called, she was told that he had been a temporary employee and had not left any forwarding information. There were no marriage certificates, housing data, or arrest warrants on file, so he was a virtual blank.

Cara decided to move on to the next person on the list. Rebecca Taylor. She had worked at the Z.J. Loussac Library for at least five years, so that was a good starting point. Cara made an appointment to speak with the head librarian. Cara was familiar with the library, which was named after a Russian immigrant who had moved to Alaska in the early 1900s and operated a drugstore before serving two terms as mayor of Anchorage. His philanthropy had led him to fund the first incarnation of the city's public library in the fifties. The current version was a monolith of concrete with a glass-covered lobby. Entering the structure, a network of spiderwebbed metal pipes and lights hanging from the ceiling made Cara feel more like she was in an airplane hangar than a library.

The head librarian, Jackie, was a soft-spoken woman who practically whispered, the way someone who had been a librarian for many years probably would. "What can I help you with?" she asked.

Cara flashed her the badge she still carried. "My name is Detective Kennedy, and I'm trying to track Rebecca Taylor's current whereabouts."

"I'm afraid Rebecca hasn't worked here for about a year and a half," Jackie said. "I'd like to know what happened to her as well. It's odd that you're here now, when I made a report back then."

Cara's eyes grew wide. "You made a report?"

"Yes, when she didn't show up for work, I called her cell phone and left numerous messages, but there was no answer. I know she didn't have any relatives out here, so I went to the address we had on file myself and knocked on the door, but no one answered. I called all the hospitals in the area to see if she might be at one of them but came up negative. I was really worried and made a report with the police. I never heard back, so I called in to check whether they had found her, and they told me that they had found a Rebecca Taylor with the same birth date who had recently moved from Anchorage to Chicago, so the case was closed. They wouldn't disclose her new contact info, and it never felt right to me. Rebecca didn't seem like the type to just stop working one day and leave without telling us. Regardless, I never heard from her again."

"Did she seem spooked before she left? Or was there anything out of the ordinary about the way she acted?"

"Well yes, actually. It's been weighing on me since. One morning, just before she disappeared, she fainted at work. Gave us quite a scare. I don't know if her disappearance had anything to do with it. Whether she had some kind of health problem. But like I said, she wasn't in a local hospital."

Cara questioned Jackie for a while longer, but there was nothing more she could tell her. Cara promised she would follow up on the Rebecca Taylor in Chicago and update Jackie if she learned anything more.

When Cara returned to her apartment, she looked up the police report on Rebecca Taylor and saw that it had been an open and shut case. Rebecca was found in Chicago, having quit her job in Anchorage of her own volition. Cara called the phone number on file, but it had been disconnected. Cara wasn't sure what to make of it all. Had the case been doctored to make it seem as if Rebecca had been found? Or had Rebecca been spooked by something and fled to Chicago? With so many more questions than answers, Cara wondered if she would have to follow her there.

CHAPTER EIGHTEEN

MIA

EVER SINCE SHE SAW THE POLICE CARS PARKED IN FRONT OF
the Lonely Diner, Mia hadn't been able to shake the feeling that the
past was about to catch up with her. Lately, Mia had been feeling lost
and at sea in Man's World. She was never interested in the sports
games shown on the diner's television, but sometimes after closing
or when the diner was empty of customers, she flipped through the
channels to see what was on the endless number of stations. The
more she watched, the emptier she felt. Perhaps it was all the people
yelling on news shows and talk shows, all the bickering, fighting,
and shootings. Or on Sundays, there were the buy-me-a-jet preach-
ers, as Mia liked to call them, trying to convince viewers they were
paying for a spot in an exclusive afterlife club. Everything was for
sale—not just goods and services but religion, hate, politics, love,

lies. Mia already felt like she was changing. Was she becoming one of them? Would things have been different if she had never gotten a job at Almagor?

A MONTH OR so after Mia started cleaning at the pharmaceutical company, she finally saw the blood donations in action. People were lined up in the blue reclining chairs in the oversized basement room. All of them had their arms splayed out on the table with needles piercing their arms—human trees being tapped for their sap. The blood coming out into the clear tubes was a dark, lingonberry red, but what was separated out of it and pulled into a plastic bag was marigold yellow. The sight had frightened Mia when she first saw it. She had seen plenty of animal blood and entrails before, but seeing so much human blood was unsettling. "They've extended plasma donation hours," Sal, one of the crew members, explained to her. "They're open 'til eight now."

"What's plasma?" Mia asked. Aaron had said they were donating blood.

"It's what they collect *from* the blood. My brother does it. Every week."

"He donates every week?" Mia's eyes widened. "You can do it that often?"

"Well, not exactly donate. You actually get paid for it. My brother says it's good money if you become a regular."

Mia started to recognize the people in the blue chairs—the same men and women coming in, twice a week, every week. The large man with the bird's-nest mustache and beard who always wore a red baseball cap. The older man with white hair and glasses who wore plaid shirts. There was the girl with the blond ponytail who always wore some kind of green uniform and sneakers that made *squick squack* noises on the marble floor. The Hispanic woman who had thick, curly hair and bright yellow loafers. They sat looking at their phones or reading books with one hand. In the other, they squeezed round rubber balls while the blood flowed from their veins through the tentacles of tubes. Mia was sure it must hurt, but they looked calm, relaxed, hardly noticing their life force being expelled through their arms.

"How much money does your cousin make donating plasma?" Mia finally asked Sal.

"He gets fifty dollars a pop. Twice a week. He comes in regular, so he makes like four hundred dollars a month. I would do it too except that the sight of blood makes me feel nauseous. But fifty dollars for just sitting there for an hour sounds pretty good otherwise."

There wasn't much that Mia needed, but an extra four hundred dollars a month could help her save up to buy a car. Diedre had sometimes given her a ride when it was snowing so that Mia wouldn't have to endure chilly waits for the bus.

"Girl, you really need a car," she had said. "It doesn't have to be a new one, but it sure beats riding the bus."

"How much does a car cost?" Mia had asked hesitantly. This was beyond the fact that she didn't know how to drive.

"Well, it depends on the car, but if you aren't picky, I've seen some beat-up old cars on Craigslist for a few thousand. You'd have to make sure they still run though, of course."

"What is *Craigslist*?"

What Mia really liked about Diedre was that she didn't judge. She didn't roll her eyes in disgust at Mia's lack of knowledge. Instead, she patiently showed Mia how to pull up boxes on Craigslist that showed photos and prices of all kinds of used cars being sold by their owners. "But don't contact anyone without me, because you can get scammed," Diedre warned, and since Mia had yet to earn any money for a car, it was just window shopping. Most of the cars they looked at in the few-thousand-dollar range were described as being undrivable or would require major repairs, but there were a few that claimed to "run and drive great."

When Mia was assigned to clean the lobby one day, she picked up one of the plasma brochures. *Donating plasma saves lives*, it said at the top. *Plasma is used to make lifesaving medicines. Every time you donate plasma, you're someone's hero.* Mia recalled her conversation with Aaron and how he had also said that what they did helped people. The thought of doing something Aaron approved of propelled her to take the step.

The brochure explained that donating plasma was safe, with few side effects, albeit a little more complicated than donating blood. Since Mia had never donated blood before, she had nothing to compare it to. To be eligible, she would have to be at least eighteen and weigh a hundred and ten pounds. Using a scale in one of the rooms at Almagor to weigh herself, she saw that she qualified. There would be a screening at check-in, and the instructions said to drink lots of water, avoid alcohol, and eat a meal high in iron and protein a few hours before the appointment.

When the office opened up, there was already a line in the lobby.

"Is this your first time plassing?" a man behind her asked.

Mia nodded. *Plassing. Is that what they called it?*

"Hope you ate a good breakfast."

Mia had eaten a bowl of cereal, her usual breakfast since coming to Man's World.

"New donors need to fill out these forms," someone at the desk announced. The rest of the donors already knew what to do and herded over to the row of self-check-in computers.

The form she needed to fill out had an extensive list of questions. She checked "no" on all the questions about diseases, most of which she'd never heard of. These were followed by more questions she didn't know the answer to—vaccinations, family medical histories, her blood type. "Don't worry about it," the lady at the desk said. "We'll do a test first."

When she was called up, a nurse weighed her and went through the form. "What have you eaten today?" Mia told her cereal, which the nurse said was not enough. So she gave Mia a bottle of horrible tasting liquid called Ensure and some crackers, then left the room, giving Mia time to down everything.

When the nurse returned, she led Mia over to one of the plastic chairs. "Did you bring a book to read?"

"No," Mia replied.

"How about a magazine?"

She brought over a cart full of magazines, and Mia sifted through the pile, picking out one with a picture-perfect house on the cover. Then the nurse rubbed something wet and cold on her arm, told her to squeeze a red ball, inserted a needle, and taped it to her arm. Mia didn't like how the lights flickered above her, and the drafty room made her feel suddenly chilled. But the nurse put a blanket on her without her even having to ask. It was as if she were being put down for a nap.

How bad can it be? Mia thought to herself, looking around the room filled with quiet, calm people. She reclined like the rest of the group and tried to focus on the magazine instead of the dark fluid traveling from her arm into a bag. Mia was truly fascinated by the houses in the magazine, which were unlike any she had seen outside of a movie—she had only known Unity huts, the women's shelter, and her apartment. Every detail entranced her. Hanging pendant lamps, colorfully patterned rugs, grand staircases, plush white sofas, fireplaces, marble sinks with gold faucets, and beautifully ordered flower gardens.

But then she started feeling hot, and she couldn't kick off the blanket with her trapped arm. Then the room started to spin like leaves in a whirlwind. She dropped the magazine and felt herself slipping from consciousness. Someone ran toward her, *clap clop, clap clop.*

"Are you okay?"

"I'm hot," Mia said. Then everything went blank, and she woke up on a flat bed with tissue paper *crinkle crackling* under her.

"It happens a lot to plasser virgins," the nurse told her. "The first time is always the worst. Next time, eat a nice, healthy, high-protein meal before you come in. Nothing greasy or high in fat. No smoking or drinking. Bring a snack too, like a protein bar."

Mia wasn't sure there was going to be a second time, but when she checked out, the woman at the counter gave her a prepaid debit card with the Almagor logo on it and told her, "You get seventy-five dollars each time for the first two donations."

So Mia returned a second time to get the other seventy-five dollars. She felt fatigued afterward, but it was worth it. She had earned a hundred and fifty dollars in just two hours.

The next week was easier. She was already in the database, and checking in was a breeze with the prefilled computer forms and automatically clicking no on all the checkboxes without pausing to read the questions. It's what she saw everyone else doing. To receive the normal fifty dollars per session, she stuck her card in a slot and the money was added to her debit card.

After about a month of plassing, Mia was told about a new program. "Repeat donors can get a hundred and fifty dollars every week for participating in an experiment," the check-in lady said. "But only select people will be chosen to participate, and the sign-up roster has been filling up fast. Want an application?"

Mia nodded. With an extra a hundred and fifty dollars a week on top of what she was already saving, she would soon be on her way to a Craigslist car.

The application form for the new program seemed even more endless than the first-time-plasser questionnaire, asking for next of kin, her previous three addresses, three emergency contacts, their relationships and addresses, the schools she had attended, and other information that Mia only had blanks for. She listed the address of the shelter as her last address and named Marla, Sonia, and Sandra at the shelter as her emergency contacts. With her numerous blank spaces, she was sure she would be rejected. But two weeks later, she was told she was accepted and scheduled for an initiation interview.

After first signing a long document called a nondisclosure agreement, which said she promised not to talk about the experiment, she was shown into a conference room. Her pulse quickened immediately when she saw, to her surprise, that Aaron was conducting the interview.

She hadn't talked to him since that day in the big room, although she sometimes spotted him through the glass door and vertical blinds of his office.

"Jennifer, right?" he said as she stepped in.

Mia could feel herself grow hot. She was elated that he'd remembered her alias name. "Yes, Mr. Kennedy . . . I mean, Aaron."

"I didn't know you were a plasma donor."

Mia nodded. "I started last month."

His expression seemed to sour as he looked over her application. "There's a lot of missing information here."

"Yes, but they told me I was accepted to the program."

"I'm afraid there's been a mistake, Jennifer."

"A mistake?"

"They missed it during the screening process, but your hemoglobin level is right at the cutoff mark. You won't be able to participate, I'm afraid."

"But I've been donating plasma all along."

"Our new program has a slightly higher cutoff rate."

"Maybe I—"

"I'm so sorry," he said interrupting her. And it was as if he were brushing her away like a fly on the window. He scuttled her out, closing the door behind her with a final *click thump* that made her heart drop.

Later she learned that the plassing times for the new program were restricted to specific evening hours that conflicted with her Anchorage Pro job, so it was for the best that she didn't qualify. And even without participating in the frequent donor program, Mia was able to save enough from her salary and the daytime plassing sessions to buy a car off Craigslist. It was a gray compact with 180,000 miles on it. Diedre came with her to inspect the car since Mia had not yet gotten a driver's license. They went around the block a couple of times to make sure that it was at least drivable. There was a dent on the left side, and the back armrest was broken, but the important thing, according to Diedre, was that it wasn't dripping oil and the motor sounded good. Diedre was already giving her driving lessons in exchange for taking care of her cats whenever she went to spend the night with her boyfriend. She'd gotten another kitten, a white one, to be a playmate to her black one. Mia didn't mind looking after them because they made her feel less alone.

ON HER EVENING shift, Mia sometimes saw Aaron examining the people hooked up to the blood collecting machines and scribbling notes on his clipboard.

Initially, there were only six people in the program. Then it doubled to twelve. Mia was on her shift inside the tube-filled harvesting room when a donor fainted, just like she had on her first day. The woman raised her free arm slightly before melting into her seal-shaped seat. Aaron and other people in white lab coats rushed over to her the way Mia imagined they had done for her. They carried her away to a separate room, probably where Mia found herself after her own fainting spell.

A week later there was another incident. This time, it was the man with the gray beard that she recognized as a frequent donor. He had finished his plasma donation and had just gotten up from the chair when he swayed the way the trees in the forest would after one of the women at Unity had chainsawed its trunk for timber, and then he collapsed to the ground, and his eyes seemed to roll to the back of his head. There was a chorus of gasps and once again, the people in the white lab coats came running. Aaron made an announcement after that. "Let's end today's sessions. You'll all still get full pay," he said, which relieved everyone.

This time, there was a more heightened commotion with the *squickety squackety* of numerous shoes running on the glossy floor. When all the donors had left, the man still hadn't come to. "We need to get him to a hospital!" someone yelled. The faces of the attendants were hewed with panic. One of them noticed Mia watching and threw her an angry look that prompted her to get on with her cleaning duties. Now she was really thankful that she hadn't qualified for the new program.

CHAPTER NINETEEN

CARA

CARA BEGAN INVESTIGATING THE NEXT PERSON ON THE LIST of photos—Jennifer Maliki. Jennifer was a pretty, Indigenous-looking woman with long, dark hair. Her photo had been shot with a telephoto lens through an apartment window. She looked to be holding a white cat in her arms. Cara called her last known employer, Anchorage Pro Cleaners. The name of the janitorial service sounded somewhat familiar. But Cara couldn't think why. Perhaps she had seen one of their ads.

The manager of the janitorial service told a somewhat similar story to that of Rebecca Taylor. "Jennifer Maliki. Oh yes, the Indigenous girl. She just stopped showing up for work one day. It's not too unusual though. We have a high turnover rate."

"I see. Was there anything unusual about the way she left? Did she display any health problems?"

"Not that I recall." He paused for a moment. "But I did think it was odd, because she was assigned to one of our better sites with higher pay. Our employees usually jockey to be on that crew."

"And where was that?" Cara asked.

"At Almagor Tech. It's a pharmaceutical company."

Then it all seemed to come together. The night when Cara had followed Aaron to the Almagor parking lot after a late-night call, she had also spotted a woman who greeted him, and later Cara demanded to know who she was. Aaron had given her the number of Anchorage Pro Cleaners to confirm his story that she was just someone on the janitorial service he was acknowledging. Jennifer was that woman. Even now, his story still held up, but the fact that both she and Aaron were missing and had both worked at Almagor had to be more than a coincidence. Did the two of them have some kind of deeper tie? Knots were welling in her stomach, and she felt the oppressiveness of the world closing around her that accompanied her claustrophobia returning.

CARA REGROUPED WITH J.B. for their second night at the motel. He updated her on his visit to APD after his PT session. He had met up with Charlie Wilkes and tried to grill him. "I didn't get any smoking guns from Charlie," he said. "He told me he didn't know anything about your case. It was before his time."

It was true that Cara had never met Charlie, but perhaps that was all the more reason he could be persuaded to impede her investigations for the right sum. Cara updated J.B. on her own findings.

His brows knitted into a furrow. "Huh . . ."

"What is it?"

J.B. paused for a moment. "It could be just a coincidence, but after you told me the name of your husband's company, the plaque kind of stuck out for me."

"What plaque?"

"You know, the plaques on the wall at headquarters? Of the big money donors? Well, Almagor's one of them. You've never noticed?"

Cara had passed the plaques hundreds of times at the old headquarters. Walmart, Boar's Head, Veritas, Alaska Rubber . . . They had helped fund equipment—body cameras, computers, tactical vests—and of course, donors had helped fund the new headquarters. "No. I'm sure I never saw an Almagor plaque. It must be a new one." Like J.B. said, it could be nothing. It seemed like most of the big companies donated to APD. Giving to the community was always good for PR. But given her latest findings, and the idea of a possible mole at APD, she had to wonder. Was there something she didn't know about her husband and his company?

Everything leads to Almagor.

CARA PARKED HER Suburban in front of the pharmaceutical tech company that her husband had worked for. She had driven by the boxy, beige building with blue-tinted windows numerous times; she'd driven into its vast parking lot and dropped Aaron off when his car was in the shop. But she had never actually gone into the building. Not even when Aaron went missing and then was declared dead. The company had sent a humorless corporate lawyer over to her house to sign papers regarding the handling of his benefits. Almagor employees had paid respects at the funeral and sent her sympathy-filled condolence cards, but only now did Cara realize that she had never once actually set foot in the building.

She told the mustached, walrus-sized uniformed guard at the security desk her name and said she was investigating the disappearance of her husband; she wanted to speak to Aaron's supervisor, Oliver Nagel. The guard's reaction was the same as the receptionist's at APD—a look that made her feel like an unwanted intruder.

But thankfully, this time, her wait wasn't long. Aaron's supervisor, a well-dressed man with slicked back hair, came down to the lobby with relative speed.

"I'm so sorry for your loss," he said. "We all miss Aaron."

"I'm still trying to find out what happened to him."

His look of confusion was fairly convincing. "Perished while hiking in the wilderness—isn't that what happened? We were all devastated."

"A mistake was made. The bodies we buried were not my husband's and my son's."

His eyes turned dark. "That . . . that can't be." His gaze flitted around the lobby. "Come this way, please."

They rode the clear glass elevators to his office. On the way, Cara saw what she assumed to be lab and testing rooms where white-coated scientists worked with tubes, machines, and plastic packs of yellow plasma, which she knew were used to make medicine that helped treat autoimmune disorders.

Once they were seated in his office, Oliver folded his hands on the desk as if he were a concerned high school principal. "I'm shocked about the mistaken identities. Are you quite certain that the bodies weren't your husband and son?"

"The DNA tests were double-checked."

"So perhaps they are still somewhere in the woods and haven't been found yet."

"Yes, it's possible," Cara admitted. "But I found photos on a known criminal's cell phone taken right before their disappearance that suggest something criminal or malicious may have occurred." Cara pulled out her cell phone. "There was a photo of someone else connected to Almagor on the same phone, who also appears to be missing."

She showed the photo of Jennifer Maliki to Oliver, who scrutinized the long-haired young woman. "She doesn't look familiar," he said.

"She worked for Anchorage Pro Cleaners."

"Oh yes, the janitorial company we contract." He looked up at Cara with a dour expression. "There's always a lot of turnover among the cleaning staff. I'm sure that young woman simply moved on to a better job. In any event, it seems a stretch to imply a connection to Almagor."

Undaunted, Cara scrolled through the photos of the others on the phone, saying, "Do you know any of these other people?"

"No, I don't think any of them worked here. Oh . . ." Oliver leaned in to get a closer look at the man with the gray beard—and then his countenance turned pale. It was as if he had suddenly seen a ghost. He looked briefly at the remaining photos, then handed back her phone. "I'm sorry, I don't know any of these people." He looked at his watch. "I've got to get to a meeting. It's a tragedy about the mistake with Aaron and your son, and I wish I could have been of more help, but I don't have any more information than you do. You know your way back to the lobby, right?" He got up and ushered her out before she could ask another question.

Oliver had been spooked, Cara was certain. On the other hand, he seemed genuinely surprised by the photos. If he knew something, perhaps he didn't have the full picture. Was there someone higher up in the chain of command she could question? As Cara headed back toward the elevator, she took her time, scanning each lab and office through its glass door or window as she passed. Nothing looked unusual. In one of the labs, she could see rows of tiny bottles of what she supposed was the medicine made from plasma Aaron talked about. Intravenous immunoglobulin, or IVIG, as he called it.

There was something about the bottles that caught her attention— their unique, mini-jug shape, filled with an almost translucent fluid and topped with a blue cap. They looked like the bottles she had spotted back at Chugach Village, with the same distinctive shape and blue cap. She had assumed they were filled with fentanyl. But she couldn't imagine why the Chugach gang would be interested in a nonaddictive medical drug. Was she stretching the connection to Almagor when there wasn't any?

Cara got back into her Suburban and headed out of the pharma-tech company's expansive asphalt lot. It wasn't long before she noticed a metal-gray van with tinted windows following behind her. She slowed, thinking it would pass her, but it held back as well. Then she hit the accelerator and veered across lanes to exit the freeway. She heard the van's tires screeching on the asphalt as it followed suit.

CHAPTER TWENTY

MIA

MIA PUSHED HER CART DOWN THE AISLE OF THE ECHOEY
Walmart store in Wasilla. She had made the special trip from Willow to load up on cases of canned soups, corned beef hash, cooking oil, chocolates, tampons, bread, pepper, vinegar, batteries, diesel oil, and other things she could think of that the women of Unity would appreciate.

Despite her new alias, her new location, and a comfortable job at the Lonely Diner, Mia realized that if she continued to live in Man's World, she would never be able to shake the fear that people were after her. She finally decided it was time to leave. She felt sorry that she wouldn't be giving her boss the usual two weeks' notice. It wasn't as if she could use a job reference for Carol Lewis, who would cease to exist when she left, but she had liked working at the diner and wished she could say her final goodbyes to her coworkers. Her intuition told her, however, that it was better to leave in stealth.

One of the wheels on the cart was off-balance, and the metal wagon shook and rattled *kachunk kachunk kachunk* down the aisles.

By the time she got to the checkout line with her haul, Mia thought the cashier would look suspiciously at her end-of-the-world-prepper's bounty. But it was just another day in Alaska, and the cashier didn't bat an eye. In one spree, Mia had nearly wiped out her meager bank account.

When she had started at Anchorage Pro Cleaners, she could never have imagined the path it would eventually lead her down.

MIA SAW AARON working in his office one night toward the end of her shift, when most everyone had gone. Reflections of letters and digits scrolled down his rimmed glasses as he stared at the monitor. She always secretly hoped that he would still be there whenever she came to clean his office.

After the man with the gray beard had fainted, she saw Aaron through the glass doors of a conference room arguing with some people in suits. One of the suits had looked over toward her, but rather than see her, he seemed to look past her. Mia was used to this look. She was almost invisible when she was wearing her uniform and holding a mop. That's why she liked Aaron. Because he actually saw her. He never failed to say hi or give her a wink when he spotted her in the hallway.

Pulling her cleanser-filled cart behind her, Mia tapped at Aaron's door. He nearly jumped out of his chair and closed his laptop.

"Oh, Jennifer," he said. "I didn't know you were still here."

"Sorry. I'm just here to empty your trash," she said.

"Of course."

As she stepped in toward his desk, he stooped to pick up the trash can and handed it to her. Mia felt her cheeks burn red. No one had ever tried to help her before.

She noticed a photo on his desk of Aaron with a woman and a child. "Is that your family?" she boldly ventured.

"Yes. My wife, Cara, and my son, Dylan."

She smiled, even though inside, she was secretly devastated. *Of course he has a wife.* She couldn't help the jealousy that bubbled up at seeing Aaron's arm around the pretty, dark-haired woman with the perfectly proportioned physique. She was holding the little boy, who had Aaron's compelling blue eyes.

"How about you?" Aaron asked. "You have family? I mean, are you married?"

She shook her head.

"What about your parents?"

"My father died," she lied. "I still have my mother, but I left home."

"Oh, I see. So, you live alone?"

Mia nodded.

"I'm sure you must have a boyfriend, though?"

Mia shook her head.

"Sorry, I didn't mean to pry."

"No, not at all."

"Did you come from a Native village?"

Mia nodded, although for some reason that she couldn't explain, she felt embarrassed to admit it. She was suddenly seeing herself through Aaron's eyes: an unsophisticated girl from a backwoods village.

"You've got to tell me all about it. I've always wanted to visit a Native village," he said. A sudden noise at the end of the hall startled Aaron again. Clearly nervous, he gathered up his papers.

"I gotta go," he said. "Thanks for cleaning up." He stood up, then hesitated for a moment. "Jennifer, would I be able to trust you with a secret?"

"Of course," Mia said without thinking or considering what kind of secret she was agreeing to keep.

Then he gave her the electric smile that made Mia's stomach do flip flops. "I knew you were the type of person I could count on."

Mia tried to calm herself.

"There are people here who are not good," he said in a hushed voice. "No, worse than that . . . they're evil."

Mia's eyes widened. She had never heard anyone in real life referred to as *evil* before. There were evil spirits in Indigenous lore, but actual evil *people*? "What do you mean?"

"It's all about this." Aaron held up one of the tiny bottles Mia had seen in some of the rooms she cleaned. "Medicine made from the plasma taken from the people you see come in here every day."

Mia was perplexed. "But I thought you said it was doing good. It helps a lot of sick people."

"Yes, it does. But there are rules, you see, about donating plasma. Most countries have stricter regulations, and that's why America's the biggest producer of plasma in the world. It's legal here to pay people for their plasma. Other countries don't think that's ethical— to make a trade out of human blood or plasma."

Literal *blood money*. Mia had never thought of that before.

"But the other problem is that there may be health risks to the donor."

Mia's eyes grew wide. "It's dangerous?" She had been giving her own plasma regularly for months. "They told me it was safe."

"Donating plasma once a month is very safe. That's what most other countries allow. In the US, it's legal to harvest plasma from someone twice a week. If the donor isn't eating a healthy diet, though, there could be risks. Our new program . . . well, it's an experiment to see if we can extract even more plasma—three times a week instead of two."

Mia didn't completely understand. "Why do you need to get so much?"

"It takes a pool of hundreds of donors' plasma to make a good batch of antigens with a broad spectrum of antibodies." He picked up one of the little vials no bigger than her thumb. It was labeled IVIG. "Do you know how much this tiny bottle sells for?"

Mia shrugged.

"Four hundred dollars retail. There are people who need regular doses to survive, and when IVIG is scarce, which it always is, it can go for twice as much on the black market."

Mia gave a little gasp. The bottle looked so small and insignificant.

"What we do here, it's big business. And we're always looking for ways to produce more plasma. In this new trial, we're studying plasma from people who donate three times a week instead of two, to see if there's any difference in quality."

"And . . . is there?"

"I don't know. Unfortunately, our company does its own testing and can manipulate the results. They're even hiding things. In this new program, some donors have been getting sick. But it's been covered up."

Mia had thought Aaron was in charge of the new program, but now it seemed like he was involved in something against his will.

"I need your help, Jennifer. You can help me bring the truth out."

"Me? But . . . There's nothing I can do. Why don't you go to the police?"

"I think the police might be in on it. I can't be sure. I just know there are a lot of people interested in keeping this business going, and the truth could bring it down."

Fear ran through Mia's veins. She didn't want to do this, she wanted to say no . . . but Aaron was trusting her, and she didn't want to let him down.

"I'm going to blow the whistle on the company," he said, "and I need to take some of these with me as proof." He lifted one of the bottles.

Mia couldn't think of what to say. This sounded like one of the espionage movies she had seen. She could only stammer, "B-but how do you want me to help?" What could she do? She knew nothing about blood or plasma or IVIG.

"The bottles from the new trial are locked in a cabinet in the room in the basement next to the one labeled 'testing.'"

Mia nodded, remembering the testing room where people dressed from head to toe in blue plastic and face masks to enter.

"The missing bottles won't be noticed, since I'm the one logging them, but no one is allowed to be in the room alone. There's a camera in the hallway and they monitor keycard entries, so if I were to go in there after hours, it would get noticed. That's where you come in." The words seemed fateful. "They'd think nothing of the cleaning crew going in after hours. So I just need you to go in with your keycard and bring out one bottle each day. I'll make you a copy of the key to the cabinet. If anything goes wrong or you run into trouble, you can text this number." He scribbled a number on a pad and gave it to her.

The task seemed wrong. Dangerous and yet thrilling at the same time. Mia had never been trusted like this by anyone. Aaron had chosen *her* to confide in, and now they had a secret that only the two of them shared. He was relying on her to do something important, something that might save lives. It was risky, but in the end, she knew she would do it. She would do it for him.

THE FIRST TIME Mia took one of the vials, her hands were wet with nervous sweat. She tried to be like *Nik'inla'eena*, the stealthy woodsman in stories Mama Unity told. He moved silently and quickly when he stole things—a fish-gutting knife or a pendant—so that no one noticed until they were gone. Sometimes he even took children in the darkness of night when their mothers weren't watching.

She swiped the door with her key card, *swish click*. She opened the glass cabinet with the key Aaron had given her. The vials were filled with clear liquid, and Mia wondered how they were able to wash out the almost neon yellow color of the raw plasma. Her fingers trembled at the thought of how much each of the tiny bottles was worth. Oh god, what if she dropped one? She wiped her hands on her uniform and reached in. *Tinkle clink*. She nearly knocked over a whole row of bottles but used her other hand to steady them. She plucked one bottle from the back and hid it among the cleansers and disinfectants of her cleaning cart, then relocked the case and left the room. The door shut automatically behind her, *faflunk*. Later, while she was cleaning Aaron's room, she hid the bottle just as he had instructed, in the tissue box on a credenza by his desk, pretending all the while to be dusting.

After a while, she got used to the nightly routine and gave it little thought. As if it were just another item on the chore list she had to check off each night. But she had the scare of her life one night when a woman in a lab coat rushed down the hallway in a hurried *clap clop clap clop*. The woman looked stern and determined, and Mia just knew she was in trouble. But the woman continued right past her without stopping or acknowledging her. That's when Mia remembered that her uniform was like a cloak of invisibility.

She couldn't remember exactly how many days had passed or how many bottles she had left in Aaron Kennedy's tissue box, but she thought it was maybe a month later when she saw another congregation of men in the conference room having a heated argument. A man with slicked-back hair was practically yelling, his face as red as kokanee salmon. Mia worked her mop back and forth, hoping not to be noticed.

"How the fuck is it possible for bottles to go missing? Where were the fail-safes?" she could hear him say.

A woman spoke up. "We need to look into it. There's too much liability."

"Maybe we should kill the program."

"You know we can't. I'm not calling the shots here."

"Heard of shit creek? Well, consider us all up it."

"Fuck!"

"Stealing is stealing. We find out who it is, give that person the axe."

"Or arrest him."

There was a moment of weighted silence, and Mia stumbled and dropped her mop. The pudgy man looked up from the table and saw her. She quickly picked up the mop and continued working as if she had seen and heard nothing. The man closed the blinds.

Arrest? The thrill of helping Aaron suddenly lost its allure at the thought of jail. Is that where this would all end?

CHAPTER TWENTY-ONE

ELLIE

IN THE MORNING, CHIEF SIPLEY RAPPED ON ELLIE'S DOOR, announcing "Sipley here!" as if he were a recruit in an army lineup. Vlad barked up a regular storm and gritted his teeth when she let him in. The police chief peered both ways.

"He's not here," Ellie said, knowing he was looking for Shane.

"Wanted to make sure you were still breathing, considering I heard your ex was in town."

Word traveled fast in the Dave-Co. "He hasn't killed me yet, but there's still time."

"So what the hell is he doing here?"

Ellie thought about spilling the beans to him, but then decided it was better to keep her mouth shut, because, as she had explained to Shane, Chief Sipley would likely try to stop them, especially if they were taking Mariko and Chuck with them on their little expedition. "He's got cancer and is feeling all remorseful after Timmy's death, so we're patching things up between us," she said.

He bowed his head. "Sorry 'bout your son. May he rest in peace. And sorry about your ex's cancer?" He didn't know how to react to the news about Shane. Whether he really should be feeling sorry or not.

Normally Ellie would have invited him to sit for a spell, but she knew that he could spend hours just chewing the fat, and Ellie had plans for the day. Chief Sipley and Ellie were alike in a lot of ways. Neither of them had exactly been star parents. Sipley had abandoned his family, though Ellie didn't know anything about his past until he brought Lonnie to Point Mettier. Old timers like herself soon figured out that Lonnie was Sipley's daughter. But Sipley hadn't exactly *announced* their relationship, so not everyone in Point Mettier was aware of the fact. Sipley paid for Lonnie's apartment and kept an eye on her but didn't interfere too much with her life. Ellie figured he didn't necessarily know how to be a father, especially to an odd duck like Lonnie.

Sipley shifted his weight and scanned the room again. "Where is he?"

"I booked him in room forty-two."

"Well, if he gives you any trouble, be sure to give me a holler," he said, and Ellie could see him mentally interrogating the room, looking for clues to what Shane might really be doing in Point Mettier.

Sipley was always much smarter than he acted, so Ellie was sure he suspected that something was afoot. For one thing, he knew Ellie would need a pretty big reason to have a change of heart about the man she'd spent her life running from. She might have visited him at the hospital, but to bring him *here*? That explanation would have to wait.

AFTER SIPLEY LEFT, Shane came down to her apartment, looking like ten miles of bad road, with bags under his eyes and what was left of his hair in a scruffy mess.

"Couldn't sleep a wink," he said. "How can anyone sleep with the goddamned building creaking and shaking and the wind howling from the elevator? Every time I started to fall asleep, I woke up thinking someone was screaming bloody murder."

"You get used to it—the noises from the wind and the ghosts."

Shane grew silent and as pale as the Pillsbury Doughboy. "So what about Chuck? Have you recruited him yet?" he asked after a bit.

"I haven't even had breakfast yet," Ellie sniped, and Vlad got so agitated by her tone that he growled and nipped Shane in the leg.

"Ow! Goddamn it!"

Ellie chuckled to herself. "Come 'ere, Vlad. Good boy." She tossed him a treat from her pocket. Vlad bounded away from Shane and caught it midair, then happily went off with his tail wagging. Ellie had never in her life had a better male companion than Vlad.

Ellie fixed them both a breakfast of eggs, sausage, and toast.

Shane almost got weepy-eyed. "Just like the old days," he said.

"Don't get used to it," Ellie said bluntly. "You're going back to where you came from after this job is done."

———

THEY CAUGHT CHUCK just as he was opening up shop.

"Marge would never let me go," he said, pretending he was busy, flipping through his receipts in the empty store. He threw a leery look at Shane, and Ellie wondered if she should have left her ex back at the apartment.

"Tell your wife you're going hunting," Ellie suggested. "Maybe you want to add another head to your wall." She hitched a thumb at the various mammal heads looking down at them.

"Whatever lie I may tell my wife, I've retired from hunting down men." Chuck was referring to his stint in the military. Ellie didn't know his full story, but she was sure that Afghanistan had done a number on him. After all, he was here, holing himself up from the world in Point Mettier. But Ellie also knew she could appeal to his soft spot: rooting out injustice.

"We're not going to kill anyone," she said. "Just scaring up answers to questions." Chuck didn't seem convinced. Time to pull out all the stops. "My son's photo was found in one of these goons' cell phones, and now he's dead. A photo of Detective Kennedy's husband and son were also in the phone. Also dead."

Chuck stopped looking at his receipts, and his brows furrowed in dismay. She could almost see the frown behind his mustache and beard. "Why don't you go to the police? Tell them what you found?"

"The police?" Shane added a guffaw to emphasize their mutual disdain. "This is Native land we're talking about. First off, we gotta have proper evidence. All we got right now is a hunch. But you gotta admit it's a strange coincidence that the Chugach gang would have photos of people who ended up dead. We already know they shy about killing people."

Chuck sat down on his stool behind the counter, and Ellie could see he was almost there.

She kept going. "You know what else we found in the phone? There was a Native woman, maybe in her twenties, a middle-aged lady, and an older man too. All of 'em gone missing, Detective Kennedy says. Maybe they're dead. Or maybe there's a chance to save them."

Chuck finally sighed. "I'm not saying *yes*," he said, "but what's the rundown?"

MARIKO AIMED HER recently purchased Colt handgun at one of the cardboard bullseyes that Ellie had put up in the spruce-filled woods as her makeshift shooting range. Ellie had cordoned off the area with neon-yellow docking rope so that Lonnie, her moose, and any of the kids would be prevented from moseying in unawares.

Mariko's shot hit the red target smack dab in the middle. She squealed in delight with a sound like a happy weasel.

"Not bad," Ellie said. She had been teaching Mariko how to shoot for a couple of months now. Ever since the incident last fall when the gang from Chugach had visited Point Mettier, Mariko had been keen on defending herself. Most folks in Alaska owned a firearm, but Mariko, being from Japan, had started with zero experience; now she was a regular Calamity Jane.

"Try that one over there," Shane said, pointing to a target higher up in the trees.

Mariko took her position, narrowed her eyes behind the safety goggles, and took a shot. It wasn't a bullseye, but still, it hit the target. Mariko let out another happy squeal and jumped up and down.

Shane, filled with doubt upon first setting eyes on the petite woman in the feathered black wig, now nodded in satisfaction.

NOBODY KNEW WHAT Mariko's real story was. She had first sashayed into town in her frilly dress looking like a frosted tiered cake. She wore those big caterpillar lashes and long painted nails, and Ellie gave her three months max before she ran back to Tokyo or wherever it was she came from. But Mariko had toughed it out and surprised them all by lasting through the winter and beyond.

She set herself up as the only entertainer in town, singing jazzy tunes in Japanese, throwing in a "Whoo!" and "Everybody clap your hands!" every now and then. She put as much get-up-and-go into her act whether there was a crowd of rambunctious tourists or just three piss-drunk patrons drowning in their beers. Mariko really got Ellie's knickers in a knot at first, but she kind of grew on her, and Ellie now considered her a Point Mettier institution.

The older letches in town used to ogle her, but Mariko never gave them the time of day. Instead, she hooked up with Ellie's handyman, Tony, who was twenty years her junior.

Even though she seemed like an endless well of bubble and cheer, Ellie had noticed three scarred lines on Mariko's wrist that told another story.

Mariko said she had been a big pop star in Japan, which seemed dubious, so Ellie paid Marco Salonga, one of Point Mettier's computer-savvy teens, to surf the Internet and dish whatever he found out about her. Apparently, Mariko was a very popular young singer in the nineties, with pimple-faced fans in her home country fawning over her like she was the best thing since the Beatles or something. In other words, she really *was* a big pop star in Japan. Then she got engaged to a top actor—a regular Asian Tom Cruise—and the paparazzi hounded and scrutinized them and dug into their dirty laundry. They discovered that the Asian Tom Cruise was having an affair, and then things really went south when Mariko got preggers amid rumors that it was someone else's baby. The impending nuptials were canceled, and her career took a nosedive. Things got so hot that Mariko had to leave Japan and escape to America. She married some nobody in California, where she was photographed with a belly bump, but then it was gone, and no one knew what happened to the baby. Some said she had a miscarriage, others that she gave it up for adoption, and still others whispered that the baby died from SIDS. Whatever the case, she had shown up in Point Mettier with no husband or child, just trunks full of wigs and glittery clothing for her act. The residents of Point Mettier were no strangers to a past that was best forgotten, so there wasn't a whole lot of judgment passed around and somehow, she fit right in.

"I'm good shot!" Mariko proclaimed after hitting another target, pumping her arms with glee.

"Question is, how are we going to keep *her* from getting shot?" Shane muttered to Ellie.

Shane did have a point there. Mariko could hit a target, but she also made an easy one. They would have to think carefully about Mariko's role and how she could be an asset rather than a liability.

———

THE WIND HAD started to pick up, so they called it a day and scuttled back to the Dave-Co. There were times in Point Mettier when the winds clocked in at 150 miles per hour and turned the building into a howling spook house. Ellie was sure Shane was not going to like it.

As the elevator began to ascend, ungodly whistles rose up through the shaft, startling Shane. She could see the hairs standing on his arm. He shivered and grumbled, "Why'd you have to pick the goddamn coldest state in the country to live in?"

Ellie smiled inside and decided to have fun with it. "You know, some people think the Dave-Co is haunted," she said.

Shane tried to laugh, but it came out like a whimper. Mariko went along with Ellie. "Yes, many ghosts," she said.

"We lose someone practically every year to the bay," Ellie explained. "Usually a fisherman getting caught in his nets. And just a couple years ago, a little girl fell in and died of hypothermia." Ellie didn't even have to make any of it up because it was the god's honest truth.

Shane turned an almost translucent blue, and Ellie thought she saw his knees wobbling. "This place sure is full of bad mojo." Then he added, "Think I can stay with you?"

"Nothing doing. You got a nice rental room all to yourself." Ellie had given Shane room 42, because it had been ransacked by the Chugach thugs, and she hadn't replaced all of the furniture yet. Even though Shane seemed to have softened with age, Ellie could still remember the alcohol binges when furniture got destroyed in his wake. To Ellie, Shane was like a big, un-housebroken dog. Let him loose, and he was bound to pee on the furniture or demolish it out-right. Ellie's actual dog, Vlad, who had been returned to her by Jim Arreak, was the only dog she would let sleep in her apartment these days.

"Good night," she said, as she and Mariko stepped off on the same floor, leaving Shane alone in the howling elevator to ascend to his rented room. With that fearful look in his eyes, Ellie almost felt sorry for him. Almost.

CHAPTER TWENTY-TWO

CARA

CARA KEPT ONE EYE ON THE REARVIEW MIRROR AS SHE EX-
ited the highway ramp, and the tinted van followed her. Cara picked
up speed, sailing through a yellow light. The van ran the red and
continued to tail. She swerved down an alleyway. Then a hard right.
It followed suit. Clearly, there was no intention of being discreet.

She wasn't sure exactly what the endgame was, but she could see
pedestrians coming up ahead in the walkway and made a hard stop
at the light. The van rolled up on her left. Though she couldn't see
beyond the smoke-colored glass, she definitely saw the passenger
window slide down to reveal the muzzle of a gun topped with a si-
lencer aimed her way.

Cara ducked just in time as bullets shattered the pane of her window. Then the van screeched past the light and drove away. But not

before Cara sat up to capture the numbers of its license plate, which she recorded in a voice memo on her phone. Was this another scare tactic? Or had she made the hit list by dint of getting too close to something?

Frazzled but unharmed, Cara made her way to an auto glass repair shop. The car would be virtually inoperable in Alaska weather without the window. She took a moment to collect herself at the auto shop, then decided to give Angelo a call. He could look up the license plate—and she was certain he would do more for her than Anchorage PD.

Angelo answered the call with a chirpy, "My favorite customer! What can I do you for?"

First, she had him run the plate of the van, but perhaps it was not surprising that it was a stolen plate taken off another car.

"Speaking of license registrations, did you find out any info on the people on our list?"

Angelo sounded frazzled. "License registrations. License registrations . . ." She could hear him shuffling through the messy heap of papers and candy wrappers on his desk.

"You did look them up, like I asked, didn't you?"

"Of course I did. Have I ever let you down?" Cara could imagine him giving her a cheeky smile on the other end of the line. "George Apernathy had a Dodge Ram," Angelo said. "Looks like it showed up in a tow yard about the time he disappeared." That was definitely a red flag to Cara.

"How about Rebecca Taylor?"

"Rebecca had a Subaru, but the registration lapsed and hasn't been re-registered in Alaska since she went missing." It was a similar story to George Apernathy's. "Neither Jorge Salazar nor Jennifer Maliki seem to have had registered cars."

It wasn't hard to fathom that Jorge, being a university student, didn't have a car, especially since the photo showed him with a bicycle. But for Jennifer Maliki not to have a vehicle would be a big inconvenience in Anchorage weather. And Cara remembered her stepping out of a car the night she had talked to Aaron in the parking lot.

After a new window was installed and calibrated, Cara decided to head toward Jennifer Maliki's last known address to see if she could ferret out any information, flitting glances every now and then at her rearview mirror for a tail.

JENNIFER'S APARTMENT WAS a relatively new low-cost housing structure. It was a three-story complex fitted with security cameras and an outdoor buzzer.

"Can I help you?" a woman's voice squawked over the intercom after Cara had pushed the button for "management."

"I'm looking for Jennifer Maliki?"

She could tell the manager was racking her brains to recall the name.

"An Indigenous woman? Possibly had a cat?"

"Well, that's impossible since we have a no pets policy. But I do remember an Indigenous woman. She doesn't live here anymore."

"I'm Detective Cara Kennedy, and I am trying to find her."

She heard a long, static-filled buzz along with a metallic click, and let herself in through the double wooden doors.

A middle-aged woman with straw-like hair met her in the lobby.

"What can you tell me about Jennifer Maliki?" Cara asked, showing the woman her detective's badge.

"She was real quiet, paid her rent on time, but I didn't see her much."

"Have you seen her in the past year and a half?"

"No, that's when she moved out. Said she had found another job. Why do you want to know?"

Cara came up with a story on the spot. "We found an abandoned vehicle that might belong to her. She could be in danger. Do you have any next of kin information for Jennifer, or the license plate number so we can confirm whether the vehicle belonged to her?"

"Oh dear. I don't have any of that information."

"Perhaps I could talk to one of her neighbors?"

The woman sighed but took her to the elevators and pressed the button to the third floor. "She was in Unit 305, I believe. I think she was pretty chummy with the woman in 302. Diedre's been here for a few years."

Cara knocked on the door of 302. A petite African American woman answered the door a crack and peeked out.

The manager introduced her. "This is Detective Kennedy. She wants to ask a few questions about Jennifer Maliki."

Diedre looked alarmed. She stepped outside, careful to close the door behind her.

Cara sneezed twice. She was allergic to cats, and the bit of white fur on Diedre's blouse was undeniable. She turned to the manager. "I'd like to talk to Diedre for a bit and I'll be right down after." She was essentially dismissing the old woman, who seemed glad to be excused and disappeared behind the elevator doors.

Cara turned back to Diedre. "I won't tell about the cats."

Diedre looked surprised. "Oh, I don't have any pets," she said, but blushed as a playful paw batted her from under the door, albeit a black one and not a white one.

"Did you know Jennifer well?"

"We hung out sometimes, but she didn't leave me a forwarding addie or anything. And when I tried to text her, her number wasn't working anymore."

"She looked after your cats?"

Diedre grew silent. Cara pulled up the photo of Jennifer and zoomed in to show the white cat.

"Who took that photo?" asked Diedre, genuinely puzzled.

"I don't know. She may have been under surveillance. Do you know why she left?"

"I know she was in a hurry to go. She wouldn't tell me why. I never heard from her again. I thought maybe she was scared of an ex." Suddenly her eyes grew wide. "Do you think something's happened to her? A crime of passion?"

"I don't know if any crime was committed at all, but I need to find her. Do you know what kind of car she drove?"

Diedre paused a moment, trying to assess Cara.

"I'm concerned Jennifer could be in grave danger. That's why I would appreciate any help you could provide."

"Okay, yeah, I helped her buy a car. It was a gray Ford compact."

That matched what Cara had seen the night in the dark parking lot. "Do you happen to know the license plate number?"

"No, I don't remember."

"Is there anything else you can tell me to help me find her?"

Diedre thought for a moment, then she lit up. "Hold on a sec." Diedre pulled out her phone. She scrolled through her photos, then finally landed on one and showed it to Cara. It was a picture of Diedre and Jennifer standing in front of a car matching the description. "We took this selfie not too long after she bought the car."

There, in the photo, was the license plate number. Bingo.

———

CARA REDIALED ANGELO. "Could you look up this license plate? D-G-X eight-two-one."

"Damn you're good."

"Aren't I, though?" She could hear him clacking on the computer.

After some moments of wordless typing, his voice came back on-line. "Boom. I've got a hit. The car was cited in Anchorage for not being registered, but the ticket was never paid. Then about six months ago, it was registered under a Carol Lewis."

"And where was that?"

"An address in Willow."

"Is it possible to get the driver's license photo of Carol?"

Angelo was almost certainly breaking some kind of law by accessing this info, but that's what made him so useful, along with their unspoken pact of discretion.

After more keyboard clacks, Angelo inhaled and said, "You're not going to believe this. I'll text it over to you."

Moments later, Cara's phone pinged, and she saw what she expected. Carol Lewis and Jennifer Maliki were one and the same.

CHAPTER TWENTY-THREE

CARA

"WE NEED TO FIND HER." CARA WAS ASSEMBLING A NEW lamp in her freshly painted living room while J.B. brewed a pot of coffee in the glass carafe he had picked up. "If these photos are some kind of hit list, Jennifer Maliki or Carol Lewis or whatever her real name is, is in danger, if she isn't already dead."

J.B. remained silent.

"What is it?" she asked trying to read his thoughts.

"If those photos are a hit list . . . well . . . you're on there too."

"But the target must have been my husband."

"You were just shot at," J.B. reminded her.

"I think if I were meant to be roadkill, I would be dead by now," Cara responded, although in the back of her mind the sentence continued darkly, *which begs the question of why* haven't *I been killed?*

"If you're going to look for her, I'm coming with you." His tone was firm.

"What about your injuries?"

"My new toes have done wonders. See?" He walked without his cane, traversing a circle. "And my chest wound is nothing but a scar." Cara had to admit that he seemed to be back to his old self. Still, she wasn't over the trauma of seeing him shot—and the grief over losing Aaron and Dylan, which would never leave her. A part of her couldn't stand to see a loved one in the path of danger ever again. Well, J.B. was a police officer, after all, and if she couldn't let go of those thoughts, she couldn't be with him going forward. The momentary thought made Cara step up to kiss him, wanting to hold on to him for as long as she could.

He took that as a sign to move them both to the unscathed bedroom. He kissed her tenderly at first, then with a hungry eagerness, finding the electric spots and crevices that aroused her both physically and emotionally—knowing when to kiss, when to hold back, when to make her want for more. Cara gave in to abandon, and it was as if she could finally release herself from all the uncertainties, the fears, and the pent-up adrenaline of the past few days that had been wound up so tightly inside her.

IN THE MORNING, they set out under an agitated sky the color of rinse water. They wrapped themselves in their parkas, and Cara packed stew in one thermos and hot coffee in another.

Willow was about an hour and a half's drive from Anchorage, not far from Talkeetna, the wilderness where Aaron and Dylan had gone missing and where their remains might still be. Even now, she held her breath, as she always did driving up this highway, trying not to relive the panic that had consumed her then. But J.B. must have noticed her tensed grip on the wheel, because he turned to her and asked, "Are you all right?"

"I'm fine," she said, steadying herself.

Along the way, Cara continually monitored her rearview mirror to make sure no one was following them. Twice, she drove off the main road and deviated down a side street just to see if anyone would pull off with her, but no one did.

Cara had been to Willow a few times to catch the Iditarod action. Every year in early March, the city surged with mushers, their dogs, and sled-racing fans from around the world. There was a ceremonial start in Anchorage, but the official race began in Willow. Cara remembered how her father had whistled and hooted at his favorite contestants, placing them at the top of his celebrity status pedestal. Those moments with her father had been treasured outings, filled with excited anticipation and spectator adrenaline. Mushers were mostly local Alaskans, but some veteran racers came all the way from Scandinavia and Switzerland. The course covered almost a thousand miles of braving gale-force winds, wild animal attacks, dog injuries, and damaged trails to make it to the finish line. The winners became Alaskan heroes.

Cara drove north on Parks Highway, and they finally passed the modest WELCOME TO WILLOW sign. J.B. ventured, "So we just go knocking on the door of this address and . . ."

"I just want to see if she's alive, for one thing." Cara's impulsive actions didn't always come with concrete plans.

The directions took them off the main road to a byway surrounded by forest. Here, the snow-packed road was unplowed in long stretches of white frosting, but luckily it was still traversable in her Suburban. On either side of the road, trees stood like erect matchsticks, blackened and bare—evidence of the forest fire that had blazed through a few years past. But farther down the road, full-branched and unscathed conifers covered in snow made for a beautiful winter wonderland. Snowcat-groomed trails for dogsleds and snow machines could be glimpsed running parallel to the road.

They drove deeper and deeper until signs of civilization were few and far between. Driveways were demarcated by PRIVATE PROPERTY and NO TRESPASSING signs.

They finally neared the address where the Ford compact was registered and the GPS indicated that there would be a house at the end of a long driveway. With the clouds thickening above, it had gotten dark and felt darker still among the dense trees, with only the car's headlights coning the way down the driveway. They came at last to a large clearing where the small house sat.

The cabin was lifted slightly off the ground, as if someone had plopped a trailer home onto the property. It had a blue, sloped roof and sand-colored siding, some of which was warped, making it questionable how much insulation it provided. Electrical wires were poked straight through the wall like an afterthought. Smoke emerged from a fireplace flue, indicating that someone was inside.

A Ford was parked in front with the right license plate—a good sign that Jennifer might still be alive inside.

There was no disguising their arrival; the Suburban's headlights lit up the house through the windows. Cara left the lights on in order to get a better look at who might come out of the house then climbed out of the car. Immediately J.B. yelled out, "Ten o'clock!" and Cara quickly swiveled to see a rifle propped on a windowsill, pointed in her direction. She lifted both her hands up and directed her voice toward the end of the rifle. "Carol? Or maybe it's Jennifer? We're not here to harm you. My name is Detective Kennedy, and this is my partner, Officer Barkowski." J.B. stepped out gingerly, also raising his hands.

"You're not in uniform," a young woman said, keeping the rifle aimed at them—or, more specifically, at Cara.

"I'm reaching for my badge," Cara said as she slowly moved her hand to her jacket pocket to retrieve it.

"Do you have a warrant?"

"We just want to talk to you. We're investigating several deaths and missing persons connected to a company called Almagor," Cara said.

"We have reason to believe you might be in danger," J.B. added.

There was a slight pause. "What did you say your name was?"

"Detective Cara Kennedy."

"Can you turn off your headlights?"

Cara turned the car's headlights off, and then the young woman beamed her own light at them so that Cara had to squint.

"You're Aaron Kennedy's wife?" It was half question, half statement.

Cara gasped. "Yes. Yes! He also worked at Almagor."

The flashlight turned off. Cara could see now that the rifle had disappeared from the window ledge.

A squeaky white door opened, and the Indigenous woman whose photo was in Michael Lovansky's phone appeared. Jennifer Maliki or Carol Lewis stood before them. With her long, dark hair and flawless skin, she was far prettier in person than in the photo.

"Come in," she said.

CHAPTER TWENTY-FOUR

MIA

WHEN THE HEADLIGHTS LIT UP HER HOUSE LIKE IN ONE OF the alien-landing movies Mia had watched with Alex, she was sure that she was a day late in her escape plan. Everything was already packed in the car, and all that remained was a good night's sleep. She had even paid up her rent and let her landlord know that she was leaving so she didn't leave a reason for the law to come looking for her—yet now they were there on her doorstep—if they actually were police, because when she peeked through the gray linen curtains, she saw a large SUV, not a patrol car. They might be the *evil people* who Aaron had warned her about. And anyway, no one, not even police, could be trusted—that's what he'd told her.

At least there were only two of them. She could easily shoot them both, if it came to that, but she would prefer not to attract unwanted attention.

When the woman announced her name as Detective Kennedy, Mia nearly dropped her rifle. She'd never imagined Aaron's wife as a police officer. But as soon as she got a good look, she could see that this woman was in fact the one in the photo on Aaron's desk—the woman he loved, with the idyllic family she had studied over and over and even imagined herself in instead. Mia would not shoot Aaron's wife. At least, not yet.

Mia tentatively unbolted the wooden door. Detective Kennedy and her partner tromped in through the enclosed breezeway and into her living space.

They both scanned the room, taking note, she was sure, of its emptiness. Nothing but a no-frills couch, a wooden crate that served as a coffee table, a secondhand square table that she had found in someone's dumpster, and a wobbly chair. She never saw the need for anything else.

Mia studied Detective Kennedy in detail. She felt she could see why Aaron had fallen for her. She was so pretty, cool, and sophisticated, with a long, beautiful neck. Mia just knew from the way she carried herself that she was much more self-assured and mature than Mia. She suddenly felt self-conscious. She wanted to run to the bathroom, brush her hair, and make herself more presentable. Which was ridiculous, she knew, since Aaron wasn't even there to compare them.

"Is it Jennifer, or Carol?" Detective Kennedy asked.

"Carol," Mia hedged, using her current alias.

"But you used to work for Almagor as Jennifer Maliki, didn't you?" Officer Barkowski chimed in.

Mia decided to remain silent. Obviously, they already had the answer to the question.

"You knew my husband, didn't you?"

Another question that they probably knew the answer to.

"Look, Carol, we aren't here to arrest you. We're here to protect you."

"Protect me?" Mia said, surprised. Maybe Mrs. Kennedy didn't know as much as she had thought. Aaron must have had a good reason not to confide in his own wife. That made her wary of the detective.

Mrs. Kennedy pulled out her cell phone and showed Mia a set of photos. Mia recognized most of the people in the pictures. Plasma donors, including the bearded man who had fainted, plus a photo of Aaron with his family. But the photo of her own face shocked her. It must have been taken through the window of her apartment by someone *spying* on her. It sent a shiver down her spine.

"Who took these pictures?" she asked.

"They were found on a gang member's phone. We don't know if he was the one who took the photos, but everyone in them is either dead or missing. You're the first person we've found alive."

Mia's stomach churned. She couldn't be sure anything had happened to the plassers, but Aaron had hinted at it. Her own photo stunned her to her core. She thought she had been so careful. This was the first undeniable proof that she had been in someone's crosshairs. The wolves had gotten her scent and were now tracking her. "Do you think . . . do you think they want to kill me?"

"We don't know," said Cara, "but . . ."

Officer Barkowski stepped in. "Could you tell us if you know any of these other people or why someone might want them to disappear?"

Mia still wasn't sure if she could trust them. Aaron had said police might be involved in Almagor's crimes. Detective Kennedy might not have even been aware herself. What if her partner was one of the bad guys?

Cara's eyes narrowed. "In order to help you, we need you to be honest. Let's start with your real name. It's not Carol *or* Jennifer, is it? I couldn't find any records for either name that made sense."

Mia stumbled over a response, then decided she would have to give them her first name at least. "I'm Mia," she finally said.

"Mia, did you know my husband, Aaron?"

"I sometimes passed Mr. Kennedy in the hall when he worked there late."

"Are you aware that he went missing on a hiking trip with my son and was never found?"

Mia knew she had to act surprised. "Oh, wow, really? I'm so sorry." Sweat began to pour down her brow, even though the room was frigid. Mia was not a good liar, and she was certain that Detective Kennedy could tell she was hiding something. She turned away from her gaze, trying to deflect. "It's getting late, so if you could just tell me what—"

Suddenly they were interrupted by an explosion of glass. An earsplitting *rat-tat-tat* and *ka-plash* of the window bursting, then dozens of *schlings* as shards flew through the air and fell to the ground.

"Get down!" Officer Barkowski yelled, and she felt Cara's arm lock onto hers, taking her down to the wooden floorboards as bullets riddled the walls.

The *rat-tat-tat* continued, blowing holes in the windows and through the wooden panels of the walls, but luckily for them, the enclosed porch added an extra layer of wood between them and whoever was trying to kill them. But her low-rent house wasn't the sturdiest of structures. Mia had no idea how long their luck would hold.

CHAPTER TWENTY-FIVE

CARA

IT DIDN'T SEEM POSSIBLE THAT SOMEONE HAD FOLLOWED them into this remote interior of the town of Willow. Cara thought she had taken enough precautions to avoid being followed. "How many are out there?" Cara gasped through the hail of bullets. She motioned for Mia to stay low and to hug the side wall.

J.B. sidled over next to the window, but it was too dark for him to discern anything. Another round of lethal projectiles had him ducking back down to the floor.

"Know how to use that rifle?" Cara asked Mia, gesturing at the gun that was still resting against the wall by the door.

"Yes."

J.B. crawled to it, grabbed it, and slid it across the floor over to Mia.

Cara and J.B. had both instinctively drawn their Glocks from their holsters.

Someone was already testing the front doorknob, making a rattle like the ghost in *A Christmas Carol*, but Mia had locked the door behind them.

"Is there a back door?"

Mia nodded her head toward a door by the kitchen.

An explosive sound of wood splintering signaled that their unseen adversary was now shooting at the lock, then a massive boot seemed to be kicking the door in.

"Do you have your car keys?" Cara demanded.

Mia pointed to a set of keys on the kitchen counter.

"Wouldn't it make more sense to take your SUV?" J.B. asked with his gun trained on the door.

"The only way I think they could have found us is if they put a tracker on my car. Besides, I need it for a distraction." Cara grabbed Mia's car key and was about to toss it to J.B. when Mia spoke up.

"I know the roads better. I can get us out quicker."

Cara paused for a moment. Could she trust her? She finally nodded and tossed the key to Mia instead. "Get the engine started. J.B., cover her."

The three of them maneuvered toward the back door just as the man at the front door finally broke through and began shooting directly into the house.

While the three of them got a running start toward Mia's car, Cara clicked the alarm button on her car key so that her SUV beeped and the lights went on. As she expected, the man with the AR-15 ran back out and headed toward the SUV, shooting in rapid succession.

He was tall—a six-foot monstrosity dressed in camouflage, with his face covered by a ski mask. *Is he one of Wolf's goons?* Cara wondered.

Of course, the window of her SUV that she *just* had replaced was once again shattered into tiny pieces, making her seethe. Someone would definitely have to pay for this later. But what Cara didn't expect was that another man, slighter in build, had been waiting in the Escalade the men had arrived in. He hopped out with his own semi-automatic when he spotted the trio emerging from the back. *Shit!* J.B. distracted him by firing off a couple of rounds from his Glock. In the darkness both of them missed their marks, but while Big Masked Thug was shooting up the SUV and Little Masked Thug was engaged with J.B., Mia had managed to get into the car and turn on the engine.

Just as Big Masked Thug swiveled around, realizing where the real action was, Cara was relieved to hear the hollow click of his AR-15, meaning they had bought some time while he reloaded.

J.B. and Cara continued trading shots with Little Masked Thug as they both followed Mia toward her car. Darkness was their friend. Then Mia's car started moving—and Cara's stomach dropped. Had she just made a huge miscalculation trusting Mia not to leave them behind? Would Cara and J.B. be able to fend off the two men despite being hugely disadvantaged in terms of firepower? But as these dire thoughts ran through her mind, the passenger door to Mia's car flung open in invitation.

Cara jumped in next to Mia, then J.B., his prosthetic toes slowing him only slightly, climbed into the back where a number of boxes and bags had already been loaded. Before shutting the door, he took one last well-aimed shot, hitting the tire of the Escalade and blowing it out. Mia revved the engine, her tires spinning on the snow, but as bullets hit the rear of the car, she let out a scream.

"Floor it!" Cara yelled and she obliged.

Cara worried how long Mia's old compact would last or how fast it could go with the extra weight, but they tore down the long driveway onto the country road, keeping an eye out for their pursuers. Mia went in the opposite direction of the way they had come, snaking through back roads that took them around a frozen lake.

"We can't go back to Anchorage. They know where you live," J.B. said to Cara.

Mia looked angry when she heard this. "I thought you said they were after me. Is it really *you* they want to kill?"

"We're both in danger," Cara had to admit.

The matchstick trees looked like thin specters, their arms outstretched in threatening poses. Mia's familiarity with the roads allowed her to speed through the wooded lanes even in the cloak of darkness, but Cara realized they hadn't discussed a destination. As if reading her mind, J.B. offered, "Maybe we should head to Point Mettier?"

Cara chewed on this before Mia volunteered, "I know a place where we'll be safe. It's where I was planning to go anyway before you showed up."

There was a raw kind of power in Mia, Cara noticed now, in the way she was driving and the confidence in her voice. Had she known someone was coming? She seemed to be on the run—and anyone who had used at least two aliases was suspect.

"When we get there, we're going to have questions. Lots of questions," Cara said.

"I know," Mia replied. "And I know you may never forgive me. Or him."

J.B. and Cara exchanged confused glances.

"Forgive who?" Cara had to ask.

"Your husband" was the meek reply. "He's alive."

Cara's vision began to swim. Had she been at the wheel in that moment, she probably would have driven them into a ditch with the shock.

CHAPTER TWENTY-SIX

MIA

THERE WAS SOMETHING IN THE WAY OFFICER BARKOWSKI acted when the shooting started that made Mia realize he was in love with Detective Kennedy. He was like a *tu-kina-jek*, the personal guardian spirit everyone had watching over them in Tlingit belief—always aware of where Cara was, trying to cover and protect her. Then, later in the car, he gazed at her with a kind of longing Mia recognized and made her think of Alex. Alex, whom she hadn't tried to contact since her first call from her new apartment. Alex, whom she thought she had moved on from, but now caused a pang in her heart. The detective, meanwhile, was the kind of person who kept all her faces on the inside and wore a mask on the outside.

Mia had briefly considered leaving the two cops behind. She could have driven off without them—she didn't owe them anything.

But in the end, she decided to take pity on Cara and allow her to see her family. Besides, the pair could be more useful than not.

MIA HAD BEEN terrified to see three men wearing latex gloves foraging through Aaron's office like wintering squirrels. They were opening files on his computer, rifling through his desk, searching every drawer, and examining the credenza. Mia had to continue mopping the hallway without letting her shaky knees give way. Finally, one of the men overturned the tissue box and shook it, and the bottle she had placed there the previous night slipped out. She could hear their excited chattering, and Mia's heart pumped in double time as she quickly pushed her cart around the corner and down the hall. She felt herself sucking for air. It would probably just be a matter of time before they reviewed the security camera footage and realized that she had been the one helping Aaron. What should she do? *Breathe. Breathe!* She needed to let Aaron know, first of all. Luckily Mia's shift was almost over. She was shaking uncontrollably, and it was all she could do to wheel her cart back to the supply room and clock out.

Once she got to her car, she texted Aaron that there was trouble. He texted back telling her to meet him in the Almagor parking lot. Paranoid, she moved her car to the darkest corner of the lot to wait until she saw Aaron step out of his car. She drove up to meet him. His eyes were wide and serious, his coat buttoned wrong. He must have put it on in haste. Despite her anxiety, she couldn't help but feel excited by the clandestine meeting. She told Aaron about the men searching his office and how they had found the bottle in the tissue box. Mia was spooked to see Aaron looking over her shoulder at something in the parking lot, and Mia followed his gaze to see a car at the far end of the mostly empty parking lot suddenly take off. Were they already tracking her as well as Aaron?

Aaron grew pale and distressed and paced for a while—a side of him she hadn't seen before. "You did the right thing texting me," he said. "I'm going to have to disappear. I'm sorry for involving you. I think you should quit your job or take a reassignment."

Mia couldn't believe his words. He made it sound so easy, to just quit. She didn't want to go back to the women's shelter. How would she explain it to Sandra, who had worked so hard to get her this job? Sandra's model beneficiary would end up being her biggest disappointment, thieving from her own employer. How had she gotten into this predicament? "Are you sure I should—"

"You may be in danger," Aaron whispered. Okay, quitting was one thing; in truth, Mia knew she couldn't stay at Almagor. But what kind of danger did he mean? She supposed she could be arrested. But was there something even worse?

Mia decided to quit the very next day. She told her boss at Anchorage Pro that her mother had gotten sick, and she would have to fly back home to take care of her.

Aaron had said he would text her again when he thought things were safe. But she didn't hear anything from him for a week. Mia started to think it would be better to go back to Unity instead of the women's shelter. Ayai would be glad to see her, but it would also mean she had failed at living in Man's World. What choice did she have? There were more important things to think about, such as staying out of jail—or just staying alive.

Mia packed up the meager belongings she had accumulated during her time in Man's World—clothes, a snow globe, an unusually shaped rock she had found, a box of batteries, an old camera, and gifts for the kids in Unity, which included candy and colored flashlights. That's when her cell phone buzzed. She didn't recognize the number but picked it up anyway.

"Jennifer." The voice was ragged and breathless. "I need your help."

"Aaron?" Mia gasped.

"They're after me and my boy. Can we go to your village for a while?"

Mia was both excited and alarmed. "What about your wife?"

"She can't know. I think the police might be in on the attempt to silence me. Better to let her think I'm dead."

Dead? Mia could think of no good scenario that required someone to think you were dead.

"I'm in Cantwell. Do you know where that is?"

Mia didn't, so Aaron gave her detailed instructions on how to get to the truck stop he was at.

"Don't let anyone at Almagor know anything and always check to see if you're being followed," he said. "I'll be waiting here."

It was a nerve-racking drive up through the vast stretches of wilderness. Of course, it was not the looming trees or the thought of wild creatures that scared her. She'd grown up in their midst. It was the actual driving. She had come to enjoy being at the wheel and the feeling of freedom, but she was still new to it, and she had never driven such a long way before. Meanwhile, she also had to keep an eye out for someone following her.

It was dark by the time she got to Cantwell and found Aaron and his son. They were huddled in dirty, oversized clothes and ski caps drawn low, so that at first, Mia thought they were vagrants. Dylan sat on a bench next to Aaron, hiccupping, in tears, and surrounded by granola bar wrappers.

Aaron took Mia aside, away from Dylan, but kept an eye on him. "They wanted to kill us, Jennifer. I was going to use this trip to look for a secluded cabin to rent—a place where I could hide out. But it was already too late. They had been stalking us, probably just looking for an opportunity when I was alone and away from a crowd." His eyes were bloodshot. "But I spotted them tailing me when I was out hiking with Dylan. I headed over to a place where I'd seen a homeless man and his son who were living rough in the woods. I paid him to exchange jackets, so I could throw them off, you know? But I didn't think . . . Oh God . . ." He started sobbing then. "They shot them both dead. I heard the screams and the gunshots. Even the kid! I never thought they would do that."

Mia's legs turned to jelly. *Shot? Dead?* And over what? Tiny bottles of liquid? "W-where are the bodies?" she whispered.

"In a ravine in the woods. We can't get them out of there."

Mia closed her eyes, imagining a father and son dead at the bottom of a gully. She thought she was going to be sick. "How did you get here?" she asked shakily, wondering how they could have hiked here, since she had passed the sign for Talkeetna hours ago.

"There's a train. A hop-on train that stops for hikers. I rode it as a kid. It took us up to the highway. Then we hitched a ride out here." He wiped the tears from his eyes as he looked over to Dylan. "They think we're dead. It's perfect."

"Where is your wife?"

He had not yet mentioned her.

"She doesn't know. She's still in Talkeetna. She'll also have to believe we're dead for now. I'll get word to her when it's safe and send

Dylan back to her. But for now, we need a place to hide out. That's why I'm asking you to take us to your village."

"It's not like a normal village," she said. "It's not registered, it's not even on a map."

"That's great," Aaron said.

Mia knew that if it were just Aaron, the women at Unity would never let him stay. But she could make a case for protecting Dylan. "They won't let you in without me. And we'll have to take a plane to get there."

"Thank you, Jennifer," Aaron said. "I know I've asked a lot of you." He put his hand on her shoulder. "I owe you my life."

Mia felt flustered by his touch. Suddenly, she felt he needed to know her real self. "My name is actually Mia," she said softly. His eyes widened, but he didn't question or admonish or take his hand away.

"I want Mommy!" Dylan suddenly cried, breaking the spell.

"Dylan, honey, I told you we won't be able to see her for a while."

More tears started to flow down the boy's face, and Mia knelt beside him. "Don't worry, Dylan. You'll be safe with us." She stroked his downy hair, trying to reassure him. Then she texted Marla and Sonia, asking for a flight home and explaining she was currently in Cantwell. Marla and Sonia gave her directions to the Chena River Seaplane Base in Fairbanks. Mia knew there were tiny airstrips and seaplane bases all over Alaska. Over five hundred, they had once told her, because that's how people got around without having to drive through the millions of acres of mostly undeveloped wilderness. They didn't fly their planes at night, though, so Mia, Aaron, and Dylan would have to spend the night in her car by the airstrip.

In the morning, they watched Marla bring the little plane in for a goose landing—skidding its pontoon feet across the water. She hopped onto the dock wearing a smile to greet Mia, but her expression turned sour when she saw Aaron and Dylan with her.

"They need our protection," Mia said hastily.

"I thought I was only bringing you back."

"I'll talk to Mama Unity. *Please*, Marla."

Marla studied Aaron and Dylan in their disheveled clothes and must have taken pity, because she finally nodded at them to get in the plane.

Mia was sad to have to leave her Craigslist car behind, but Marla said that she and Sonia would come back for it and Mia could decide what to do with it later.

NOW, MORE THAN a year later, it was like déjà vu, bringing two more refuge seekers. Mia had already texted Marla and Sonia that she was coming back to Unity. But after the armed men arrived, it was too risky to stay in Willow overnight, so Mia drove with the two cops to Big Lake, twenty-five miles away. She took the Parks Highway south back toward Anchorage for a short while, but then turned onto a country road. There was a stretch of desolate and unlit but thankfully paved road before a pocket of civilization appeared that was well lit. They passed a pub, a fire station, a library, and a grocery store, then finally came upon the airport. Mia was relieved that she hadn't seen anyone following them, and texted Marla and Sonia the new location. With the lakes iced over, she knew they'd be flying out the bush planes instead of the float planes. Mia said a silent prayer to *Agloolik*, the spirit under the ice, to keep them safe.

In the parking lot, waiting for daylight and unable to sleep, Mia's thoughts wandered. She discreetly studied the detective the way she would observe animals on a hunt. The detective had exactly what Mia had sought but never found. She was loved by not one but two men. What was her allure? Did she love J.B. or Aaron?

Mia spotted clues that gave Cara's feelings away—the tender glances toward J.B., and the way she leaned toward him, as if drawn by an invisible magnet, whenever he spoke. Subtle, intimate motions. *This is what Aaron needed to see*, Mia thought. That Cara no longer loved him, and she should just take Dylan and go back to Man's World with J.B. Then Aaron would be free to be with Mia.

CHAPTER TWENTY-SEVEN

ELLIE

ELLIE, SHANE, CHUCK, AND MARIKO NO DOUBT MADE FOR one of the stranger posses in the history of posses. An innkeeper, a storekeeper, a Japanese lounge singer, and a cancer-ridden geezer. They were all past their prime, and none of them had hit the gym in the last decade or so. In fact, it was a bit of a miracle that Ellie and Shane had talked them into infiltrating the lair of known criminals and tattooed drug dealers. But at the end of the day, that was the charm of Point Mettier, thought Ellie. Sure, everybody had their demons and vagaries, but there were folks you could count on to have your back.

AFTER ELLIE MADE them all some coffee and breakfast, they went to visit Kai, whose room was filled with the smell of wacky tobaccy coming from his purple bong.

"Dude!" It was his standard greeting. He didn't think it odd that the four of them suddenly wanted to rent snow machines. He wasn't the type to ask questions—or maybe it was just that he was stoned silly.

Ellie had wrapped her weaponry in cloth so it wouldn't be too obvious as she walked around the Dave-Co, but it did little to fool Kai. "Going hunting?" he asked.

"That's right. Maybe we'll get us some caribou." Well, they *were* going hunting, but what they were searching for was information, not wild game.

They signed their waivers and decided they only needed two snow machines because they could ride tandem. Mariko would ride with Ellie at the wheel, and Chuck would take Shane since he was familiar with riding snow machines.

"Good luck!" Kai chirped as they left.

ELLIE RODE THE lead to Chugach, retreading the path she and Detective Kennedy had traveled just a week ago. But this time, Ellie instructed Chuck that they needed to park their mobiles a ways back before they reached the village so the roar of their engines wouldn't alert anyone that they were coming.

Shane cased the joint first, using the binoculars Ellie had given him. It was as if they were back on one of their old bank heists. Ellie pointed out the two-story monstrosity with the animal-bone decor sitting atop the hill. The house wouldn't have made the cover of *Better Homes & Gardens*. Shane tried to suss out how many people were inside. The ship that Ellie and Cara had spotted on their last visit seemed to have disappeared, but she didn't know if that was a good thing or bad. Were the reinforcements still there? Or had they gone out with the ship?

Shane spent a long time staring and hemming and hawing as the rest of them froze their asses off in the bitter cold.

"Well?" Ellie asked impatiently.

Shane declared that he couldn't see any signs of life through the windows other than the flicker of a television set. "There could be one person inside, there could be twenty."

"Well thanks, Sherlock. That's some real useful intel," Ellie said, dishing out the sarcasm.

"This ain't as easy as peerin' through clear glass windows at a bank," Shane grumbled. "But there's a back door, and that's going to be where Chuck and I break in while you two ladies head to the front for the distraction."

The plan was for Mariko to knock on the front door pretending to be someone from the census bureau. She was the least suspicious-looking of the four, and no one in the gang had seen her before, so they would think she was harmless. Meanwhile, Chuck and Shane would enter through the back. Ellie would keep herself hidden with an eye on the front in case anything went sideways with Mariko.

They had prepped the lounge singer with a name tag and a clipboard. They had also written up a script for her to read off. She made her way up the hill toward the front, looking all businesslike.

Shane picked up the AR-15 and led the way through the trees and foliage to get on the backside of the house. Ellie was amazed at how spry Shane still was for his age. It was almost as if the adrenaline gave him not only energy but agility as well. The two of them scuttled their way over, hunched low with their weapons, with Ellie trailing them. Shane had come prepared with a set of bump keys—

something every good thief had to pick locks with—but when he crouched and slowly tested the knob, he found that it was unlocked. He nodded to Chuck, who, of course, had military-grade weaponry, and they slipped their way in.

Gripping Woodie and with Bessie in her holster, Ellie kept moving toward the front, hugging the exterior wall. Mariko had already reached the door and rapped at it like a woman on a mission. Ellie held her breath.

One of the tattooed hooligans with his arm in a cast answered. "What the fuck do you want?" It was a different man from the one Cara had called Victor. This one also had a bandaged leg, so Cara and J.B. must have roughed him up good. That made Ellie relax a skosh.

Mariko read off the script. "Hello, sir. I am a census taker with the US Census Bureau."

"Fuck your census and go to hell, lady."

He was about to close the door, but Mariko was a firecracker. "'Scuse me. I came from very far. If you don't answer questions, I just make guess. You don't look like Native people, so I just write down white people seem to be living here in big house with many rooms in Native village." Ellie wasn't sure that's what census takers did, but it seemed to work.

The man narrowed his eyes. "Hold on." He hollered into the house behind him. "Shari!"

A Native woman appeared—the same one who had given her backhand to Cara.

"What is it?" Shari asked with the same unwelcoming tone.

"I am from the US Census Bureau. I would like to know how many people live here." Mariko read her part beautifully.

"My husband died so now it's just me and two kids," the Native woman said with a steely eye.

Mariko gave her a look of disbelief. "So who is that man?"

"He's a relative. Just staying here temporarily. Now I've answered your question so you can fuck off." Shari started to close the door, but Mariko planted her foot in the way.

"I am not finished with questions," Mariko persisted, and Ellie had to hand it to her for her fearlessness.

Shari gave her a look that could have ended all nine lives of a cat, and Ellie was afraid she was going to slap Mariko like she did Cara when all of a sudden, an explosive *BOOM* shook the house and shocked the bejesus out of all of them. Somebody's firearm had just gone off, but the question was whose.

"Fuck!" Shari said turning to look behind her.

"Goddamn it!" Ellie echoed to herself. She had a bad feeling and made a snap decision on what to do next.

Mariko still had her foot in the door, so Ellie sprinted up there quicker than a hiccup, whacked the lights out of Shari with the handle of her Glock, and headed in, telling Mariko, "Stay close behind." And into the lion's den they went.

CHAPTER TWENTY-EIGHT

CARA

A SLEW OF THOUGHTS AND FEELINGS CASCADED THROUGH Cara when she heard Mia say that Aaron was alive, but the first was joy. "And Dylan?" she burst out.

"Your son is alive too."

That's when the tears welled uncontrollably. J.B. put his hand on her arm but seemed not to know what to say.

"Where are they?" Cara asked shakily.

"I'm taking you now," Mia said. "But we need to fly there."

"What did you mean about me not forgiving him? For what?"

"For not contacting you earlier."

There were more questions than answers. "Why *didn't* he contact me earlier?" she asked pointedly. *How could he keep her child away from her for so long?*

"They were trying to kill him," Mia replied. "So he decided it was better to stay dead."

"Who was trying to kill him?" J.B. asked the obvious question.

"The same people who were shooting at us earlier. The people from the company."

"You mean Almagor?"

Mia nodded.

"Why would they want him dead?" J.B. took the interrogator role.

"Because of the experiments. The experiments where people died. He didn't want to do it anymore."

Shock rippled through Cara. *Experiments where people died?* Aaron hadn't mentioned any of this to her. She was his wife and a detective. Why would he confide in this young woman instead of her? Cara recalled the night when Aaron met Jennifer-now-Mia, in the parking lot. He had claimed he was just making friendly conversation, but clearly there was more going on if he was sharing secrets with her.

"Did you and my husband . . ." Cara couldn't get herself to ask the rest of the question.

J.B. looked at Mia, who didn't seem to comprehend. "Did you and Aaron have an affair?" he asked.

"No," Mia said, turning red. "I . . . I just helped him because he asked me to."

Cara wasn't sure what to believe. She was thrilled Aaron was alive . . . but she had a lot of hard questions to ask her resurrected husband.

———

FOR CARA, THE night in the parking lot was excruciating. To be promised a reunion with her husband and son and then to not be able to see them for another day felt like the ultimate cruelty.

Mia nodded off, her head slumping against the side window on the driver's side.

J.B. stepped out of the Ford to stretch his legs in the lot of the tiny airstrip. He looked at Cara in a way that begged her to step out with him. It was bitingly cold, but it still felt good to get some fresh air. J.B. led her to an area near the maintenance hangars and put his arms around her. "It must be a terrible shock. What you're going through."

She nodded, feeling confused and overwhelmed all at once. His warmth was comforting, and it felt good to stay locked together for a moment before he finally lifted her face to get a better look at her expression.

"I'm here for you, and I'll do anything to help you find answers . . . but if Aaron is still alive . . . where does that put us?"

"I don't know," she responded honestly. "I don't even know if I'm legally still married."

J.B. pursed his lips. She knew it wasn't the answer he was looking for. But Cara felt like a marionette with strings of her past, her present, and her future pulling in different directions. Her love for J.B. had blossomed, but she also loved Aaron . . . and there was Dylan to consider. "I haven't even processed the fact that my husband is still alive," she said.

"I know I've come on pretty strong," J.B. admitted. His voice went down to a whisper, and he hesitated. "But I don't want to play second fiddle. I've gone through that before." J.B. had suffered deceit in his past relationship, and she owed it to him to be honest.

"I don't know how I'll feel when I see Aaron, but I just know that I . . . need you . . . want you now more than ever. That's the truth." Cara could no longer imagine life without J.B. It almost scared her how much he had come to mean to her. Even now, knowing that her husband might be alive, with the way J.B. looked into her eyes, she had an urge to kiss him, have sex with him right there in the parking lot up against the siding of the hangar.

Headlights suddenly flashed as a vehicle entered the parking lot. He quickly moved her out of the light as they both held their breath. The van made a U-turn out of the lot and headed off in the opposite direction, and they both sighed in collective relief.

When daylight broke, a small bush plane sputtered in, and a woman in overalls and a pixie bob climbed out from the pilot's seat. She and Mia exchanged hugs.

"This is Sonia," Mia said to Cara and J.B. Then, "These two people need a safe place to stay." When Sonia frowned, Mia quickly added, "Temporarily."

Sonia finally broke out a smile. "Mia, you can't keep bringing people home with you like stray pets," she joked. "I'll let Mama Unity decide whether they can stay."

Mia didn't mention Cara's relationship to Aaron and Dylan; Cara didn't know if that would end up being a positive or a negative, so she refrained from mentioning her connection.

They each carried some of the supplies that were packed in the trunk of Mia's car and loaded them onto the plane. The aircraft took off, and with each gust of wind that lofted them, Cara's stomach lurched. But the winter wonderland was breathtaking as they soared over white-frosted forests and frozen lakes. She had ridden in light planes before, but the vast stretches of wilderness framed by majestic mountains always made Cara feel small. After about an hour or so, they finally landed on the snow-packed ground at the edge of a lake necklaced with beached fishing boats in various states of repair. The adjoining village consisted of a dozen or so wooden huts, smokehouses, woodpiles, a yurt, and a large central structure. Unlike Chugach, the village felt warm and inviting, the houses painted in cheerful colors and adorned with wind chimes and wooden decorations—a fairy nook in an area otherwise devoid of civilization.

TWO OLDER NATIVE-LOOKING women were waiting for them on the ground. One of them immediately ran to hug Mia, while the other stood still, looking none too happy to see that she had brought guests.

"This is Mama Unity," Mia said introducing the older woman. Despite whatever age her white hair belied, she seemed formidable, with a muscular, stout frame. "She's the leader of the village. And this is Ayai Upash, my mother." Ayai's hair was long and black, like Mia's, but lightly streaked with silver.

"This is Detective Cara Kennedy and Officer Barkowski."

On hearing that Mia's guests were police officers, both of the women looked alarmed. They took Mia aside, and a heated argument ensued.

Cara could only glean bits and pieces.

"They won't be staying long."

"She's Dylan's mother!"

"I thought you said she was dead."

Dead? Cara gave Mia a daggered look. Why would she have told the women she was dead? It seemed like another hint of an affair. There was more back-and-forth before the older women begrudgingly seemed to relent and turned back to Cara and J.B.

"Please—I want to see my husband and son," Cara said impatiently.

"First, we'll need your weapons and cell phones," Mama Unity said icily. Cara nodded to J.B. They seemed far enough from the danger that had met them at Mia's door back in Willow, and she was willing to comply with any demand in order to see her family. Ayai and Mia took the guns and phones that Cara and J.B. produced from their pockets and holsters.

Mama Unity pointed her finger toward a hut painted blue with smoke rising from its flue. Cara's breath quickened as she ran toward it. She glanced back to see J.B. standing rigidly with the other women, a cloud seemingly passing over him. Before she reached the hut, the door opened and Aaron, with a grizzled beard and unkempt hair, appeared before her. They stood frozen, not saying anything as the shock of it all registered.

Cara wondered whether the Aaron in front of her was just another dream like numerous ones she'd had before.

Then Dylan ran from behind Aaron to nearly knock Cara over with a hug. "Mommy! Mommy!" he squealed.

He had grown so much! She bent down to squeeze him until he gasped, then she peppered his face with kisses, tears pouring forth uncontrollably. "Dylan! Thank God!" She alternated between hugging him tight and examining him, making sure he was completely intact—his arms, his fingers, his ears, his little nose.

"Cara . . ." Aaron finally said, almost in a whisper. His eyes were moist with tears when he stepped forward and wrapped his arms around her. It might have been a breeze that kicked in or the doubt she felt about his fidelity, but she felt a sudden chill run through her.

CHAPTER TWENTY-NINE

CARA

AARON'S CABIN WAS A FAR CRY FROM THE TWO-STORY, TWO-thousand-square-foot house they had once shared in Anchorage with all its modern conveniences and trappings, but the hut was cozy and warm, with a wood-burning furnace, small windows, and a separate bedroom. Secondhand chairs and other pieces of furniture, perhaps boated in or salvaged from the lake, gave the place an old-world charm. Even the unfinished wood gave the place a homey feel.

"I got lucky," he said noticing Cara inspecting the hut. "They started building this hut before we got here, for a woman and her child who were staying in the yurt until the hut was ready. But she couldn't take life off the grid and left before it was finished. I've gotten pretty handy finishing it off. I put those windows in and I made the table," he said, proudly pointing to the large slab of wood that was carved, stained, and varnished, serving both as a dining table and a work desk.

Cara had never known Aaron to be handy around the house but couldn't find words to praise him for his newfound skills. Because now that she was past her initial shock, she was seething with rage. She concentrated on hugging Dylan, breathing him in, and kissing him so much that he finally squirmed out of her embrace. It pained her to lose sight of him for even a second now that they were reunited, but she asked him to go outside and play so that she could talk to Daddy.

Aaron clearly knew what was coming next, because he looked down at his mud-stained shoes.

"Do you know what I went through? With no contact for over a year?" Although she tried to keep herself calm, her voice was trembling. "I thought you were dead. I thought *my child was dead*! I buried strangers and put headstones over them. *Beloved husband and son.* I was put on disability because of the emotional mess you left me in. I failed my psych evals."

"I'm so sorry, Cara, but killers were after me. It was important for everyone to think we were dead. I had to protect Dylan . . . and you. There are ruthless men out there who are willing to murder all of us. This is not the easiest place to communicate from, especially since there's a no cell phone policy. I did try to contact you a while back just to let you know we were okay. It was when the women finally trusted me enough to go into town to buy supplies. I got a burner phone and called you that night, but I got spooked and tossed it when I spotted someone I thought was following me."

"Why didn't you tell me what was going on? And how did you manage to have the DNA results altered?"

Aaron looked sheepish. "My college roommate worked at AADC. He agreed to do it—for a price, of course. And he said he could make it hard to trace the report."

So, he had confided in more than one person about his plans, just not her.

"And what about our little friend out there, huh, what was her price for helping you? Damn it, Aaron, were you having an affair with her?"

"No, we were not having an affair!" he practically yelled back at her, then he lowered his voice. "I know what it looks like. I'll admit I wasn't honest about a lot of things, but I swear I did not cheat on you."

"You were stealing from Almagor, though, weren't you? And you were making Mia do your dirty work without her even knowing."

Aaron's face registered genuine surprise. Whether it was because she had figured him out or that she would dare to accuse him of such a thing, she wasn't sure. He sat down on one of the mismatched chairs and motioned for her to do the same. "I'll explain everything." He had that look. His hand in the cookie jar. "We have to start from the beginning."

Cara saw it was going to be a long story and sat where he motioned.

"You know about the medicine we make at Almagor?"

"IVIG." Cara had heard Aaron fling the term around a million times. "To treat immune disorders."

Aaron nodded his head. "Thrombocytopenia, Kawasaki syndrome, and now, possibly, Alzheimer's."

Cara hadn't heard that before. "Really? Is that true?"

"It's not FDA-approved, and more tests need to be done, but there have been promising results."

"That would be a major breakthrough. That could change a lot of lives."

Aaron nodded. "It could change the world, really. More and more money is going into research. People were just throwing research dollars at us."

"That sounds incredible." Cara paused a moment. "But I'm assuming there's a downside?" Otherwise, what would lead him to run?

"Remember how I told you that our biggest bottleneck is getting enough plasma?"

Cara nodded. She knew it's why they paid donors.

He rubbed his chin—something he often did when he was nervous. "I spearheaded an experimental program to see if it was safe to extract plasma three times a week instead of two."

Cara was surprised. "Almagor was allowed to do its own clinical trials? Not an outside lab?"

"Yeah, little-known fact. Pharmaceutical companies can do their own testing despite bias and financial incentive. We slap a different name on the testing division, of course. Ours was Alaska Plasma Testing."

Cara was stunned by the deception. "So, what did you find? Is it safe to extract that much plasma?"

"Theoretically. But we use sodium citrate, a blood anticoagulant, to make extraction faster and easier, and it depletes calcium." He buried his head in his hands again and Cara had the awful feeling she knew what he would say next. "We underestimated the side effects. Patients were fainting and one of them threatened to sue. Then . . . someone died."

"So you stopped the program, right?" Aaron didn't answer right away. Cara said it louder. "Aaron, you stopped the program?"

"I wanted to stop, but it was difficult."

It was not the answer she wanted to hear. Cara narrowed her eyes at her Frankensteined husband. A man she had thought was dead but had been brought back to life as a more frightening version of himself.

"Honestly, I thought I could stop it. I tried. We did halt the program for a few days. But then the person who threatened to sue suddenly disappeared, and any record of the fatality seemed to vanish as well. And the tests were back on again."

"Who is responsible for the cover-up and the disappearances? Almagor?"

"I don't know for sure, but I think pressure might have been coming from anonymous donors."

"Anonymous donors?"

The story was getting thornier and more heinous as he went on.

"As I said, there are people who have invested a ton of money in this, and they don't just want profits, they want to be first in line for the IVIG."

"First in line? If they were sick, couldn't they just get a prescription?"

"IVIG is always in short supply, even as a prescribed treatment. Plus, even though the drug is not yet proven effective or FDA-approved for certain conditions, like Alzheimer's, plenty of people are willing to take the chance. The company was selling IVIG under the table."

"At a premium price."

"Yes."

"Why didn't you report it?"

Aaron looked away and was silent. Cara braced herself for an admission that he had crossed the line. "We were making money . . . A lot of money . . ." His voice trailed off.

Now Cara knew that Aaron had definitely crossed the line. It was probably why he hadn't confided in her. Working at Anchorage PD, Cara had encountered a lot of drug trafficking cases, but that was for recreational drugs; plasma trafficking was something entirely new to her. And never in her wildest dreams did she think Aaron would be any part of it.

"Was the whole company in on this, or just you?"

"There were key people . . . and most of the higher-ups."

Cara thought about the tip-offs to the Chugach gang and the message on her wall after her visit to Anchorage PD. "What about the police? Are the police involved?"

"I have my suspicions. These people have resources, Cara, not just money. They were able to cover up a death and make the lawsuit go away. It's very possible the police are working with Almagor. If I had gotten you involved, your career—even your life—could have been jeopardized."

"They were jeopardized regardless," Cara snapped at him. Could she trust Aaron about any of this? "You still haven't explained why you were making Mia steal bottles of medicine."

Before Aaron could answer, Dylan bounded in through the door. "Are you done talking yet? I missed you, Mommy."

"I missed you too, honey." The tears welled again as she went to hug him. God, she had missed stroking his hair. When Aaron put his hand on her shoulder, she stiffened and nearly jerked away from him. "We'll continue our discussion later," Cara said.

"Okay, but I just want to know one thing. The man you came with . . ."

"Joe Barkowski."

"Is he . . . ?"

He didn't finish the sentence, but Cara could sense by his tone what he was groping for. "I don't know," she said slowly. "I don't know yet. But I thought you were dead, Aaron. He and I . . . we had . . ." Cara corrected herself. "We're in a relationship."

Aaron looked as if he had been slapped in the face, but he collected himself and said softly, "We have to think of our son, Cara. It might not be safe for you or for Dylan to be back in Anchorage. We need to stay here in Unity. But there's no need to involve that man."

Aaron couldn't even say his name. He was right, though. It was safer for them here until they found out who was behind everything. But her mind was reeling with questions. Should she and J.B. go back to Anchorage and leave Aaron and Dylan to hide out in Unity? No, the thought of having to part from Dylan again after she had just found him was unbearable. But to drag J.B. into this mess was unfair. What would he think if she suggested he go back alone? What would he say if she asked for time to figure things out with Aaron? Would he wait for her? For how long?

CHAPTER THIRTY

MIA

WHEN CARA DISAPPEARED BEHIND THE DOOR OF AARON'S cabin, Mia glanced at J.B. and recognized his crestfallen look. The look as if his world had fallen off a cliff and down a crushing waterfall. It was the same cratering feeling she'd had when she heard the girl tittering in the background on her call with Alex.

She took pity on him. "Mothers will always love their sons," she said, offering a scenario in which Cara wanted to be with Dylan more than with Aaron. "Are you hungry? I'm sure my mother's cooked up enough to feed an army."

This seemed to wake him from his trance.

"I could use a bite," he said and let her lead him to Ayai's hut while the women and children gawked at him just like they had with Aaron and Dylan at first.

———

BACK THEN, MAMA Unity had been even more unwelcoming. "You know the rules," she had said. "He can't stay here." She jutted her chin at Aaron.

"But his son," Mia protested. "His son is in danger. The people who are after them have murdered others."

"Murdered?" Ayai looked more than alarmed.

Mama Unity barely softened. "We can take the boy in, but not his father. That's all I will allow," she said adamantly.

Aaron shifted uncomfortably as they debated his fate directly in front of him.

"Dylan is too young to be without his father," Mia argued.

"Where is the mother?" Ayai asked.

"Dead," Mia said. Aaron shot her an unhappy look, about to object, and Dylan started crying. But the lie was necessary. She tried to convey with her eyes that Aaron had to trust what she was doing, and he closed his mouth.

"Mama Unity," Ayai jumped in, "we must help them. You created Unity to protect people, didn't you?"

Seeing the boy's tears finally swayed Mama Unity. "All right. But no one can know they are here. They cannot leave, and they cannot contact anyone, or it will endanger all of us."

Mia looked at Aaron, and he nodded his assent.

Mia had hoped that their time together at Unity would bring them closer—that he would see her for her true self, beyond the Anchorage Pro Cleaners uniform. She helped him adjust to life in Unity, where he was clearly out of his element. He had sat in a shiny building in front of a computer and eaten food out of plastic packages and containers without giving a thought to where it came from. Now she brought him smoked salmon and salted reindeer to help him last during the harsh winter and taught him the ways of subsisting—how to catch fish, how to hunt, and how to trap. Dylan even participated in the annual ice fishing just as Mia had done at his age. All of the women in the village doted on him—happy to watch over the blue-eyed boy, singing songs to him in their native languages or engaging him with games and handmade toys.

Aaron and Mia were chopping supple willow branches in swift *schiff schoff* movements to make their rabbit traps, shaping nooses with snare wire, when he halted and put down his axe for a moment. "Thank you," he said warmly, "for teaching me how to hunt, for letting me stay in your village. For everything. I couldn't be more grateful."

He looked at her in the way she'd been hoping for. A look that said he finally recognized her inner being and her soul. It brought a bass-like thrumming, an urgent beating of drums, from somewhere deep within her. There was a momentary silence except for the triple whistle of a yellow warbler. She reached up to Aaron and kissed him on the lips, basking in the warmth of it. It wasn't like kissing Alex, full of flame and fireworks, but it was a more adult, restrained kiss she thought he would like. Instead of reciprocating, Aaron pulled back. He looked flustered and apologetic. "Mia, I'm sorry. I-I may have misled you. I'm still married."

Mia felt her cheeks burn in embarrassment. She couldn't believe that she had misread the signs. She took off running, feeling foolish, confused, and heartbroken. Her boots left a trail of craters in the snow as she bounded as quickly as she could through it, tears inexplicably streaming.

"Mia!" she could hear him calling out, but she didn't stop. By the time she got home, she was breathing hard, exhausted from the physical and mental exertion. She lay on her bed, sobbing, until it was time for dinner and Ayai finally came and sat down next to her.

Her mother had already guessed what it was about. "This man is still mourning the loss of his wife," she said, and Mia had to remember that she had told everyone Aaron's wife was dead.

"Why is it so hard?"

"Time will heal. You are so young. You think that you love this man, but it is *hatsukoi*. Puppy love."

"It's not puppy love," Mia insisted, but she didn't know if it was supposed to feel any different.

"Once he is out of sight and out of mind, you will forget him," Ayai said.

Mia thought that there might be truth to this. Maybe if she didn't have to see Aaron, she would stop thinking of him. She supposed Ayai would prefer it if Aaron left, but instead Mia made the decision to go back to Man's World. Away from Aaron, away from the hurt and embarrassment that surged whenever she saw him.

NOW THAT SHE was back in Unity, Mia admitted to herself that she had not forgotten Aaron, but at the same time, she wasn't consumed with a bonfire of emotions whenever she saw him. Now it was tamped to a flame of jealousy. Still, if Cara didn't love Aaron, then she didn't deserve him. Her plan was to make him see that J.B. and Cara were in love.

The opportunity came at supper when she and Ayai prepared to celebrate her return and welcome the new arrivals in the Clan

House. Mia knew she needed to win over the elders of the village, so she also invited Marla, Sonia, Mama Unity, and her sister, Niki, to accept her thanks with a feast.

It was a cloudless night, and the moon sat luminous in the sky. The table was spread with butternut squash soup, oysters, farmer's bread, and reindeer sausage. Mia had bought Alaska oysters while in Wasilla.

"Oysters don't grow in Alaska due to the cold," Marla had once said.

"On the contrary, people have discovered how to grow them in a lab first and then transplant them to Kachemak Bay," Sonia rebutted.

Marla gave her a disgruntled look. "But they're not growing there naturally."

Mia didn't usually eat oysters because they were so expensive, but she knew that Marla and Sonia loved them regardless of how they were grown. Since she was cleaning out her bank account anyway, it seemed like the right way to repay the pilots for bringing her back home. They had always told her that the best way to eat oysters was with a loaf of bread, some pepper, and vinegar, so these were items that had made their way into her account-emptying splurge.

Marla and Sonia made a toast thanking Ayai for the bounty they had enjoyed. Cara and J.B. lifted their glasses of mulberry wine and gazed at each other for a moment. Cara's cheeks turned crimson, and anyone could tell by the way they looked at each other then that there was a connection between them. Like the eagle and raven moieties whose halves balanced and completed each other, they were intertwined. Mia looked at Aaron and knew that he saw it. But she suddenly realized the mistake she had made. Jealousy only drew him even more strongly toward Cara.

Mia suddenly felt powerless. She was not in the same league as Cara. She was not worldly. She was not graceful. She was not beautiful. She got up from the table and went to sulk outside, despite the biting cold that *Silla*, spirit of the sky, the wind, and the weather, brought upon them.

Ayai came out after her, zipping up her coat. "Mia-chan, my sweet daughter, I know you went to Man's World to be away from Aaron, and when you brought his wife back with you, I was sure you had gotten over him."

Ayai put her arms around her daughter. Mia rested her head on her mother's shoulder, trying not to cry, and said, "I didn't expect to bring his wife back, and I didn't expect to feel so rejected again."

She let herself be held and rocked for a while until she felt Ayai stiffen. Mia looked for what Ayai had seen. In the dark, ever expansive sky above, she saw the blue-green lights of the aurora overhead. The agitated way they were dancing seemed particularly menacing tonight, especially with the cry of a wolf in the distance. There seemed to be something that Ayai could read in the skies—a bad omen, secret signs from the *kamuy*.

"Are the men who murder still after Aaron?" Ayai asked.

Mia still wasn't sure if they were after Aaron, herself, Cara, or all three. All of them had been in the photos, after all. Mia felt a shiver up her spine. Had they brought the threat of danger to Unity's door?

CHAPTER THIRTY-ONE

ELLIE

WITH THE WOMAN NAMED SHARI OUT OF COMMISSION, EL-
lie and Mariko made their way into the house, guns drawn. Ellie's
eyes had to adjust to the lack of light. Why did hoodlums always like
to be in the dark? You never saw gang members in houses with sky-
lights, big windows, or sunny atriums. They always lived like rats in
some basement-like hovel.

Ellie motioned for Mariko to follow her as she pancaked herself
against the wall of the hallway and inched forward, leading with her
rifle. It was unnervingly quiet. Only the sound of their own boots
treading the floorboards.

Ellie pointed to an open doorway beyond a stairwell ahead on
the right. She paused beside it like they did in those television crime
shows, then she threw herself into the doorway with her rifle pointed

in. It was the kitchen, empty of people but filled with crap. Just like the rest of the house, it was dark, with warping wood cabinets and counters crowded with bags of chips, sippy cups, thermoses, a microwave, pots, and a roll of toilet paper. Half-empty glasses of beer and ashtrays filled with spent butts sat on a table. When she was sure there were no hooligans hiding in the room, she beckoned Mariko in out of the hallway until she could decide what to do next.

"I'm going upstairs, but you cover me, okay?" Ellie whispered. "Stand right here. If you see anybody following after me, shoot 'em."

Mariko nodded, holding her pistol out like an eager beaver.

Ellie was back in the hallway, ready for business, when she spotted something at the other end of the corridor. It looked like a fax machine sitting on a table. She recollected Cara saying that's how the men communicated with their head honcho. If Shane couldn't get the men to talk, maybe there would be some answers there. She raised a hand and whisper-called to Mariko, "Hold up. Let me check this out."

Ellie put her rifle down and picked up a set of faxes that had come through. On the top page were numbers that Ellie couldn't make heads or tails of, and there were a couple of wadded pages on the floor that she decided to scoop up as well.

A series of POP POPs, thumps, banging, and growls made Mariko gasp, and Ellie quickly folded the pages and stuffed them inside her jacket. Mariko forgot about holding her position and came out into the hallway waving her gun around.

"Get back!" Ellie warned her just as a creak in the floorboards alerted her to the goon with the arm cast coming at them. Without a moment to think, and with adrenaline-fueled strength, she ripped the fax machine out of the wall and threw it at the man's face before Mariko even thought about pulling the trigger on her gun. The thug fell on the floor with a groan. Now he'd be able to add a concussion to his injuries.

Boots stomped on the stairs and were coming down the hall toward them. Ellie engaged her rifle and pulled Mariko back into the kitchen, stepping over the goon's fax-bruised body.

It was Chuck and Shane practically stumbling down the stairs in a hail of bullets. "Get out! Get out!" Shane was yelling.

Behind him was a man Ellie had never seen before. He was not the de facto leader, Victor. In fact, he didn't look like a man from the village at all. He was too clean-shaven, with a proper haircut and a shirt and jeans that looked expensive. Ellie recalled what Timmy's landlady had said about a visit by bookish-looking men the night before he died. He didn't look like a Chugach gang member, but clearly, they were in cahoots. There wasn't time to ponder, though, because he growled and pointed his gun at her. Mariko finally chose this moment to put her months of training to use and took a potshot at the man, catching him in the leg. He went down like a felled tree.

The danger wasn't yet over, though, because just as Chuck and Shane busted out the back door, Shari came back to life, feeling the bump on her head, then angrily crawling toward the clean-shaven man's dropped gun. Ellie thought about maiming her, but instead grabbed Mariko and hightailed it after Chuck and Shane. They stumbled toward the parked snow machines.

Behind them, Ellie could hear Shari screaming, "I'm going to fucking kill you!" followed by shots that hit the snow behind Ellie's heels.

Shane looked completely tuckered out by the time they got to their machines. Ellie wasn't sure if it was the cancer or his old age, but he suddenly looked weak, so she helped him onto his seat. All that adrenaline had finally been spent.

"Did you find out anything?" Ellie asked.

"Yeah, we all sat down and had a nice chat over tea, and they spilled everything."

Well, at least he still had his sense of humor.

Chuck stepped in. "A young Native woman there told us we were too late, and that everyone was already gone."

"Too late for what?"

Chuck shrugged his shoulders. "Two of 'em snuck up on us, and we got into a scuffle and traded some shots. The one that Mariko got, and there was one with a patched-up leg."

"It wasn't a nest of bees like you made it sound, though," Shane said.

"Yeah, maybe that's what she meant. Everyone was already gone."

The disappointment of another unsuccessful Chugach run fouled Ellie's mood. At least she had managed to grab the fax pages.

They'd ridden about a mile when Chuck spoke through the headset in the helmets Kai had given them. "Ellie, I think something's wrong with Shane." She heard his motor slow to a stop, and Ellie made a U-turn to see what was going on.

Chuck had gotten off the machine to check on Shane. Ellie was shocked to see her ex slumped in the back, looking almost as pale as the snow they were driving on. His breath was labored, and pain was evident in his grimace. Ellie pulled his hand from his abdomen when she saw gummy red liquid seeping between his fingers.

"Jesus H. Christ!" Ellie fumed. "Why didn't you say you got shot?"

"I didn't know he got hit," Chuck said mournfully, like he had let down one of his war buddies.

"I'm sorry," Shane gasped, except he wasn't talking about the botched job or the fact that he had gotten hit. "I know I wasn't a good husband. And I wasn't a good father. I've had a lot of time to think about how I wronged you both."

Ellie wasn't sure now whether he was gasping or sobbing.

"Shut your trap," Ellie said, trying to hide the shakiness in her voice. "Chuck, we need to get back as soon as possible. Nurse Lindbaum will know what to do." Nurse Lindbaum had saved J.B. after he was shot, so she could surely save Shane, or at least get him patched up enough to send to Anchorage.

They sped toward Point Mettier, kicking up powdery white fountains. Ellie's vision was blurred with hot tears. The way seemed to stretch on for forever now that they were in a hurry.

They finally made it back to Point Mettier, but instead of driving up to the warehouse where the mobiles were stored, Ellie led them straight up to the entrance of the Dave-Co and climbed off. She thanked the gods that it wasn't a street-plowing day.

Chuck made a quick call on his cell phone to Chief Sipley now that they were in range of a signal. "We need help!" he yelled into the phone. "Get Nurse Lindbaum to the lobby ASAP."

Ellie, Chuck, and Mariko helped lift Shane out of the snow machine, but he motioned for them to set him back down. "I was too late for Timmy. But I'm asking you now. To forgive me." His ragged voice was barely a whisper.

"I forgive you. Now save your breath and shut the fuck up!" Ellie said.

Shane grew quiet as a mouse and for a moment, the three of them simply knelt over him, a bitter wind picking up and the light turning gray. Ellie tried to shake Shane to life, but she could feel him slipping away.

Chief Sipley, who was still unaware of their escapade to Chugach Village, rushed out of the Dave-Co and surveyed the group, his gaze turning to Shane's body and his blood-soaked clothes. "Did you finally kill him?" he asked Ellie, his eyes wide.

"Maybe I did," she said, wiping away her tears.

CHAPTER THIRTY-TWO

CARA

"I'M LEAVING TOMORROW," J.B. SAID AS THEY MOVED FROM
the log-fired warmth of the Clan House into the frigid chill of the
Alaskan woods surrounding the village. Cara's eyes had to adjust to
the darkness; without the ambient glow of city lights, the night was
black as pitch.

She looked at him in surprise. "So soon? I don't know if it's safe
for us to leave yet. I think we should stay for a while longer until we
come up with a plan."

"Yes, you and your family are better off staying. But I don't know
if I have a role here. I'll be back to work soon. I can run ops from
Anchorage. Try to find out who's behind all of this."

Cara knew she was being selfish by asking, "What about us?"

"I believe that's my line." He threw it right back at her. "Are you going to divorce Aaron?"

Cara was rattled by the bald question. "I'm still getting used to the idea that he's not just a ghost of my imagination. And there's Dylan." Her mind was a jumble. Could it be possible to love two people at once? "I know it's asking a lot, but I want you to stay . . . until I sort everything out."

Clearly her response was not what J.B. wanted to hear.

"Cara, it doesn't feel right to be here."

"But . . ." What exactly was she going to ask of him? *I need to be by my husband and child, but in the meantime, can you also be here to comfort me?* Cara knew it was too much to ask.

"I'll ask Marla or Sonia if they can fly me back to town in the morning," he said while she left her sentence hanging. "Maybe it's best we say our goodbyes now."

Cara didn't like the way J.B. made it sound final. She felt numb, as if she were about to lose someone all over again. Something inside her had changed ever since the day Aaron and Dylan went missing in the woods, and perhaps it was that terror of loss that made her want to cling to all of them—Aaron, Dylan, and J.B.—as illogical and insane as the thought might be. Tears began to well. Did her exhaustion explain why she had recently been a puddle of emotion? She didn't consider herself someone who easily turned on the faucets, but it was as if she had been holding back so many emotions for so long, and now that the walls she had built to protect herself were crumbling, the whole of her was spilling out uncontrollably.

"Well, I should go now," J.B. said, looking toward the yurt where the women had told him he could stay.

"Wait," she said, making him turn back toward her so she could see him better. "I'm sorry, J.B. I didn't think . . . I don't know how . . ." There were no words that could encapsulate the well of feelings—the combination of sorrow, love, hurt, regret, desire, contrition, and adoration—so she closed the gap between them and kissed him. Kissed him in a way that was almost desperate on her part—knowing that this would have to be a terminal moment of time, a parting impression that would have to last maybe forever. It was the final goodbye before she went back to being Aaron's wife and, more importantly, Dylan's mother. He seemed to shudder beneath her lips.

"Cara" came a voice from behind.

They turned to see Aaron emerging from the Clan House with Dylan. Despite the darkness, Cara could read from Aaron's stance that there was something simmering inside, about to explode. But it was the look on Dylan's face when he came into the moonlight that devastated her as she and J.B. pulled away from each other.

"I'm just leaving," J.B. said and, without another word, headed in the direction of the yurt.

CARA FOLLOWED HER family to their hut as if she were heading toward the principal's office. She had the terrible feeling of having let Dylan down.

Once inside the hut, the tension was cut by Dylan asking, "Can you tuck me in?"

"You go on ahead, honey. I'll be right there," she said.

As soon as their son had left, Aaron sat down and looked grimly at Cara. "Are you in love with him?"

"Yes," she said, surprised to hear herself answer so quickly and decisively. She saw the hurt in Aaron's eyes.

"I didn't think that you would betray me like this."

"Betray you? I thought you were *dead*. Which was *your choice*, Aaron!" But it was more than that. There was the web of lies he had spun. Whatever their future held, their marriage could never be the same again. "I think it's me who's been betrayed," she went on bitterly. "You manipulated Mia into stealing bottles of IVIG for you? What's your explanation for that?"

With the tables suddenly turned, Aaron was on the defensive. "I was going to blow the whistle on Almagor," he began, "but I needed solid proof of the experiments we were conducting. She had access that wouldn't be questioned."

Cara hated that she didn't know whether her husband was lying to her. "You said the bottles were worth a lot of money. Where are they now? And where's the exposé?"

Aaron couldn't look her in the eye when he said, "Yes, I sold some before we went to Talkeetna in case I needed to run and needed cash. The rest are in a safe place for when the time is right to send to an investigator along with my confession."

"It's been over a year. When was it going to be the right time?"

He faltered. "I . . . I admit, I'm still afraid, but it was going to be soon, I swear."

Cara's rage got the better of her. "You could have come to me. You could have told me everything instead of . . . this."

"No," Aaron said. "You'd have become a target too."

"But I am a target now. You put your life on the line, our son's life, my life. How could you have involved Dylan in all of this?"

"I didn't intend to. They caught up to me while we were on the camping trip. I couldn't leave him behind, and they killed a homeless man and his son thinking they were us. Killed them in cold blood! Once they thought we were dead, I thought it would be better to keep it that way."

That explained who the remains belonged to. Had the homeless man and his son really been killed by whomever *they* were? Or was it a convenient explanation for Aaron to start a new life with the money he would make selling stolen bottles of IVIG?

"I was going to try to forge a new identity for me and Dylan. And then I was going to come back to you. God's honest truth."

Cara was enraged at herself that she—a detective—had had no hint of what was going on. Perhaps she had been wearing personal blinders to protect herself.

"Look, I don't expect us to go back to the way we were," Aaron continued. "But maybe, now that we're together again, we can pick up the pieces. Or start a new life together when it's safe to leave."

"I don't know, Aaron. The choices you made—I disagree with almost every one of them . . ."

He ran his fingers through his hair. "I know, I haven't been honest with you. I've let you down in so many ways. But I want us to start over."

In that moment it hit Cara that she no longer felt the same about Aaron, but a part of her wanted her happy family back—the two of them and Dylan. *Could* they start over? Should she try, for Dylan's sake? He had already gone through so much. "We'll talk in the morning," she finally responded. "It's been a long day."

With that, she went into the bedroom and curled up next to Dylan.

"Who's the man you were kissing?" he asked sleepily, making Cara feel guilty.

"He's a friend," she said. What else could she say to explain?

Nothing came to her. "No matter what happens, Dylan, remember that I always love you." Then she felt her exhaustion wash over and she was asleep before she knew it.

IN THE MORNING, the sky outside was tinged yellow by light from an invisible sun.

Dylan was already up and tugging at her feet. Cara decided a walk along the lake would do them good.

Leaving Aaron to sleep, she quietly crept out of the hut, holding her boy's hand. A slow mist was rolling in, but undeterred, Dylan seemed excited to be having some alone time with his mother after being apart for so long. He let go of her and ran out ahead, laughing and daring her to chase after him. It put a smile on her face. Before she knew it, they were beyond the huts and on the frozen pier at the vast, iced-over lake.

"Come on, slowpoke!" he was yelling. The vaporous clouds had seemingly swallowed him so that she lost her bead on him, though she could still hear him laughing in the distance.

"Dylan, don't go too far," she called, struggling to regain sight of him, when all of a sudden, a splintering noise filled the air. A jagged crack in the ice grew larger, traveling from the lake's edge toward the center and directly at Dylan, growing larger and louder as it zig-zagged its way to him and split the ice in two.

"Dylan!" she screamed, but in this crucial moment, her feet felt like cement blocks, as if they had suddenly been glued in place. Her heart beat wildly as Dylan's high-pitched scream echoed across the lake. "Dylan!" she cried.

Cara bolted upright in the bed. She looked over to see Dylan still sleeping beside her. Just a dream. But somehow, the scream persisted into her waking world.

She finally realized it wasn't a scream after all but the sound of whistles. There was a bang on the bedroom door before Aaron barged in with a look of alarm.

"Get ready" was all he said.

Cara followed him to the living area where he grabbed his rifle off the wall. Seeing this, she instinctively looked for her gun belt before remembering that she had surrendered it to Mama Unity.

All the while, the high-pitched whistles persisted.

"Stay in the house," Aaron told Dylan before stepping out of the hut. Cara grabbed her parka and followed.

J.B. was emerging from his yurt with a similarly confused look on his face. Women were gathering outside.

Cara followed their gaze toward the skies. Time suspended as a sinking feeling washed over. Tiny black dots blighted the sky, growing larger as they approached the village like an angry swarm. There were five propeller-driven planes.

The women had been signaling danger by means of whistles they all wore around their necks, awakening the village and sending them into action.

"They're here," Aaron said with a tone of dread.

They had been found.

CHAPTER THIRTY-THREE

CARA

"EVERYBODY, GET TO YOUR STATIONS," MAMA UNITY COM-manded as the women and children gathered outside, their faces etched with fear. The women immediately set off in different directions, as coordinated as a hive of bees with Mama Unity its queen, while Cara and J.B. stood fixated in the snow. Cara was secretly glad he had not yet left. Aaron lingered only to say, "Mama Unity will tell you what to do. I'll take care of Dylan," before he disappeared.

Mama Unity turned toward Cara and J.B. and gave them an accusatory glare. "What have you brought to my village?"

Cara looked up at the dots in the sky, then exchanged glances with J.B. *Had* they brought them? Whoever they were, they seemed to have an uncanny ability to find them. She had thought maybe there was a tracker on her car, but they had been traced to this remote village even after she ditched it. Who could have told them where they were? She supposed that her cell phone or J.B.'s, which were still in Mama Unity's hands, could have been used to track them. Or maybe there was someone inside the village who had contacted the outside world.

But now wasn't the time for questioning. "We'll need our guns!" she said.

Mama Unity paused for a moment before calling out to Mia and tossing her a key. "Let them have what they need."

Mia led them to Mama Unity's cabin—one that had clearly been there for a while, sprouting from the ground as if it were part of the forest. Even its sloped, corrugated roof and the metal flue had oxidized green in a way that blended with the background. Mia went to a locked cabinet, opening it to reveal Cara's and J.B.'s guns as well as a cache of rifles and cartridges of ammo. Mia began grabbing them all while Cara and J.B. strapped on their gun belts.

"You should each take a rifle too," she said, handing them the weapons.

"Anyone else know how to shoot?" J.B. asked.

"We hunt to survive, so yeah," Mia said practically rolling her eyes.

Cara assessed the boxes. "Is that all the ammo you have?"

Mia nodded and simultaneously seemed to recognize the dire lack of it.

After they had emptied the cabinet, they quickly followed Mia back to Mama Unity.

J.B. was already in police mode. "What about the children? Is there a safe place for them?"

"They know to go to the Clan House," Mama Unity replied,

taking up one of the rifles Mia had brought. Aaron and a small group of women had returned to the center of the village and took the rest of the ammo and guns. There was clearly a rehearsed plan in place.

"Aaron, where's Dylan?"

"Don't worry, he's safe."

Thank god, Cara thought. Aaron must have already taken him to the Clan House. He and the women split off in different directions, climbing onto the roofs of huts on either side of the central clearing.

The buzz of propellers churned louder, and their silhouettes were growing larger by the second. There was no time for J.B. or Cara to question the line of action. "I'm a sniper in the National Guard," J.B. offered.

"Head to the roof of the Clan House with Niki," Mama Unity ordered. "You'll be our last line of defense. Keep everyone inside safe at all costs." J.B. nodded and followed Niki and Mia, who were already headed toward the Clan House. Mama Unity turned to Cara. "You come with me."

They headed to the huts across from those Ayai and Aaron had climbed. Cara now realized that there was an order to the huts' layout. To get to the clearing in the middle of the village, and the Clan House beyond, anyone had to walk between the huts forming the periphery. The sloped metal roofs were designed not only to drain snow and rain but also to act as shields.

Mama Unity climbed to the top of a hut with a ladder already propped against the wall and pointed Cara toward a neighboring hut to follow suit. Once atop, they each pulled up their respective ladders.

It was then that the propeller planes came in to land like a wake of vultures that had spotted their prey.

THE AIR WAS thick with anticipation. Mama Unity made a sign to all who were watching from the other rooftops to hold their fire. They froze in their positions, seeming to hold their collective breath in the quiet before the storm.

The planes disgorged men dressed in camouflage and ski masks. It was hard to discern one man from another, but there was something familiar about the swagger of one barking orders. Cara believed it must be Victor. She almost regretted having patched him up when she and J.B. had first visited Chugach Village in the past. She should have let him bleed to death.

When they had all emerged, perhaps twenty-five men in all, the man Cara believed to be Victor yelled out in the direction of the huts. "Come out, come out, wherever you are," he said. "Or we'll huff and we'll puff and we'll blow your pretty little houses to bits."

One of the camo'd henchmen cackled in response and shot his gun into the air before Victor put his hand up for him to stop.

Cara looked over toward Mama Unity, who remained composed and unmoving. The unexpected silence made the men mill about uneasily.

With no one in sight, Victor signaled for his men to advance in front of him, while he remained where he was. They moved forward, starting to fan out toward the huts, when suddenly the first row of men disappeared, the ground beneath them giving way, followed by a cacophony of screams. Cara gasped at the realization that a wooden platform camouflaged by snow had given way, dropping the men into a pit below lined with elk antlers. From her vantage point, Cara could also see Marla and Sonia scurry behind the huts, presumably after releasing the catch that kept the platform in place.

All hell seemed to break loose after that. Men who looked to be padded with Kevlar vests found their way around the pit and shot their AK-47s at every hut. It sounded like the chaotic finale of a Fourth of July celebration. Still, Mama Unity showed amazing restraint, waiting until the entire group had made their way to the central area.

Only then did she finally raise her hand and point toward the men, giving the signal to all the rooftop snipers to begin shooting with their rifles. The men were once again taken by surprise as one after another was picked off. Amid the noise of their own rapid gunfire, they couldn't tell where the shots were coming from. But Victor, perhaps being the only brain among the brawn, finally realized he should be looking up. He sprayed the nearest rooftop, which was the one Mama Unity was sprawled on, mowing the roof as if he were watering a lawn with a hose. Cara heard a yelp of pain from Mama Unity, who fell back. Cara did her best to keep up the barrage against the men below, but they too eventually caught on and began shooting at the roofs on either side of them or ran to take cover. Caught in a hail of gunfire and shaken by the reverberations and the heat of bullets all around her, Cara covered her head and inched backward. Was it just a matter of time before she and the village residents would all be dead?

"Wait!" came a distant voice. It was Aaron.

Cara ventured a look and saw that he had climbed down from his rooftop and thrown his weapon to the ground. He held his hands up in surrender as men swarmed around him, their guns trained.

"No!" Cara forced herself not to scream, so that it came out more as a gasp. What was Aaron thinking?

Two of the men frisked him for weapons then shoved him toward Victor.

Cara could scarcely breathe as she watched Aaron face Victor. "I know I'm the one you're after," he said. "Leave everyone else alone, and I'll go with you."

Victor chuckled. "Well, hello, Doc. So you got your grubby little hands dirty, and now you wanna be Mr. Superhero. Isn't that big of you? Offering to sacrifice yourself. You know, if you had done that from the beginning, you'd have saved a lot of lives. But it's a little too late now. Now you've got your wife, your girlfriend, and everyone else here involved. And they're all going to have to die for that. But lucky for us, that means we triple our fees."

Cara felt panicked. It was impossible for J.B. or anyone on the Clan House roof to get a bead on Victor with Aaron in the line of sight. With Mother Unity injured or possibly dead, Cara was probably the closest to the pair, albeit at an angle. She wasn't the crack shot that J.B. was, but if she kept a steady hand, she was sure she could take Victor out. She aimed at his head through the scope, took a deep breath, and pulled the trigger.

Click. Her heart sank with the hollow sound that told her she was out of bullets. She had no extra ammo. She had her Glock, but without a scope she didn't trust her aim from this distance, not with Victor in Kevlar and Aaron standing so close to him.

"Please," Aaron said. "I can pay you double whatever they're paying you. Tell them you shot us and walk away. We'll disappear and no one needs to know."

Victor seemed to consider the proposition. "I can appreciate that we're both money people, you and me. But where is it?"

"I have, uh, bottles of IVIG," Aaron stammered. "It's not all here, but I can give you what I have now and the rest later."

This was news to Cara. Victor seemed dubious as well.

"Show me," he said.

Aaron turned toward his hut, but as he did, Cara watched in horror as Victor called his bluff, lifted his gun and fired three times. Aaron collapsed to the ground, blood tarnishing the snow red.

CHAPTER THIRTY-FOUR

CARA

CARA COULDN'T HELP BUT SCREAM. SHE SHOT OFF A ROUND of her Glock at Victor, but it went wide, and he scuttled for cover in Aaron's hut.

Now the rest of the posse was advancing forward in the direction of the Clan House, spraying empty village huts along the way. Cara wasn't sure if Ayai had also run out of bullets or if she had been hit, but the sniper action on the other end had also gone quiet, leaving only J.B. and Niki trying to pick off the approaching men.

Cara was still in a state of stunned stasis, struggling to breathe, when another barrage hit her rooftop, bullets coming dangerously close. She slid back away from the edge.

"Cara!" She was startled by the strained voice of Mama Unity on the roof next door. She had managed to crawl to the edge nearest

Cara. The older woman was holding her arm, from which a dark red blotch bled through her coat. "The Clan House," Mama Unity managed to say. She lifted her rifle as if she wanted to pass it to Cara, but it was clear she didn't have the strength to toss it across the divide.

Cara knew she had only moments and told herself to pull her shit together. "Hold on," she said, and, willing herself into action, she slid her ladder back down, descended, then ran beneath the eaves of the neighboring hut. "Down below!" she rasped.

Mama Unity let go of the rifle, dropping it to Cara. Her ammo belt followed, landing in the snow, and Cara strapped it on. "Go!" Cara could hear Mama Unity's weak command.

She doubled back to grab the ladder, not wanting it to land in the hands of the enemy, when she spotted two of the men making their way through the thick woods behind the huts. She only had time to shoot one in the arm with her Glock. She closed her eyes as a second shot rang out, fully expecting to feel the sting of metal, but when she opened her eyes the second man had gone down with a hit to the neck.

Cara turned to see Sonia standing behind her, still aiming her rifle.

"Come on," Sonia urged, heading toward the Clan House where J.B. and Niki were doing their best to stave off the horde. She helped Cara carry the ladder with them.

Once at the Clan House, Cara could see that Marla had similarly arrived to help in its defense. Cara and Sonia had come from the west flank where Niki was, while Marla was on the east flank where J.B. had staked his position. Sonia scuttled up the ladder to join Niki. Cara unstrapped the ammo and handed it up to them. Cara had a pressing urge to check on Dylan first. "Everybody okay in there?"

she hollered through the log slats of the gathering place. "Is Dylan safe?"

"We're okay," she heard Mia say, "but Dylan isn't here. We don't know where he is. I think maybe Aaron took him somewhere else."

Panic set in. *Damn it!* Where had Aaron taken him? Clearly, he hadn't trusted the safety of the Clan House. Was he in Aaron's hut? The hut that Victor had gone into either to keep out of bullet range or to search for the promised IVIG bottles?

Cara moved toward the other end of the Clan House. J.B. spotted her and pulled back from the ledge to speak to her.

"There's no more ammo," Cara said apologetically. "But take this." She tossed him the extra rifle.

"I'm sorry about Aaron."

Cara couldn't find the words to respond to that. She had to focus on her son. "I have to find Dylan."

His expression filled with surprise. "He's not in the Clan House?"

Cara shook her head.

"We'll hold the fort," Marla jumped in, grabbing the ladder to join J.B.

"Be careful," J.B. added. The final look they exchanged seemed pregnant with unspoken words. They could have been "I'm sorry" or "I love you" or "I wish we had had longer." Maybe it was just one word.

"Goodbye."

Then Cara was off, grateful for the cover J.B. and Marla gave her as she dashed through the trees behind the huts toward Aaron's lodge. She could feel the adrenaline coursing through her veins.

She did not expect the man who emerged from behind a tree and blasted a shot that ripped through her upper left arm. She knew she was already too far from the Clan House rooftop for anyone to give her cover now. But before the man could take a more lethal shot at her, he fell to the ground, struck by an arrow that had pierced his Kevlar.

This time it was Ayai, who stood behind him with a bow and arrow. Her rifle, which had probably run out of ammo, had been abandoned. Despite her steadfast and unapologetic demeanor, Ayai knelt on the ground next to the man and put her hands together in a short prayer. "May your spirit forgive me for taking your life in exchange for another's, and may you find peace in the next life."

Cara glanced down at her own wound and saw that it wasn't deep despite hurting like hell. She had to keep going. Ayai looked on in surprise when Cara continued in the opposite direction of the Clan House, toward Aaron's hut.

She used her good arm to hold up the Glock as she entered.

Chairs and tables were upended, a sign that Victor had searched the place for the medicinal bonanza. Whether he had found anything or not, he was nowhere in sight. It was eerily quiet.

Cara looked back at the Clan House for a moment; Victor's men were using a fallen timber to try to break down the door. The sniper action from the rooftop had all but stopped. Were they all dead, or had they run out of ammo?

She felt anguished by the thought that she had brought Armageddon upon the village. They were clearly outgunned and probably doomed. But she was grateful she had been able to spend her last days with Dylan. Her only hope was to see her son one more time before she died. Or if he had found somewhere safe to hide, that he would find a way to survive without them.

"Dylan?" Cara called out with tears in her eyes. "Honey. It's

Mommy." She checked under the cot and in the closet, but Dylan was nowhere.

The door creaked open. *Dylan?* She whirled to find herself staring at Victor and the barrel of his handgun. His AK-47 was strapped to his back, as if he were taunting her by saying he didn't need it.

"I saw you sneaking this way like a little mouse," he said. "Too afraid to watch the massacre of your friends?"

Cara whipped her Glock at him, but he was quicker on the draw, and she felt a searing pain as he shot her right hand and the gun dropped to the floor. Blood poured forth from the new wound, and he seemed pleased, satisfied to maim but not kill.

"You think you're so tough with your army of men and semi-automatic weapons ambushing a tiny village full of women?" Cara rasped. "You must be so proud of yourself."

Victor kicked the Glock far out of reach. "Proud? No. Soon to be rich? Yes. You and your husband, I know your type. Thinking you're better and smarter than everybody else. Surprise! I'm the smart one, bitch! I gave your husband a quick demise, but for you, I'm going to go slow. I've been waiting patiently for the go-ahead to kill you, you fucking whore! It's going to be long and painful."

He holstered his gun and pulled a hefty hunting knife from his waist belt. One that could skin and carve a 250-pound buck.

Cara looked for something, anything, that she could use as a weapon. Aaron's kitchen tools were too far away from where she stood, but she spied an awl on the table where he had been working on a leather belt.

She lunged for the tool with her left arm, ignoring the pain, but before she could reach it, Victor slammed his knife into the back of her hand. Cara screamed. This time, the sensation of a hot coal singeing her hand spread into fire ripping through her entire body. She was pinned to the table now, both of her hands rendered useless. With the pain starting to numb all her senses, it was a struggle to stay conscious. Was this how it was going to end? With Victor ripping her to shreds with his knife? She screamed again and, as he pulled the knife back out, crumpled to the floor.

"That was for Wolf," he said. "But I'm going to take a finger off for each of the others." He grabbed her wrist and slammed her bloody palm on the table, readying his knife as if her hand was a slab of steak.

She knew she would bleed to death.

It was funny how time seemed to move at a different pace when on the edge of death. She closed her eyes, remembering the electric feeling that had buzzed through her when she first met Aaron at the grocery store. His awkward but still romantic proposal. The hilarious sensation of her baby's hiccups in the womb. The taste and the warmth of J.B.'s carefully siphoned coffee that had started to melt her defenses. Dylan's delighted smile as they made snow angels together. Everything in the space of a heartbeat. She welcomed the sights, the sounds, the emotions in her memories—anything to take her up and away from the room of impending torture. *I'm sorry, Dylan*, she thought. *I'm so sorry I won't be there for you.*

She heard the faint sound of rapid *pop pop pop*s from somewhere far away. When Cara forced her eyes open, she saw Victor on the ground and . . . Ellie standing at the door with her AK-47? "Find Dylan," she gasped to what was probably a wishful hallucination. Then everything faded into darkness.

CHAPTER THIRTY-FIVE

ELLIE

SHANE HAD BEEN PRONOUNCED DEAD ON ARRIVAL AT THE hospital. She wasn't sure which address of the afterlife he would end up at, but she hoped the Lord would take into account the good in him, like the way he'd come to make amends with her. Despite their regular knock-down, drag-out fights, she mourned his loss and thought it was a damned shame that he'd died. Still, she knew he would have preferred to go out like he did—with a literal bang rather than a slow, whimpering death in a hospital bed.

Technically they had broken into the Chugach Village house, so the thugs had every right to shoot Shane dead. Sipley was none too happy about the whole thing but did Ellie a favor by going along with the story to the cops that it was a hunting accident. That was

Point Mettier for you—living in the gray zone and looking out for your neighbors.

She knew she owed Mariko a heap of debt. "Anytime you need those chips cashed, you come to me," Ellie told her. She wasn't sure if her gambling analogy landed with the Japanese Madonna, but Mariko smiled like she got the gist of what she was saying.

Now Ellie spread the sheets out on Chuck's dining room table. His apartment was much like his shop—cluttered with tchotchkes and taxidermied animals but organized in a fashion, thanks to Chuck's wife, Marge, who made tea for them but gave Ellie the stink eye. She was none too happy about Ellie getting Chuck into a hornet's nest of trouble.

There better be something in these damn fax papers, she thought. Something to make Shane's sacrifice worth it. Ellie pointed to the numbers that looked like some kind of secret code. She figured Chuck could sort out what it all meant, being ex-military.

"Those look like GPS coordinates," Chuck said.

There was also a page with a list of names—Aaron Kennedy, Cara Kennedy, Jennifer Maliki, Timothy MacCullum—and grainy photos next to them. "That's Detective Kennedy's husband," she said, pointing, "and that girl was on Lovansky's phone as well." Next to the names were numbers that Ellie recognized as sums of money—1M, 500G, 50G.

"Looks like a bounty list," Chuck said.

"That's some hefty reward money. Maybe we should beat 'em to it."

Chuck gave her an exasperated look.

"I'm just joshing," Ellie had to spell out.

"But I thought her husband was already dead."

Ellie had to mull over that one. "Maybe they already took him out and collected?"

The shopkeeper shrugged. "I'm less clued in to what's going on than you are."

Ellie smoothed down the crumpled papers she had found on the floor. Men arriving with good faith shipment read one of them. Do not murk CK until other targets found read another. Ellie decided "murk" was gang-speak for "murder or kill" and "CK" meant Cara Kennedy. But the one that made Ellie's hair stand on end was Body moved from Almagor. Set up as OD. $50G. It was followed by an apartment address.

Chuck noticed the way Ellie had tensed up, her eyes turning to hot coals.

"Do you know what this means?"

"That was my son's address. It means that Timmy didn't OD. He was murdered. I'm going to kill every one of those sons of bitches!" Ellie growled.

"How about we call Anchorage police instead?" Chuck offered.

"We're way ahead of the police, Chuck. And you know as well as I do that they're not jumping into action based on these faxes, especially once they find out how we got them."

Chuck must have agreed because he was quiet.

"We oughtta call Detective Kennedy, though, and tell her about the bounty on her head."

Chuck agreed and went to get his cell phone. "If this really is a hit list, we may be too late. There weren't many people there at the village. You said there was a virtual army there the time before, so maybe the men have already set off to find the people on the list." Chuck dialed Cara's number but it went straight to voice mail.

"Try J.B.," Ellie offered.

Chuck tried J.B.'s number, and again there was no answer. "It's not looking good," he said gravely.

Even though Chuck was an aloof kind of guy, he had an uncanny way of making people do what he wanted. He could charm the socks off a snake if he had to. So Ellie wasn't too surprised that he was able to convince a buddy to fly them out the next day to the coordinates on the fax. Lots of folks in Alaska had seaplanes or bush planes. Made it easier to go hunting or fishing, which was a big reason people from the lower forty-eight came to Alaska. Lots of wilderness, but not too many ways of getting there.

ELLIE GRIPPED THE armrests of a rickety old Cessna, certain the heap of mechanical junk was going to fall apart midair. She was never fond of heights and even less fond of flying. She wasn't sure if the never-ending vibrations were coming from the plane's engine or from the way she was shaking in her boots. The plane dipped down suddenly, and she felt herself flying off her seat, even with the goddamned seat belt wrapped over her lap.

"Damn you, Shane! I ain't ready to join you yet!" she said, raising her fist in the air.

That's when Chuck's pilot friend, Doug, yelled, "I think I see it there!"

They all looked out the window into the distance toward dots of color that looked like houses in a tiny village on the edge of a frozen lake.

They finally buzzard-circled in for a landing to the village the GPS coordinates had pointed them to. As they got closer, she saw what looked like tiny ants advancing toward the biggest hut in the village.

"Holy shit!" Doug yelled. "There's definitely something going on down there."

The plane landed in a clearing next to a group of other planes. Ellie wrapped her gun belt around her. Not knowing what they'd find, they had decided to pack a lot of firepower. Chuck had brought more than one military-issue gun and wore a flak jacket, as did Doug, who threw her a Kevlar vest. "Better put this on," he told her.

Then they were climbing out of the plane. Doug and Chuck went into military mode, hunching low and using hand signals that were probably ingrained in them for life. Ellie did her best to copy them.

Bodies already littered the ground, and multiple shots were being fired in a general-mayhem kind of way. The three of them leap-frogged from one tree to another heading to the center of the action.

One of the bodies on the ground looked vaguely familiar to Ellie, and then she realized that he had been in Cara's family photo—her husband. Things were looking grim. "We might be too late," Ellie said.

They crept up to a berm and started picking off members of the gang. They had the element of surprise and amid the confusion no one even seemed to be looking back toward them as they fell in the snow, oozing red. The gangsters had Kevlar vests, and Ellie realized that they needed to aim strategically. Luckily, shooting to maim was her specialty, so hitting an appendage or two wasn't a problem.

Most of the men were gathered around the largest hut, trying to break the door down. "People must be holed up in there," Chuck said. "We need to get to them quick!"

The three of them started in that direction when a hair-raising yell of agony came from a hut closer to them. It sounded like Detective Kennedy. "You boys get to the big house," Ellie said. "I'll check this out."

They split up. Some of the men in camo had finally started to get wise that they were being attacked from the rear and began shooting back at them. Ellie hightailed it over to the hut.

There was blood everywhere. On the floor, on the table, on Detective Kennedy's clothes, on the man Ellie instantly recognized as Mister Evil of the village hooligans. Victor, he was called. He looked like he was about to saw off one bloody hand while Cara's other bloody hand tried to push him away from her. She was as pale as cotton; she would soon be a goner if Ellie didn't act quick. She shot Victor in the thigh, twice. He swiveled around, his eyes filled with hellish rage. He lunged toward her as if he'd received nothing but a mosquito bite, roaring like he was a goddamn Viking or something.

"This is for Timmy!" she shouted—and put a couple of bullets through the son of a motherless goat's forehead.

"Ellie?" Cara looked up at her with a mix of shock and relief. "Find Dylan," she murmured before losing consciousness.

Dylan? Who the hell's Dylan? Then it suddenly dawned on Ellie that it was the name of Detective Kennedy's son.

She ventured back out with her semiautomatic in front of her, ready for action, but it had gone eerily quiet. Was everybody dead?

There were bullet casings everywhere. Some CSI type was going to have a field day, she thought to herself. If Dylan had hidden in any one of these little huts, he was probably dead. But something told Ellie that the boy wasn't in any of them.

"Dylan?" she called out. "I'm your mommy's friend." There was nothing but the sound of wind whipping up mini snow cyclones.

Remembering Timmy's childhood days when they used to go hunting for rabbits in the snow, Ellie scoured the ground for a trail. There was a whole mess of adult-sized prints near the front of the hut, but when she walked around toward the back, she spotted what looked like little child-sized prints that disappeared into the woods.

Ellie continued calling out Dylan's name. There was no answer, so she headed farther into the woods. She kept talking, trying to reassure the boy. Or maybe it was more for her own sake than his. "Your mother would be looking for you, but she can't right now. See, the truth is, she's hurt, but she's gonna be okay." Ellie knew she was rambling, but she couldn't stop. "She's a better mother than I ever was, but she asked me to look for you so here I am instead. I'm doing my best." There was a rustle of brush, and Ellie spun her weapon toward it, but it was only a bird flitting off. "When you lose your only son, it messes with you," she continued gabbing. "Makes you all sad and bitter. I was already a bitter old woman when my son died, but your mom's still young, so please don't be dead and come out, little boy."

Ellie stopped to take a moment. Maybe it was all that adrenaline finally catching up. Maybe it was all the death and hurt hitting her all at once, but she sat on a fallen log and started to sob.

"How can I trust you?" came a boy's voice.

Ellie quickly wiped her tears and spoke out in the direction of the voice. "Your mom, Cara, she's a great detective. And I know she loves you very much." Ellie racked her brains for some tidbit, something to reassure the boy that she really did know his mother, then finally recalled something the detective had said back in Point Mettier. "She told me you used to ride a blue tricycle. Mr. DooDoo?"

"No, silly. Mr. Dodo," the voice corrected.

Ellie heard a movement from the woods, and then a little boy with blond hair emerged from inside the hollow of a tree.

"Dad told me this is where I needed to go if bad men ever came," the boy said.

"Come on, let's go back," Ellie coaxed, but Dylan continued to hesitate.

"I have things Dad said I could only give to Mommy."

"Mommy can't come out right now, but how 'bout I take you to her, and you can give them to her yourself then?"

The boy finally nodded and showed her what else was hidden inside the tree—a little drive, not the old chunky kind or the square floppy disks that Ellie was used to, but a tiny one that was smaller than her thumb, and a bunch of small bottles full of clear liquid.

Ellie gave him a hug, wrapping her arms tight around him as if he were her own—the son she had failed to save.

CHAPTER THIRTY-SIX

MIA

AS FAR BACK AS MIA COULD REMEMBER, MAMA UNITY HAD been preparing the village. At first, Mia didn't fully understand what they were preparing for. She assumed this was just a normal part of life, the way their various religions had rituals and superstitions about warding off danger. But as she grew older, she began to learn what Unity was really a haven from—what loomed beyond the lake were not evil spirits or mythical creatures after all, but other humans. An abusive ex, a family member who might try to rip a child from their mother in a custody dispute, the police, or a government official threatening the very existence of their village. Despite the years of anticipating and planning, the danger had come in a manner that no one could have predicted, with a force that no one could have imagined. Had Mia even the slightest notion, she would have brought ammo and weaponry back to the village with her.

Mia and the others had done their best to calm the children while they huddled in a circle in the Clan House, but they couldn't stop the crying and whimpering as the never-ending *rat-a-tat-a-tat* continued outside. Then the bullets stopped and there was just the *thump thump thump* of people trying to break down the door. Mothers hugged their little ones in fear. Each *thump* reverberated through the Clan House, shaking its solid timbers and bringing down particles of dust. She heard a crack, like a splinter of wood, and believed it was just a matter of time before they were all dead, expiring together like the group of salmon that had washed up on the creek one summer after a debilitating drought.

But then the thumping stopped, and there was nothing but quiet and emptiness.

"Everybody okay in there?" an unrecognizable voice asked.

"Don't open it!" Lorraine had hissed.

But then she heard J.B.'s voice. "It's safe, you can open the door."

Mia and Lorraine went to move the thick wooden slat that kept the door in place, and the hazy winter sunlight streamed in. Aside from J.B., there were two older men—an African American man with a gray mustache and beard and a man with white hair tied back in a ponytail.

Later, when all was said and done and a swarm of police helicopters filled the air, Mia sat in a pool of blood and tears, cursing the *kamuy* for not being able to protect Aaron. Ayai came to embrace her, rocking her until Mia had quieted to a state of numbness.

"I'm sorry, Mia-chan," she said. "You should never have had to go through all this. Maybe we should have stayed with your father. Maybe I was wrong to bring us here. I'm so sorry."

Mia pulled back from her then and looked into her eyes, which were brimming with tears. "No, Mama," she said staunchly. "You were right to bring us here. You made the right decision."

Ayai looked puzzled.

Mia continued, "I don't want to go back to Man's World. This is my home. This is where I want to be."

BEFORE MIA HAD entered Man's World, she sometimes wondered about her father and why Ayai had run from him. She ran through scenarios in her mind of how the conversation would go if she ever had the opportunity to meet him. He would say, "What a fine woman you've grown into, just as pretty as your mother." Then he would apologize. "I'm sorry I wasn't there for you. I've been looking for you and I'm so glad you're back in my life." Or maybe it wouldn't go so well. He would ask, "So what exactly is it that you want from me?" And then she would be stumped because she didn't know what she wanted. She never did follow through with the idea to look for him. After all, she didn't even know his name and was afraid to ask Ayai, because she knew her mother would never give her approval to go look for him.

When families came in to eat at the Lonely Diner, Mia sometimes imagined they were the complete set she never had—a mother and a father and maybe even a sibling or two instead of just a mother and an overwhelming set of "aunties" in Unity.

A "complete set" family had walked in one evening. The father had a flop of gray hair, bushy eyebrows, and a dark mustache. He wore a plaid flannel shirt and long boots. The older son was a teenager with acne growing pains, dressed in a dark hoodie and jeans, and there was a younger daughter as well, who was quiet and with-drawn. The mother had hair the color of straw and wore an over-sized sweater and puffy vest. At first, the conversation centered around school and the son's hockey team.

But when Mia came back to the table to fill their glasses with wa-ter, the tone had changed, and everyone looked agitated. "Don't you give me cheek," the father yelled. Then he angrily reached across the table and grabbed his son's wrist.

"Ow," the teenager yelped.

"The next time you talk back to me, you'll get the worst beating of your life. Understand?"

The daughter's gaze flicked between them with fear, and she tried to make herself smaller.

It seemed as if an alter ego had just been unleashed, and the man whipped his head toward Mia, who stood frozen with the pitcher in her hand, wondering if she should turn around. She couldn't under-stand why she suddenly felt afraid when she had faced wild animals before and knew she could defend herself. There was something about the fear in the children that was contagious.

"What are you looking at, missy?" he growled. "Do your job and mind your own business."

Mia stepped forward, but her hand shook, and she spilled water, making a mess.

"Fucking Jesus Christ, what's the matter with you?" The man shot up as water cascaded over the edge of the table onto his lap. His face went completely red, and everyone in the diner turned to look. He was a powder keg ready to explode.

"I'm so sorry," Mia said.

"The fuck! Don't you know how to do your job?"

His wife tried to calm him, pulling him back down. "It's just water."

Mia turned to look at the children, and she understood now that their father was the wolf and they were the prey. The café grew suddenly quiet, all eyes on the father before he finally settled back down in his chair.

It was then that Mia realized what Ayai had done for her. She didn't care anymore about her father. It was better that they'd lived without him if he was anything like the man in the diner—the kind who needed to control others. Mia would never let anyone have that kind of power over her. Because of Ayai, she was free.

MONTHS AFTER THE invasion of Unity, when winter had thawed into spring, one of Marla and Sonia's planes sputtered in. Although it had been a while, the villagers still looked up apprehensively whenever they heard the buzz of a plane's motor. They relaxed when they saw the familiar logo of the tour company and gathered at the pier to watch it skate in.

Sonia was all smiles as she opened the pilot-side door and waved her hands excitedly. "I've brought a guest!" she exclaimed.

A young man with long raven hair climbed out after her. Lorraine gasped and ran forward, calling, "Alex!" Alex caught his mother in a bearish hug.

Mia thought he looked somehow taller and bigger and possibly more handsome than when he had left.

After hugs and words of glee were exchanged, Alex finally picked her in his sights. "Whoa, is that Mia Upash?" Mia felt her cheeks go hot. "I thought you were still in Anchorage."

"I found my way back home, and now I'm here to stay." Mia understood that now. She once was embarrassed to be from a village that others might consider primitive, but she now believed it was just the opposite, even though she *had* been in the dark on the ways of Man. Mia had been searching for *someone* or *something* for fulfillment, when what she needed, she already had. Love—love was overflowing in Unity. The change she needed was in her own mindset, and she knew that Unity was the place where she belonged.

Alex's smile was electric. "I got a grant to document life in Unity, to show how it's possible to incorporate various Indigenous cultures into one society. So I guess I'll be here for a while." He paused and looked at her again. "You look different. Something's changed. Like you've become Bear Woman."

"Bear Woman?"

"There's an Ojibwe story about a girl who had visions of a great bear coming toward her. As it got closer, it got smaller, and when it was right beside her, she became the bear. The girl overcame many obstacles in her life until she became a woman with a strong heart and the courage of a bear."

Mia smiled. She was reminded of her mother's stories about *Iomante*, an Ainu ritual in which the bear god is liberated from its bear form after its mission in the human world is over and is sent back to the Land of the Gods, back to its own world where its families and friends awaited. The spiritual beliefs seemed apt. She had become Bear Woman, and she had come home. *"One' gganaa',"* she said, speaking to Alex in Koyukon. "Let's go eat."

CHAPTER THIRTY-SEVEN

ELLIE

"DO YOU WANT TO SAY A FEW WORDS?" DOUG YELLED TO EL-
lie over the sound of the propeller. She was thankful that this ride
was smoother than the first go-round. They had picked a soft-cloud
kind of day without the wind tossing them about like Bingo balls in
a hopper.

Chuck's military bud had come to the rescue once again when
Ellie decided what to do with Shane's ashes after she had his body
cremated. It was actually Chuck's suggestion to scatter them at sea,
and Ellie thought that was proper since Shane had been a nomad for
most of his life—or at least when he wasn't in jail. Doug agreed to fly
them out over the Gulf of Alaska for the impromptu ceremony.
Chief Sipley said he was coming along for "emotional support."

Ellie hadn't thought about saying anything. She was never really good with words. "Well, Shane, you're a man people will miss more now that you're dead," she began, but the men in the plane gave her a puckered look so she added, "I know there was good in you at the beginning and at the end, even if the middle wasn't so good. Make amends with Timmy while you're up there. I loved you both despite all the grief I got."

Chuck, who was maybe the most priestlike of all of them, added a short prayer. "The Lord lift up the light of his countenance upon us, and give us peace, this day and forevermore. Amen." Ellie was no churchgoer, but she appreciated his blessing.

"Amen," she chorused.

Jim Arreak was afraid of heights, so he hadn't come along, not that there would have been room for him, but he had helped out by instructing Ellie how to spread Shane's ashes from the plane. He had looked it up on the world wide web and found out that she couldn't just toss them out the window without Shane flying back in her face. So he had moved Shane's ashes into a paper bag and closed it with a rubber band. He told Ellie to remove the rubber band just before tossing the whole bag out the window.

Now Ellie opened the window and did as Jim had instructed. The bag opened up as it descended, and the trail of ashes fell like smoke into the ocean. The empty paper bag kicked up on its own into the wind and wafted back down like a lost, ownerless kite before it disappeared. It was beautiful and sad all at once, and Ellie couldn't help but tear up at the sight.

J.B. EXPLAINED TO Ellie what they believed had happened to her son. The dirty pharma company that Cara's husband used to work at was into conducting experiments on hapless souls who weren't warned of the most serious possible side effect—death. They recruited people like Timmy for the experiments, because it would be easy to cover up the deaths of people who had a history of drug use by making them look like overdoses.

While Cara was getting patched up at the hospital, Ellie looked after Dylan. Debra Blackmon, the schoolteacher, brought over some clothes, books, and games that her sons had outgrown. Even Amy came by with free Chinese delivery. She was graduating soon and heading off to California for college, and Ellie fully expected her to come back with a new pronoun.

Surprisingly, Vlad didn't have a problem with Dylan. Her terrier seemed to sense that the boy had seen some rough times and only yapped at him in the beginning, then warmed up to him and was soon sleeping in his lap.

Dylan reminded Ellie of Timmy, but she was glad to hand the tyke back to his proper mom after a few days when she got out of the hospital. At least one of their kids had come back from the dead. J.B., meanwhile, was clinging to the detective's side like a tacky dryer sheet. All the din at the Dave-Co was starting to get on her nerves, so Ellie was glad when things finally started going back to normal and she could participate in the weekly "board meetings" at the Salty Pub.

MARIKO MADE HER usual swishes and sashays as she sang a jazzy tune onstage, seemingly unfazed by her Chugach Village venture. Ellie's smoke rings wafted up toward the nicotine-stained ceiling as she considered her poker hand. Chief Sipley, Jim, and Chuck were in their usual seats.

"Well, at least I've got less of a workload these days," Jim piped up as he rearranged his cards.

"How's that?"

"There's not a whole lot of people for me to look out for with everybody's exes being dead."

"Now maybe you'll stop spying on people with those binoculars," Chuck threw out in Ellie's direction.

True, her original intention with the binoculars had been to keep a lookout for Shane in case he got out of prison. But she had to admit that she liked to be kept informed of the whole building's comings and goings. "I'm not looking out for myself anymore," she responded. "I'm looking out for everybody else. After all, we're short one officer."

"Speaking of which, when are we getting our new guy?" Jim asked Sipley.

"Interviewed a man yesterday who might be willing to take J.B.'s place."

"We'll make sure to give him the Point Mettier welcome," Ellie said, and the four of them cackled like a bunch of drunken vultures.

CHAPTER THIRTY-EIGHT

CARA

UNDER THE FAMILIAR GLOW OF LED LIGHTS IN ANGELO'S monitor-filled back room, Cara caught the tech whiz engaged in a game of virtual chess.

"Cara," he said brightly, switching it off and looking up at her. "Want a Rolo?" No matter how many times she had refused his offer of candy, he never stopped asking.

"No, thanks."

Only now did he notice the white bandages covering her hands like a pair of bike gloves. "Wow! What happened?"

"Someone tried to kill me," she answered matter-of-factly.

"*What?*"

"Don't worry. He's dead." Her placid demeanor continued, making Angelo visibly nervous.

"What can I do you for? More photo searching?" He pulled up a software window and began typing.

While recovering from her injuries, Cara had had time to think. She kept coming back to the question of how someone had always been able to track her whereabouts. The idea of a locator on her car was ruled out after she ditched it at Mia's. She put aside the idea of someone with her at the village being a mole since everyone there had been a target. That left her cell phone. Someone could have enabled her phone's GPS location tracking. Someone who had had access to her phone. A hunch, however, was not evidence.

"No, I have some questions I'd like to ask you."

Angelo stopped typing. "What about?"

There was something Cara had tucked away in her visual memory that was suddenly spotlighted when her suspicions grew. It was something she needed to confirm, and she walked over now to the area that was dedicated to machinery from bygone eras, tucked off into a corner of Angelo's shop. Old computers, disk drives, CRT monitors . . . and there it was. "I see you have an old fax machine."

"Yeah, I have a lot of old-school stuff. Didn't I tell you that I've got some older customers always looking for outdated parts?"

Cara bent down to examine it. "Yours seems to be plugged in and working."

"And that's a problem because . . . ?"

But Cara could detect a tiny inflection of Angelo's voice that betrayed him. "I believe you've been using it to give orders to the gang in Chugach. And you've been tracking my phone, Angelo."

"What? Why would I do that?"

"I trusted you with my phone several times, which gave you the opportunity to enable location sharing. You knew I would lead you to Mia and then to my husband."

Angelo scoffed. "I've never even met your husband. I thought you said he was dead."

Cara scrutinized him. "You're one of Almagor's donors."

"Almagor? Where your husband worked? Why would I be donating anything to them?"

Why indeed. That was the puzzling part. Trying to understand what Angelo's motive was. "Was the medicine for your father?" Cara pointed to the photo of Angelo posing with his father. "I remembered your story of how you got on the wrong side of the law to pay your father's medical expenses." This is what Cara had decided to look into after her initial hunch. "I know he's in a facility for Alzheimer's patients. Maybe you thought you could help him by buying black-market IVIG."

Angelo seemed to fog over with silence.

Cara turned her attention back to the fax machine. "I'm afraid I'm going to have to take this back with me so we can check its memory for every fax sent and received."

"You'd need a warrant for that."

Cara unfolded her warrant and showed it to him.

"Oh, come on, Cara. I know you're on disability."

"*Was* on disability. I'm back on the job. Light duty."

Angelo's expression turned to surprise.

"I'm also going to need you to step away from the computer." Cara watched as Angelo mentally weighed his options before he yanked a drawer open and pulled out an M17 Sig Sauer, pointing it toward her.

"I don't think so," he said.

"Angelo." She looked at him with disappointment. "I thought we were friends."

"Hey, I sent you plenty of warnings. In fact, I specifically told the operatives not to kill you or the deal was off. They were just supposed to scare you so that you'd stop looking into the case. If your husband had stayed dead, we could've let sleeping dogs lie. But once you stuck your nose in, I realized you were going to bring back Aaron. The man who could shut everything down."

"You had my husband killed. You had other innocent people killed. And now you're willing to kill me? For what? For medicine that may or may not help your father?"

"Not him. Me."

Now Cara was the one to balk in surprise.

"I have early onset. I'm starting to forget conversations. I have to leave all these notes to myself because I keep forgetting what I'm supposed to be doing. Yesterday I had trouble tying my shoes. I have mood swings, too, and right now, I'm pretty riled up. I might shoot you and then forget that it happened. You have no idea what it's like to know you're slowly losing your faculties."

The growing mess of Post-its and piles of paper made sense now. It must have been frightening and frustrating for someone with Angelo's acuity. Cara felt only a beat of sympathy, outweighed by the depth of his treachery. "That's no excuse for what you did and the lives that have been lost."

Angelo looked contrite. "It was never meant to go this far."

"Where did you get the money to pay those hefty bounties?"

"I wasn't the only one who wanted black-market plasma. There are a lot of rich motherfuckers willing to pay to keep the operation going. I was just the go-between. And we all used code names, if that's what you're asking. Even I don't know who they really are. IP billionaires, Russian oligarchs, or people getting wealthy on political conspiracies. Alex Jones–type shock jocks who suck off of people's tragedies for all I know. Whether they needed the medicine for Alzheimer's or some phony elixir that promises eternal life, I also don't know."

"So these billionaires were paying the thugs at Chugach for IVIG?"

"No, not them specifically. There are always go-betweens. Their doctors, their pharmacists, or whoever rich people usually pay to be their high-class drug dealers. That's probably as far you'll get, if you can even dig that far."

Cara believed Angelo in this sad truth. She looked down at his 9 mm handgun, which was still pointed at her. "I didn't come alone with nothing but the warrant," she said. "I think it would be best to put the gun down."

Angelo hesitated. "I think you're bluffing."

"Angelo, have I ever lied to you before?"

Angelo faltered. He studied her like a scientist through a microscope.

"I've always been two steps ahead of you, Cara."

"Except this time." Cara didn't blink.

Angelo finally lowered his gun. Smart move.

The door opened and officers from Anchorage PD rushed in. J.B. was in the lead. He had just made the transition from Point Mettier to Anchorage.

"Step away from the computer, sir," he said, flashing his new badge, while others stepped in to cuff Angelo. Maybe it was her imagination, but it seemed to Cara that he gave her a nod, acknowledging that she had won the chess game.

AARON'S DATA FILES on the thumb drive and the IVIG samples Ellie had found in a tree at Unity provided enough details to shut down not just Almagor's experiments but Almagor itself, at least until the investigations were concluded. Cara was also able to get the state to file missing persons reports for the plasma donors who had disappeared and to reexamine every death among Almagor plasma donors.

Like Angelo, she doubted that the wealthy people at the top of the food chain behind the illicit plasma-harvesting operation would ever be revealed. She sighed between sips of morning coffee, contemplating the injustices of the world.

"Dylan, you're going to be late for school!" came a voice from behind her. It was J.B. looking handsome in his pressed uniform as he came around to kiss Cara's cheek and then the scars on her hands.

They were both working at Anchorage PD now, but the inherent awkwardness, teasing from coworkers, and still-lingering doubts that had clouded Cara's relationship with the force had propelled her to apply for a job with the FBI. If she was accepted, her goal was to land a position with the Anchorage field office.

Aaron had had a second burial ceremony. The police were trying to match the poor souls whose remains had been in the ground under the wrong headstones with any of the thousands of missing persons reports filed in the last few years. It was a sad reality that so many people were lost in the vast wilderness-covered state of Alaska every year.

Still, Cara had to be thankful that J.B. and Dylan had managed to fill the void in her life. Her cup was full again. She no longer felt as if she were teetering in an unsteady boat but was now standing on a rock-solid foundation. She gazed at J.B. and her son. Her memories around the events at Unity were spotty, but things had felt almost perfect since then. She sometimes wondered if everything had been but a dream, or if she was dreaming now.

ACKNOWLEDGMENTS

There are so many people I wish to thank for their support in writing this book. I am in awe of each of you who has buoyed me in so many ways and given me the courage to keep writing and pursing a lifelong dream.

First, on the research end, I am so grateful to the Alaska Native Women's Resource Center, particularly to founding member Tia M. Holley, who generously looked over passages and pointed me in the right direction. Alaska continues to have the highest homicide rate in the nation for women killed by men, and Alaska Native women are particularly vulnerable. The AKNWRC empowers tribes and strengthens local responses to domestic violence. More information about this worthy cause can be found at www.aknwrc.org.

I recently had the incredible good fortune of getting to know fellow mystery author Wes Blalock, who kindly zipped through my manuscript and gave me amazing notes and insight on police matters. I also need to thank Officer Carol Poon for taking the time to answer questions in the early research stages. Still, there are certain details that I have chosen to finesse for purposes of the story.

I'm constantly flummoxed by how many talented and amazing advocates there are in the writing community. Special gratitude must be given to my eagle-eyed fellow writer friends who never fail to add an encouraging word along with their helpful notes—Daniel Benjamin, Jimmy Tsai, and David Ariniello. Other accomplished colleagues have given me a stage, welcomed me on their vlogs and podcasts, shared advice, or otherwise given me a leg up. While the list is never-ending, I would like to spotlight certain facilitators who also happen to be leaders and female writing dynamos. Fellow Japanese-American mystery writer Naomi Hirahara, an icon in the AAPI community, has never failed to respond to my questions and requests for advice. She always seems to be in three places at one time. I must thank the lovely Hank Phillippi Ryan, who has been exceptionally kind and welcoming to the world of mystery writing. Despite her numerous accomplishments and awards, she manages to stay grounded and somehow finds time to help other writers through podcasts, author panels, and writing workshops. What an incredible inspiration! Writer/producer Maria Elena Rodriguez has been a friend for over fifteen years and has always been a staunch advocate of the AAPI creative community. Thank you for always pushing to have our voices heard. The gorgeous Leslie Zemeckis, with whom I have been fortunate enough to rub elbows in my screenwriting career, has been more than kind. She is a tireless facilitator and promoter of book authors.

Tracy Bernstein, my editor at Berkley, not only has been responsive to all my needs, but her intelligent comments, sharp wit, and rigorous edits have improved my writing tenfold. She is tireless, patient, and goes above and beyond to get notes to me in a timely manner.

My incomparable agent, Lucy Carson, continues to guide and assist me on every front and at every step. I am so lucky to have her and her assistants on my team.

I cannot say enough about the stellar publicity and marketing team, especially Loren Jaggers and Jessica Mangicaro, who have helped give me every opportunity to succeed. The audiobook team at Penguin Random House Audio has also been topnotch.

I am so grateful to the staff at the *Rafu Shimpo* newspaper, with special mentions to J.K. Yamamoto and Kathee Yamamoto Fleming. The *Rafu Shimpo*, which serves the Japanese American community of Los Angeles, has always been so kind in its coverage, even before I made the move from screenwriting to novel writing.

I thank my lucky stars that I have such supportive family members. As always, my husband, John Chan, has been a trouper, listening to story rants, helping me solve problems, and even designing marketing items! My sister, Satsuki Yamashita and my extended family of in-laws—the Louis, the Feitelbergs, and the Ngs—have all acted as my unofficial sales and marketing team. While we lost Betty and Jesse, I feel they are still rooting for me from the hereafter. My cousins Alice Tayama-Kerley and Grace Tayama have also cheered me on and spread the word even when they were going through their own difficult losses and circumstances. I so appreciate you all.

Last but not least, I would like to thank the people of Alaska, with special recognition to its Indigenous population, and you, the readers—your kind emails and notes light up my day and continue to act as an incentive to keep writing.